Shades

KEN HUBONA

ISBN: 9781097996261

DEDICATION

To Lieutenant Junior Grade Quentin Gunn, USNR

ACKNOWLEDGMENTS

Like a motion picture, a novel is a collaborative effort involving many hands. The hands that shaped this book belong to Donna Sullivan, William F. Charles, Paul E. Creasy, John Granderson, Denise Woods, Kathryn Carson, Randolph Braccialarghe, Theora Braccialarghe, Whitney Roberts Hill, Greg Smith of *Agile Writers,* and Tiffany White of *Writers Untapped.* My thanks to each of them.

CHAPTER 1

David Quinn led his troops against tyranny. Never one to yield to the slavery of groupthink, he blazed his own trail and was proud that his people were prepared to pay the price. But why couldn't they pay on time?

Dave raised his bullhorn. "People, please. Get the lead out." He raised his arm and gave the air a wide follow-me sweep. "At this rate, we'll never make it."

He turned and resumed the march. A general leading his ragtag guerrilla band, he tilted forward as though into a headwind. His combat boots thumped against the pavement as he advanced toward the battle. Sergeant stripes on his arm and a red bandana on his forehead were his insignia of command, but he knew it was his eyes that radiated authority. Blue and deep set, they shone with a determination that inspired his soldiers, whose sandals flapped against naked feet as they struggled to keep up. He could have been a revolutionary, leading machete-wielding peasants toward the dictator's palace—were this not Ohio, that is.

After fifty paces, he turned back toward his straggling retinue: a gaggle of torn jeans, tie-dye T-shirts, and protest signs resting on shoulders.

He sighed and raised the bullhorn again.

"You don't need that thing, Dave," Abbie said. "We can hear you." With skin as pale as her flowing white muslin dress, Abbie wore a placid smile that suggested a deep inner peace—or perhaps braless comfort.

"But if we don't shake a leg, Abbie, the press will be gone when we get there." He squinted at the daisies she carried.

She withdrew a flower and held it out. "For their rifle barrels. When the soldiers block our path. You know, to show them the power of love."

Dave looked into her serene eyes. "There are no soldiers."

She reached out and touched the peace medallion on his chest. "Violence never resolved anything."

Her hands moved up and cupped his crimson beard, a DNA remnant of a Viking warrior who pillaged England in the ninth century and donated the seed that became Dave forty generations later. But instead of the battle sword wielded by his Norse ancestor, Dave clutched only the bullhorn.

"We should all just love each other," she said.

Dave had to smile. Loving was something Abbie did well and often.

Behind her, a thin man jabbed his "peace now" sign in the air.

"Make love not war," he chanted as he bobbed his protest placard up and down. "Make love not war."

Dave raised his palms. "Darryl, what are you doing?"

The man stared back through the round lenses of purple-tinted John Lennon glasses, a veil of stringy hair, and the folds of Play-Doh that once formed a good mind. "Protesting, man." He jabbed the air in short bursts as though harpooning Moby Dick from below.

"But we're not *there* yet, Darryl." Dave swept his arm across the horizon. "Do you see any people?"

Maple seed pods swirled in the Indian summer breeze, helicoptering toward the vacant brick street. Only the brief wail of a distant factory whistle disrupted the peace.

Darryl's head tilted. "So?"

Dave rested a hand on Darryl's shoulder. "So, if no one sees it, it didn't happen." He watched Darryl's brow crinkle as though the words were searching for meaning in the misfiring synapses of his drug-furrowed brain.

Darryl's eyes widened. "Ohhhhh." He raised his hand. "Right on."

Dave drooped his head with a groan and slapped Darryl's upraised hand rather than letting it go un-fived.

This was what he had to work with, a motivated bunch with good intentions but bumbling execution. And though he could have culled the herd, a general needed all the troops he could muster, even the walking wounded.

He glanced at his watch and raked both hands through his thick mane. They were late. He'd have to pull out the big gun. He didn't want to. It smacked of siccing a police dog on nonviolent civil rights marchers. But what choice did he have? They had to get there before the clock ran out. He turned to his second in command.

"Tanya," he said, nodding toward his tattered army, "tighten it up."

She looked back, muttered a curse, and broke from Dave's side. A ferret of a woman, compact and eager, she attacked the troupe's flank in a staccato of rapid steps, barking at the laggards.

"Close it up," she said, scowling and waving her arms. "We have a war to end."

An Angela Davis wannabe in a Che Guevara T-shirt, Tanya's well-practiced scowl was fearsome, but her Afro a disappointment. With hair as straight and light as her Irish features, even an hour of pre-march frizzing had failed to achieve the desired effect, the result being less Angela Davis and more Phyllis Diller.

She raised her white arm in a black power salute. "Come on, people. Men are dying."

Tanya was her activist name. Her real name, Bunny, just didn't provide the gravitas of a serious radical. Dave shook his head. Poor Darryl cowered under the onslaught. Tanya glowered as if she might swat him with her "peace now" sign.

Beneath a canopy of ancient shade trees glowing in reds, oranges, and yellows, the general and his moral warriors resumed their trek toward campus. The clock tower chimed from the square as the aroma of burning leaves wafted by.

When an object ricocheted off Dave's shoulder, he winced in surprise. The tossed beer can clattered harmlessly on the sidewalk at the feet of the marchers as a pickup pulled alongside. In the bed were three young factory workers, just off shift.

"Peaceniks," the big one called out.

"You tell 'em, Buck," another said. "My brother's in Vee-it Nay-yam."

Tanya raised a defiant fist, revealing her unshaven armpit.

"Check out the gorilla," Buck said to the laughter of his friends. He jumped to his feet. "Hey, lesbo, you should try some of this." He arched his hips forward and grabbed his crotch. "You might like it." He ran the other hand over his flat top.

Dave watched Tanya's raised fist become a single finger. *Oh, christ.*

Buck's eyes grew wide and his face reddened. "Why you little bitch." He flicked his cigarette to the ground and jumped from the truck. His friends followed.

The marchers recoiled.

Buck took several steps toward Tanya, his fists clenched by his side.

She stumbled back.

Dave glanced at his frozen soldiers, slack-jawed and wide-eyed. No help there. He took a deep breath, jumped in front of Tanya, and puffed out his torso to shield her from Buck and his pals. The men froze in a silent standoff. Dave steadied his quivering legs so the others wouldn't see. He wasn't up to the challenge. After four years of majoring in beer, the meat on his six-foot frame was largely blubber.

He inspected Buck's thick arms and neck, sweat-matted hair, and soiled hands, and the equally muscular factory workers on each side, severely toned by youth and a life of physical labor. He looked at his pot-smoking army. This could not be won on the field of battle. It required cunning. He took a deep breath and modulated his voice so it wouldn't crack. "I think what she means is . . . she would *not* like to try any of"—he grabbed his crotch—"this." He winked at Buck. "But I would." He pursed his lips and kissed the air.

Buck's face morphed from rage to bewilderment at the intensity of Dave's cold blue stare. He eyed Dave's long hair and medallion, then took a step back and spit on the ground. "Fuckin' homo." He turned and waved his chiseled arm. The townies jumped back on the pickup and departed to the sound of squealing tires and shouted profanities.

Dave found himself hyperventilating. He stood motionless, leaning forward and calming his breathing.

"Sorry," Tanya said, her eyes downcast. "I couldn't help myself."

Dave nodded. As the stress waned, he straightened up. "Let's go." He chopped the air toward the college on the hill and resumed the ascent.

He led his battalion beneath an ancient arch, its engraved stone heralding *Gladstone Academy, Est. 1831*. A conservative college of long tradition, Gladstone attracted students of privilege.

The gang passed the library where Dave had recruited William just that morning. Of the army of nine, only William had a brain not addled by drugs, or rage at the world, or a colossal ignorance of human nature. But he was also the only one Dave had to bribe. The lone black protestor wore tropical garb, a necklace of beads, and a large hair pick. A black beret would have been more intimidating, but Dave couldn't find one, so he had settled for the pick. He had tracked down William deep within the stacks, sitting erect and wearing slacks and a white-collared shirt.

"It's a moral imperative, William," Dave whispered among the towers of books that deadened all sound.

"I'm here for an education," William said, "not political activism."

"What about the draft?"

"I can't be drafted, Dave. I'm Jamaican."

"But we need a black face. What can I do?"

Since *supply and demand* was the lynchpin of Econ 101, the answer came as a bright smile blossoming on the only ebony face on campus. They settled on a price of twelve hours of tutelage in freshmen calculus.

As the protesters approached the quadrangle, the cadre's demeanor morphed from passive to passionate. The makeshift signs came off their shoulders and bobbed in the air. The chants began.

"No more war. No more war."

They marched to the center of the mostly vacant quad, a rectangle formed by academic buildings, the student union, and the chapel. Dave marshalled the nine into a tight circle. They grew louder and their signs jabbed the air violently. "Stop the war now."

Protests were unheard of on this affluent and conservative campus. Maybe at radical Berkeley, but not here. The few passing students looked on with bemusement. One raised a clenched fist in a black power salute of mock solidarity.

"Yo, William," he said to the Jamaican protester, "what's your beef, mahn? You got no dog in dis fight."

William averted his eyes.

The protesters responded with more enthusiastic air jabs and louder chants.

"Make love, not war."

"Peace now."

"Hell no, we won't go."

They tried to provoke confrontation, but the sparse gauntlet offered little resistance. Being mid-hour and classes in session, only a few students entered and left the library and student union on the tranquil quad.

Dave looked around. "Where is everyone? Where are the reporters?"

"Tanya's in charge of the press," Abbie said.

Dave turned to Tanya. "Where are the cameras?"

"WGUB is here," Tanya said. She nodded toward a chubby, acne-faced kid approaching with a mic and cassette recorder.

"Campus radio? That's it?"

"Thanks for the appreciation. Next time, *you* let Homer cop a feel to get him over here."

"Hi, Bunny," Homer said, smiling shyly.

She scowled. "It's *Tanya*."

Dave shook his head. With no meaningful press coverage, enthusiasm devolved into lethargy. The marchers propped their signs against the wall and lay in the grass or sat on the bench and smoked cigarettes. Tanya teased her hair. William studied a text book. Even the smitten Homer, his infatuation leading nowhere, lost interest and wandered off.

Dave sat on the low stone wall, his head drooping. He fished his notes from his pocket. What a waste. He had prepared two versions of what he might say—the version in which he played the thoughtful analyst of geopolitical affairs, and the other, the antiwar rant. He could go either way. Much of the privileged class supported the war, but the draft loomed over most of the men. He had planned to read the crowd and assume the persona which would better sell his message—principled man of conscience or antiwar zealot.

He snorted. With no audience, it didn't matter now. The papers slipped from his fingers onto the brown grass.

A van screeched to a stop in the admin building parking lot. When a reporter leaped out, followed by his cameraman, the protesters scrambled to their feet. Their enthusiasm returned with signs higher, chants louder, and steps quicker. Dave led the choir with his bullhorn, his voice carrying half a mile, though the farthest protester stood only feet away.

The young reporter pulled a blue blazer over his white short-sleeve shirt and narrow black tie. His patch read *WOHO News*. He opened a pocket mirror for a final makeup check, ran a comb through his hair, and made a beeline for the bullhorn. Thrusting a microphone in Dave's face, he looked up.

"Skip Perkins, Action News," he said. "And you are?"

"Field Marshall Quinn," Dave said, amused by the irony that military rank inspired his antiwar troops. "David Quinn."

A bell rang and students poured from the classroom buildings. The sight of the reporter and camera drew a crowd of the curious. Dave stood taller, his shoulders broader and chest pumped out.

"And why are you here?" Skip said.

"Yeah, Field Marshall. Why?" one of the onlookers called out. "You run out of dope to smoke with your hippie friends?"

A jock in a lambda delta sweater guffawed. Two sorority girls tittered. The gathering crowd laughed.

That helped Dave decide. He'd go with the rant. He donned his scowl of outrage. "We're protesting the immoral and criminal war our government is waging against the sovereign nation of Viet Nam."

"But what about the Reds, the domino effect?" the reporter said. "Don't we have to stop the tide of communism?"

"It isn't a tide, it's a swamp. It's 1967. We've been sinking in this quagmire since sixty-one. First, we sent in equipment, then advisors, then in sixty-five, combat troops." He paused and turned to the camera. He could see the lens zoom in on his face. "Ever since, our boys have been coming home in body bags." Dave shuddered, appearing unable to mask his passion. "I refuse to kill small brown people for LBJ and McNamara." Then, in his best Mohammad Ali impersonation, "I ain't got no quarrel with them Viet Congs." A masterful performance. He should have been an actor.

"So if called, you'll refuse to serve? Like The Champ?"

"Serve? I don't call killing people *serving*. And by *called*, you mean *conscripted*. Johnson is drafting five thousand men a week to fight his war."

"But they're from farms and factories and inner cities. No one here is getting drafted. You all have student deferments."

Dave shook his head. "It's only a temporary reprieve, not a pardon."

The cameraman rolled his finger in the air. Skip glanced at his watch. "Thanks," he said, "gotta meet deadline." He hurried off, and the crowd of onlookers promptly dissipated.

"Okay, that's a wrap," Dave said. "Mission accomplished."

An athlete in a letter jacket slapped a pal's chest with the back of his hand. "Hey, Chad, it's a wrap," he said. "We got a movie director here, a regular Cecil B. DeMille."

As Dave led his troupe back across the quad, he turned to William.

"Too much?"

"You did fine, Dave." William put his hand on the taller man's shoulder, then broke into a jog.

"Wait," Dave said, "come have a beer with us."

William shook his head and cut toward the library. "I have to study," he said. "Not everyone has a job waiting."

Dave nodded. Yes, in six months he would graduate into the family insurance agency. But only for a few years, until he saved enough to buy a plot of land in the gently sloping foothills of the Blue Ridge mountains and could grow grapes and start a winery. And if he had to be a caged office rat first, he would at least be out of this enclave of privileged yahoos, where bone structure and fraternity affiliation defined the measure of a man. Only one thing on this campus would he miss. And there she stood, among friends, her back braced against a mighty oak tree. A sweater draped over her shoulders, its sleeves tied loosely around her neck. As he passed, she folded her arms across her chest. Her gaze pierced into him, boring down to his bedrock. Jennifer shook her head, and Dave looked away.

CHAPTER 2

Jennifer Pruitt caught herself shaking her head as David and his army-of-the-broken passed by. She hadn't meant to be judgmental. It was his life. He could do with it as he wanted. Including throwing away his unique gifts. He could have been a mathematician, a physician, a physicist. Instead, he chose to enlist all those lost souls in his search for attention. Such a shame. He didn't used to be like that.

Three years earlier when Jennifer arrived at college, she felt like Julie Andrews spinning through an Alpine meadow of flowers. A yoke of oppression had been lifted. She was out from under Daddy's thumb for the first time in her eighteen years, independent and free to control her own life. She loved Daddy and Mother, of course, but she would never live at home again. Never.

She'd given her escape to college a lot of thought. Though she could never confront Daddy head on, she'd use her education to get what *she* wanted. She'd study hard, become a teacher, and spend her life molding young minds and loving her work. Heck, it wouldn't even be work. It'd be a joy.

But she probably wouldn't ever marry. Marriage was a trap of servitude. Mother was practically Daddy's slave, and that wasn't going to happen to her even if it meant she wouldn't have her own children. She'd just love the children in her class all the more. But she would never again be dominated by a man.

Then, a gangly boy approached her at the freshman mixer. He had drawn her name for the first dance. "Are you"—he looked down at the card in his hand, then held it up—"she?"

Though his grammar caught her ear, it was his dazzling blue eyes that mesmerized her, drawing her gaze like a black hole captures light. There was no escaping them. Intelligent, contemplative, beautiful. A whole universe dwelt in those eyes.

Without further words, he led her in a dance unlike any other, not a waltz or foxtrot or cha-cha, but a series of random footfalls executed in complete silence. It unnerved her.

Finally, he spoke. "Do you believe in God?"

Startled, she drew back, but his blue eyes awaited an answer.

"Of course." She tried to follow as they stumbled across the dance floor. "Do you?"

"I don't know," he said. "I'm trying to figure it out." His forehead furrowed. "But it's like Asphalt trying to solve a differential equation."

He gazed into the air as though pondering the question. He must have seen the confusion on her face.

"Asphalt's my dog," he said, blushing, just as the music ended. He thanked her and ran off, leaving her alone in the middle of the dance floor.

For an hour, she danced with young men who talked about their cars, their clubs, their connections.

"I'm in pre-law," Chad said. "Going to join my dad's firm."

"My ride's a T-Bird," Thad said. "She's cherry."

"I'm into lacrosse," Chip said. "Go team." He held up a fist.

She'd had enough. "Chip," she said, "do you believe there's a God?"

Puzzlement twisted his face until he caught on to what must have been a joke. "Oh, sure," he said, grinning. "He's the coach."

She dropped into a folding chair against the wall and watched the dancing and laughing and puffing and flirting and thought about the boy who pondered divine existence. She sighed and gazed out the window. A lone figure sat on the low brick wall surrounding the patio. He faced the forest, his back to the building. Piercing the darkness, the ember on his cigarette glowed. A cloud of smoke billowed toward the woods.

"Want to dance?" a voice said.

She looked up. "Thank you," she said, grabbing her purse, "but I have to leave."

As she opened the door, the warm September air hit her. He still sat on the wall. As she approached him from behind, a column of smoke rose from his up-tilted face.

"Those aren't good for you," she said.

He turned his head toward her. Those blue eyes again.

"That's what my mother says."

Her mind raced for something to say. "Are you enjoying the mixer?"

He took another drag and expelled a long breath. "I am now."

Her face flushed. When he motioned for her to join him, she sat, but facing the opposite direction toward the building, her feet on the patio. His dangled over the other side, pointing into the darkness. He offered her a cigarette. She shook her head.

He nodded toward the window. "Why aren't you in there with the swells?"

She smiled. "An hour of listening to the Chads and Thads and Chips talking about themselves wore me out."

"Isn't that your clan?" he said. "I'd bet you were captain of your high school cheerleader squad."

"Certainly not." They sat inches apart on the wall, staring in opposite directions. The balmy evening breeze caressed their faces. "I was *co*-captain."

His eyes regarded her as he nodded almost imperceptibly.

They sat in silence.

"Why did you ask me about God?" she said.

He shrugged. "It's one of the things I wonder about."

"What are the other things?"

He peered deep into the forest. "Am I my brother's keeper? Is morality absolute? Are there universes inside of atoms?" He took another drag. "Or is our universe just an atom inside a larger universe?" He snubbed out the cigarette on the side of the wall, sending orange embers cascading into the grass. "If existence is a machine set in motion eons ago, is everything preordained? And if so, why should we struggle?" He gazed up at the celestial black velvet dome that showcased the sparkling diamonds of light. "Do men have free will?"

She stared, entranced. When he turned toward her, she shook her head to break the spell. "In my experience, they don't," she said, "but women do."

His gaze penetrated to her core. Then his face blossomed into a smile.

They talked for hours. Math and science fascinated him, but he would major in philosophy. She loved children and wanted to teach third grade. He wasn't religious, but the more he learned about the nature of matter, the more wondrous and mysterious the universe became. Her father wanted her to be a lawyer, but she would study education and a couple of business courses. She'd teach for ten years, save her money, and start her own school to foster confidence and independence in girls. Dave made his own wine from grapes he tended on a neighbor's arbor. He wanted to dig in the soil with his hands, to be close to the earth, grow food for his own table, lead a simple life, ponder the big questions, raise a family, love a good woman. She watched his eyes sparkle with intensity as he spoke. He was unlike anyone she had ever met, a beautiful man-boy groping with transition.

When the lights inside the dance went out, he walked her to her dorm. They saw each other every day for two months. They studied together in the library, picnicked in the grass on the quad, and spent evenings under the stars.

"That's Orion, and that's Ursa Major and Ursa Minor, and that's the North Star, and that's Sirius, the Dog Star. That light we see left eight years ago. That's when I got Asphalt." Dave's eyes shone with love. "He's always been my best friend." His calm authority and beautiful eyes filled her with peace, and she was about to suspend the above-the-waist-only rule when the trouble began.

"You're going to pledge Chi Delta?" she asked.

He stared at the ground. "*You* pledged a sorority."

"Because they're my friends."

"You have mixers. With fraternities."

"Dave, we're together. You don't have to worry about that."

But he did worry about it. His sad eyes radiated his fear of loss. So on pledge night, he buried his principles and lined up at the door of Chi Delta with twenty other freshmen hopefuls.

"They put me on the loser bench," he said the next day. "I sat there half an hour as the brothers schmoozed Thad and Chad and the rest of them. Then I walked out."

"What others think doesn't matter, Dave. *You* know who you are and *I* know who you are."

But it did matter. The next evening, he slurred his words. "Darryl snuck a case of beer into the dorm. That's good stuff. I feel a lot better."

She watched his downward spiral with dismay, unable to alter his course. He started drinking regularly, missed their library dates, and cut classes. When Asphalt died, he disappeared for three days. He withdrew from her and became guarded about expressing feelings he had once shared. He no longer talked about the big questions. He lamented the evils of society and the dark side of man's nature. A veil had fallen between them.

The final straw came just after Christmas break.

In the year 1758, Reverend Phineas T. Gladstone arrived in the wilds of central Ohio to teach Christian values to the savages. When Gladstone Academy was established on the hill above the village and named in his honor, a statue was erected atop the knoll and inscribed with his principles. *Faith, tolerance, love.* A century later, the monolith stood in the center of the women's complex, a grassy field with dorms on three sides and the dining hall on the fourth. Since half the dorm windows faced inward, the quadrangle became a stage and often attracted the hijinks of the men on campus.

So when Jennifer heard the blaring of kazoos and the banging of a washtub, she didn't even rise from her desk. Her roommate went to the window, and girls from across the hall ran in to catch the action. Jennifer shook her head and focused on her book.

The coeds giggled at the show.

"Jen," one said, "isn't that your boyfriend?"

Jennifer jumped up. Six ski-masked men marched in a circle around the statue, chanting with the discordant racket. In the center, tied to Reverend Gladstone, Dave hunched over, wearing only sneakers and a look of humiliation. Giggling girls filled the windows of the dorms surrounding the stage.

Jennifer's jaw dropped. "No, I don't think so."

The circling band became a single line and marched off the quad, leaving only naked Dave as the focal point of four hundred pairs of eyes. He turned toward the reverend in a futile attempt to cover himself, but like a theater in the round, there was no shelter.

Her roommate nodded. "Yeah, that's him."

Below their window, Doris, the matronly housemother, shuffled out the front door shaking her head. It took her five minutes to undo the knots, giving all the girls in the college a good look. When released, Dave bolted into the darkness like a wild animal whose cage door had opened, and Doris returned to the dormitory, abandoning the statue of Reverend Gladstone and his unfinished ministry to bring Christian charity to the natives.

"I finally cracked," Dave told her later. "I told this Chi Delt jock to quit hassling Darryl on the quad." Wow. Dave was never confrontational. "He came back with a van load of his friends. After Doris untied me, I had to run across campus to my dorm. I'm going to transfer at the end of the semester."

But he didn't. His father prevailed on him to "tough it out." An alumnus, he wanted Dave to be "a Gladstone man."

Instead, Dave began railing about the evils of social injustice, the corruption of power, and the "criminal" military, even though he knew his views were antithetical to her conservative nature. But she was willing to compromise, to understand his point of view.

"Can't we just accept our differences?"

"I won't abandon my principles."

"I'm not talking about pledging a fraternity, Dave. I'm talking about respecting my views."

But he couldn't. Or wouldn't. He wasn't even willing to sacrifice for *them*. His life had become about *him*. What *he* wanted. It broke her heart to lose such a remarkable friend, but she could no longer be with someone like that.

"I'm sorry, Dave. I don't think we work anymore."

He ultimately found his home with the disenfranchised, a small cadre who kept to themselves, smoked marijuana, and dressed like homeless teenagers. Dave became the king of the outcasts, the one-eyed man in the valley of the blind, seeking to right the wrongs of the world. And he used these broken people for his own selfish ends, treating them like they were children and he was some sort of cult leader. He had grown into a pudgy, shaggy, slovenly man. Instead of excelling in academics and preparing for graduation, he was spending his senior year protesting the war. And though she admired his willingness to stand up to authority—a trait she didn't share—she knew he would never support her dreams. Like Daddy didn't. No, a selfish man like that didn't fit into her plans at all.

As she watched him lead his troupe down the hill, she sighed. Such a waste.

CHAPTER 3

"It's starting," Tanya called out.

The words echoed through the old wooden house. Footsteps clattered across the floor and down the stairs. The residents assembled in the parlor, its large bay window overlooking Main Street. The proud Victorian had endured years as a small-town college rental, but decades of hard-living residents had taken their toll. Her walls and woodwork were shabby, her furnishings secondhand, and her perfume the stale musk of cigarettes and marijuana. The Grande Dame had faded into seediness.

A small black and white TV sat on a wooden crate. An overstuffed sofa with threadbare fabric filled the opposite wall. Two upholstered armchairs and several folding chairs lined the perimeter. The central piece, a large round coffee table, was littered with ashtrays, books, and beer cans.

Dave sprawled horizontally between the sofa and the coffee table, a human suspension bridge drinking a beer. Abbie leaned against him, her hand on his thigh. He was drained. Jennifer's glare of disapproval that afternoon had stabbed him like a blade.

Tanya, in the archway, called out again. "Hurry up," she said as the last stragglers filtered in. "It's on."

The TV flickered. "And now," a deep baritone oozed, "Action News at Six."

As the stern news anchor appeared, the room fell silent.

"Our lead story tonight," he began. "A Granville high school student won the blue ribbon for her prize bull, Bobo, at the Licking County Fair today. . . ."

Dave lit a cigarette. Fifteen minutes droned by. The farm report. High school wrestling. Susie Sunshine, the weather girl. Finally, a graphic of the Gladstone Arch appeared.

"In other news, Gladstone University students rallied today in protest against the ongoing conflict in Viet Nam. Protest leader Donald Guinn promised more action to come." The anchor looked up from his copy and smiled. "And now, the sports roundup. Coach Woody Hayes said today when the Buckeyes meet Nebraska this Saturday . . ."

The room was silent.

Tanya raised her palms. "That's it?"

Darryl stroked his beard. "Who's Donald Guinn?"

In the silence of their collective disappointment, the national news came on with graphic war footage of the usual carnage. Huey gunships fired rockets into the jungle. Marines dragged the limp bodies of their comrades. A Buddhist monk torched himself in a public square. Body bags aligned in perfect rows on a tarmac next to a C-130 transport formed the backdrop for the weekly death count. It was the new warehouse fire of TV news—exciting, dramatic, and photogenic—and so it aired every night.

Dave stared, sickened by the slaughter. These men weren't faceless troops. They were Eddie Thompson.

Eddie had been Dave's next-door neighbor and playmate since kindergarten. They'd frolic on the porch swing, ride their tricycles along the sidewalk, and celebrate each other's birthday every year. They shared the rites of passage through adolescence. In high school, they double dated and confided their secrets. Eddie showed him how to make wine with the grapes from the arbor that latticed up the porch. One day they would open a winery and make the finest wine in the state.

Eddie's talent as an artist was apparent early on. He was always drawing, coloring, creating. He even painted a mural in city hall their senior year. He would be famous for sure. Other boys often razzed him about his gift. "Are you a fruit, Eddie?" And Dave laughed along with them. Eddie didn't seem to mind. But after graduation, instead of art school, he joined the Marines.

Last summer, Eddie came home from the war with both arms amputated at the shoulder and a leg above the knee. He got a prosthetic leg, but with no arms to use for balance, he spent most of his time in his wheelchair.

Dave sat on Eddie's mother's porch swing with a lump in his throat, watching Eddie paint with his mouth. He painted scenes of freedom—birds soaring, clouds floating, lovers dancing. Dave knew it wasn't his fault, but he couldn't shed the guilt. Or the anger. Ignorant politicians bloviated about the tide of communism and falling dominos and sent young men into mayhem and death. This wasn't WWII. This wasn't a fight for survival. It was a civil war in a small country eight thousand miles from home. *How could our government be so stupid?* He clenched his teeth. Because it was run by petty politicians.

"In a related story," the blow-dried anchor said, "NBC News has learned that General Lewis B. Hershey, head of Selective Service, has recommended to local draft boards the revocation of student deferments for college students who deface their draft cards or interfere with military recruiting on campus."

Dave's eyes grew wide.

"Hershey said student deferments are given only to serve the national interest. Anyone who violates the Selective Service Act will be subject to immediate induction into the armed service."

They stared at each other in stunned silence.

Tanya raised her trademark finger at the screen.

"He can't do that," Darryl said. "Can he?"

"Maybe we should slow down," Abbie said.

Dave's face flushed. Bloated old men in comfortable offices in Washington sent boys to be mangled and die in the mud. This couldn't stand.

"No," he said, trying to modulate his voice. "We're not going to slow down. We're going to take it to the next level."

"Radical," Darryl said. "Let's hang him in effigy."

Dave shook his head. "We're going to occupy the administration building."

Tanya's fist shot up. "A sit-in."

Dave nodded. "We'll present our demands."

The ensemble joined in.

"Co-ed dorms."

"Beer on campus."

"No eight a.m. classes."

Dave raised his hand. "Political demands, like abolishing ROTC on campus."

"Far out."

"Or that Hershey be fired."

"Yeah."

"Or make opposition to the war official school policy." Dave fell back on the sofa and drained his beer. "I'll make a list."

"Make it tomorrow," Abbie said, squeezing his thigh. She hopped up and offered Dave her hand. He rose and followed her through a door, flipping the hanging sign from *Vacant* to *Occupied.*

As the morning sun peeked through the parlor bay window, the TV flickered an image of Wile E. Coyote, perched on a precipice, an empty Acme-Anvil-Company box nearby. Above, the anvil dangled from a crane. And below, on the canyon floor, an X marked the spot where the Road Runner pecked at a pile of birdseed.

Dave rallied the troops for their next act of civil disobedience. "We'll meet in the administration building at noon. Tanya, you call the press. Abbie, get more signs ready. And I'll work up some chants that will be dynamite on TV."

"Awesome."

Dave nodded with resolve. "We'll claim the moral high ground with the courage of our convictions."

Abbie cooed in admiration.

He held up the notepad of scribbled demands. "Non-negotiable."

"Right on," Tanya said. "I'll get T-shirts."

Darryl wandered into the room with a handful of letters. "Mail call," he said, and passed them out. "Dave." He handed him a letter.

Dave looked at the envelope. His stomach knotted.

Wile E. pulled the lever and wheezed with delight. As the anvil fell, the attached rope ensnared his foot and pulled him off his perch. Wile E. and the anvil fell together, down, down, down toward the X and the Road Runner. Wile E. floated beneath the anvil. "Uh, oh," he squeaked. Just before impact, the Road Runner took one step aside, off the X. Wile E. landed on the X in the growing shadow of the anvil. His Adam's apple bobbed with an audible gulp. He held up a tiny umbrella.

Dave inserted a finger under the flap and popped open the envelope. With trembling hands, he removed the single sheet of paper and unfolded it. His gaze crawled across the text. *Greetings from the president. In preparation of the upcoming expiration of your 2-S student deferment and consequent eligibility for induction into the Armed Forces, you are hereby directed to report for a physical examination at . . .*

The anvil flattened Wile E. and a cloud of dust billowed up.

"Beep, beep," the Road Runner said and disappeared in a puff.

Everyone roared. Except Dave. He dissolved into the overstuffed upholstery, the letter dangling in the fingers of his limp hand.

CHAPTER 4

Lt. Ron Nelson lay on his back, his face hot, heart pounding, and chest heaving in rapid breaths. The scar on his chin pulsed, and a mist of perspiration covered his bare torso. He stared at the ceiling as his breathing slowed.

"They want me to push the students through," he said.

A sigh came from the other side of the bed.

"They want me to compromise safety. Nobody will say it. They can't. But that's what they expect me to do."

The bed springs squeaked, and a naked back appeared as a young woman threw off the sheet and sat on the edge of the bed.

"The XO complained I didn't certify enough students to solo." He raised his palms. "Hell, if they're not ready, they're not ready."

The young woman sighed again and reached for a pack of Newports on the nightstand. She shook one out, lit it, and inhaled deeply.

"So what does that get me? He said I'm not a team player. What is this? Basketball? No, it's life and death. I'm not going to certify an inept student as ready to solo and let him go up and kill himself."

She snorted, took another drag, and blew a column of smoke across the bedroom.

He turned his head toward her. "Do you have to do that? It stinks up my whole apartment."

She smacked her lips, stubbed out the cigarette in the glass ashtray, and turned toward him. "When are we going to Expo 67 in Montreal? It closes soon and you promised."

"Oh, yeah," he said. "I'm not going to be able to make that."

Her voice hardened. "You promised, Ron."

"I know, but I'm getting new orders soon and have to get ready."

"So you can't take a long weekend?"

"Not with this alimony sucking me dry." He pulled the sheet off himself. "I have to get to work." He showered, shaved, and put on his flight suit. When he returned to the bedroom, she stood with hands on hips, wearing only panties, a lit cigarette hanging from her pouty mouth and a bra dangling in her hand.

"You're always complaining." She pulled on the bra and fastened it. "Your ex-wife, your job, your students. How about your attitude? Maybe that's the problem."

He stared at her. Even women no longer relieved the ache. The pleasure of sex was fleeting and the après conversation devoid of intimacy, leaving his only emotion a desire to race out like he was fleeing the scene of a hit-and-run.

He sat on the edge of the bed and pulled on his flight boots. This one wouldn't last either. And he was right. When he got home that evening, she and all her stuff had vanished. His third girlfriend in a year. Each bailed after a few months. Just as well. He'd be leaving Pensacola soon, his new orders due any day. And this time had to be a charm. After thirteen years in the Navy, he had yet to get a good flying billet. When he first earned his wings, he got a non-flying assignment, three years pushing papers around a metal desk in a Quonset hut in Maine. Then a ferry squadron out of Mississippi, flying beat-up heaps to the boneyard. Then NAS Adak, in the middle of the Aleutian Island chain.

"I'm not going," his wife had said when the orders arrived. "That's the end of the world."

When he returned after enduring eighteen months of chastity, she filed for divorce and moved in with her twenty-three-year-old boyfriend on the beach.

"You're such a downer," she had said as she packed. "You need to get over it."

It meant the incident thirteen years ago, the one he couldn't put aside, the source of all his problems.

"You need therapy." She closed the door, suitcase in hand.

No, he needed good orders.

At his current assignment at Training Squadron One, he taught students how to fly the primary trainer. And he hadn't made many friends. To his ex-wife, he was "Ron Alimony-Check," to his fellow instructors, "Mr. Personality," and to his students, "Lt. Hardass."

And while he had logged lots of flight time, a career naval aviator would want to be elsewhere after thirteen years.

Later that morning, he sat across the desk from the squadron executive officer, a commander not much older than Nelson. At thirty-seven, Nelson should have been a lieutenant commander by now, and just two years shy of full commander. But he'd remained a lieutenant for a decade with no realistic prospects of being promoted. All because of the incident. At least they let him remain in the Navy. Even damaged pilots have value, especially now with a war on.

The XO pushed a set of papers across the blotter.

His orders. Nelson held his breath. He'd requested a fighter squadron, or an attack squadron, or even P-3s. He picked up the documents.

"Fleet Composite Squadron Five? Where's that?"

"Cubi Point. The Philippines."

"Target towing?"

"Primarily. But you'll probably be doing mostly training given your background."

Nelson's face burned. He should get up and leave right now. Resign his commission and quit the Navy while still young. He sighed. And then what? Fly for some regional airline? He'd just be a glorified bus driver. No, he wanted to serve his country.

He stood and saluted. "Thank you, Commander," he said, and went home to pack.

CHAPTER 5

Dave reclined in a back-row desk. Almost horizontal, he watched the second hand on the wall clock jump from one mark to the next. His eyelids fluttered. Up front, Professor Lighthouse preened before the coeds, his beacon sweeping across barren shoals. Serious front-row students basked in the glow, scribbling notes to record each erudite observation that flashed by. But in the back, on a distant shore, the light dimmed, and the pearls of wisdom faded to a droning monologue. Dave lowered his gaze to the back of Jennifer's alabaster neck. Her ponytail bobbed as her slender fingers guided her pen across the notebook pages. He could actually feel his heart and count the beats. He had never stopped loving her, since the moment he had seen her at the freshman mixer. She smiled with the beautiful, sweet innocence of a child, but her eyes penetrated to his soul, the eyes of a knowing woman. He loved the way she threw her head back when she laughed at his wit, the way she appreciated and valued his knowledge and intelligence, his point of view, his reasoned arguments. He loved how she knew what she wanted and went after it.

And she understood him. Perhaps too well. She was class, and he was a mess. So they could never be together. They were two different people. She had been right. They "didn't work." She was wedded to her studies and her teaching future, seemingly content in the status quo, while he just wanted to survive the lunacy of the world.

He looked down at his notepad. A doodle of *The Scream* howled in pain.

A sudden commotion alerted him that class had ended. Students popped to their feet, gathered their books, and shuffled toward the door. Dave didn't stand but turned to a fellow back-row slacker.

"Hey, Brad," he said, straightening up as though a thought just occurred to him, "I heard you got a draft notice." He watched

Jennifer walk away. She glanced back as she passed through the door. "Is that right?"

"Sort of," Brad said. "They ordered me to report for my draft physical."

"Did you pass?"

"You have to be dead not to." Brad stood and gathered his books. "But I won't actually get drafted until graduation when they pull my student deferment." He started toward the door.

Dave jumped up and followed. "What about grad school?"

"They don't give deferments for grad school. Four years and that's it, unless you're going to medical school."

Dave sighed. "So what are you going to do?" he asked. "You going in?"

"Hell, no. I'm going to Canada when I graduate. Toronto, I think. It'll piss my dad off, but . . ." He shrugged.

Dave nodded. His own father often spoke with great pride of his service during *The Big One*, World War II. "Some other boy died in his place," he'd spit, anytime he heard about a draft dodger. The memory sent Dave's gaze to the floor.

"I'm going to claim political asylum," Brad said. "They don't deport anyone for draft evasion. The Canadians know it's an immoral war."

"What about your family?"

"I guess I won't see them for a while. But it's better than getting my legs blown off in the jungle. Or worse."

Dave pondered, then tried his last escape route. "What about conscientious objector status?"

"Nah, the draft boards wised up to that scam long ago. They make you prove it now. You have to belong to a pacifist church and get letters from your clergy. And I'm not Amish."

Dave hadn't been inside a church since he turned twelve.

"You can't just say you're against killing," Brad said. "Hell, who isn't against killing?" He eyed Dave. "Why are you so interested?"

Dave glanced away and shrugged.

Brad shuffled out the door. "Well, I tried everything. There's no other way out." He scowled. "And I'm sure as hell not going to claim I'm a homo."

Dave forced a laugh that came out a croak. Trapped, the only way he could avoid the Army was to enlist in a less-dangerous branch of the military. So that afternoon, he drove to Columbus and parked in an alley. With the collar turned up on his long coat and a baseball cap pulled over his eyes, he scurried into a nearby storefront. Its poster challenged passersby to *Fly Air Force.* Moments later, he pushed open the glass door, hurried out, and strode briskly down the street. Three blocks later he entered another storefront. *Serve in the National Guard,* the poster read. When leaving, he checked an address on a slip of paper and hurried to the next recruiting office. After another rejection, he straggled out past their sign. *Join the Navy and See the World.* Dave was only seeing Columbus, Ohio.

"Where were you?" Abbie stood over Dave, her hands on her hips and slender frame illuminated by the streetlight beaming through the bay window. "The sit-in bombed."

From his usual pose deep in the sofa, he tossed a just-emptied beer can into the pizza box on the table. "I was busy."

"Seven people," she said. "That's all we had. College staff moved around us like we didn't exist."

He looked up, gazing at her womanly figure.

She sighed. "Okay, okay, it's behind us. So what's our next move?" She stared at the ceiling briefly, then pointed at Dave. "There's a Navy pilot recruiter in the student union. We should picket him. They drop Napalm on babies, you know."

As her pouty lips awaited an answer, he inspected the frayed jeans clinging to the folds of her southern hemisphere and the *Ohio State* T-shirt, the o's of *Ohio* lifted by the rise of her nipples.

As he stood and took her hand, she sighed in acquiescence that the conversation was over. He led her across the room, flipped the door sign to *Occupied*, and descended the rickety basement steps. Ancient un-mortared stone walls and a potent musty odor made it more a dungeon than a cellar. A bare mattress lay in the corner.

"How about a glass of your homemade wine first?" she said.

He nodded, opened a cooler, and removed a twenty-six-ounce glass Coke bottle, its green hue masking the color of the wine inside. A cork stuck from the top of the bottle. He produced two crystal wine glasses, finery well out of place in this basement. He pulled the cork, filled the glasses, and handed one to Abbie.

"To wine," he said, holding up his glass in a toast. "One of the great pleasures of life."

As Dave swirled, smelled, and sipped slowly, Abbie downed her drink quickly.

"Yummy," she said. "This is really good." She lowered herself to the mattress and sat facing a small table. She lit a bamboo incense stick, flipped a switch on a portable record player, and set the needle on the turning disk. A scratchy sitar played. She folded her legs into the lotus position, her thumbs and forefingers forming small circles, and closed her eyes. Sounds emanated from deep within.

"Oooommm," she crooned, "oooommm."

"Abbie," Dave said, dropping to the mattress. "Is that really necessary?"

Her eyes opened lazily. "We have to summon the spirits. The vibes have to resonate."

When the vibes finally did resonate, she lit a joint, took a deep drag, and held it in. After exhaling, she offered Dave a toke.

He shook his head.

"You're a strange one, David Quinn," she said, "a philosophy major who won't share a joint. You need to reach your spiritual core. Everybody must get stoned."

Dave put his hand on her shoulder. "Abbie, philosophy is about Nietzsche and Kant and Camus." He guided her down onto the mattress. "Not Bob Dylan."

Dave found himself in a jungle clearing. The warm air, steamy and motionless, clung to his face like a gossamer web. Nearby, Skip scribbled on a pad. He wore black pajamas and a porkpie hat with a *PRESS* card protruding from the headband.

"You should choose your metaphors more carefully," Skip said. "You could be playing dominos instead."

Dave looked down. Up to his knees in a pool of quicksand and sinking fast, he reached out. "Help me." The warm goo rose up his thighs.

"I *am* helping you," Skip said. "You wanted a way out. This is a way out."

As the gritty sludge reached Dave's waist, Brad pulled up in a small, two-seater MG convertible, the trunk rack stacked high with suitcases.

"Hey, Field Marshall, how about a road trip to Yellowknife, eh?"

"Can't do it," Dave croaked. He raised his arms as he sank to his chest. The pressure built. He strained to breathe.

Skip stuck a microphone in his face. "Any final words?"

The swamp bubbled over Dave's shoulders and climbed his neck. He turned his face skyward.

Skip shrugged. "That's a wrap."

Dave's ears submerged. Sound became muffled. He gagged as the gritty oatmeal oozed into his mouth and nostrils and filled his windpipe.

He bolted upright on the mattress, gasping for air. The clammy T-shirt clung to his skin. Incense still burned as Abbie snored next to him. He reached for a cigarette, lit it, and lay back down.

Abbie twitched, then opened an eye and stared. "I sense you are not present."

Dave watched a large smoke ring wobble upward and a small one penetrate it.

She put a hand on his chest. "I feel discordant vibes. You're not living in harmony with your true nature."

He stifled a snort and took another drag.

She snuggled against him. "I know we have to stop this immoral war. But sometimes"—she traced a finger to his navel—"I think you care more about the Vietnamese than about me."

Dave rolled on his side and stubbed the cigarette out on the dirty concrete floor. "This isn't about the Vietnamese."

Her brow furrowed. "Then what's it about?"

He stood and pulled on his jeans. "It's about *me*." His face grew warm. "Don't you understand? I'm not risking my life so they can eat their fish heads and rice under a government in Saigon instead of Hanoi."

Her lower lip quivered. "You don't have to be mean."

He sighed. "Look, Abbie, I graduate in May. That's seven months. Then my deferment goes bye-bye."

She wiped a tear. "Maybe the war will be over by then."

"And if it isn't, I'm going to get drafted, and by this time next year I'll be in the jungle dodging bullets and picking leeches off my butt. Or worse, wrapped in one of those body bags." His words grew hoarse. "The most immoral thing about this war is me getting dragged into it."

She inspected his face. "I see," she said and turned her back.

He headed for the steps.

"By the way, Dave"—her voice was tight—"fish heads and rice is a Japanese dish."

CHAPTER 6

Jennifer and her roommate watched the festivities from a picnic table. Revelers filled the crowded meadow by the pond below, enjoying the fraternity-sponsored beer blast under a warm autumn sun that belied the calendar. But the once-brilliant leaves had faded to drab brown, the song birds had fallen silent, and the smell of change filled the air.

She lifted the plastic cup and took a sip of the warm beer she'd been nursing for half an hour. Jennifer didn't care for these things, certainly not as a senior. She'd rather be studying now that she was in the home stretch. But her roommate wanted to come, so Jennifer tagged along to enjoy the last beautiful day of Indian summer before the cruel Ohio winter arrived.

Two boys buzzed around them like bees seeking to track in some pollen.

"Let's go for a swim, ladies," one said.

"Yeah," another said. "Let's play Marco Polo."

"You can mount us," the first said. "On our shoulders."

The boys guffawed and gulped down more beer.

Jennifer's roommate rolled her eyes. "You boys go ahead," she said. "We'll join you later."

"How about you, Jennifer?" the first boy said. "Care for a dip?"

"Thanks, Chad." Jennifer stretched her lips across her teeth and tried to smile. "But I'm leaving soon. I have a lesson plan to prepare."

She wasn't lying. Her student teaching started on Monday. Third grade. Exactly what she'd requested. She should be preparing.

"Okay, ladies," Chad said. The boys headed down toward the lake, each tossing a football with one hand and spilling beer with the other.

Jennifer's roommate shook her head. "The boys are cute, but they get a few beers in them and they're fifteen again."

Her friend's words faded as Jennifer watched a lone figure straggle along the lakeshore. His crew, huddled around the beer table, saw him and beckoned. One held out a beer, but Dave waved him off. Another started toward the lake and gestured for him to follow. He shook his head, his eyes scanning the crowd.

His searching stopped when he saw Jennifer. He turned toward her and maneuvered through the crush of beer drinkers and beneath the flightpaths of frisbees and footballs. She looked away and back at her chattering roommate.

". . . So I told him straight out, 'Chad, I'm not interested. . . .'"

Dave appeared behind the roommate, standing in silence, his shoulders hunched and his hands stuffed into his pockets.

Jennifer's gaze locked onto his beautiful blue eyes. But they no longer twinkled. She shook herself. *Stop it.*

The roommate saw the shudder and stopped talking. She turned to follow Jennifer's gaze over her shoulder to Dave.

She looked back at Jennifer, then again at Dave, and the silent stare between them.

"I think I'll take a dip," she said, rising.

Jennifer grabbed her wrist, but she gently twisted free.

"See you later," she said and scurried off.

Dave broke Jennifer's gaze and stared at the ground. Finally, he took a deep breath. "How are you?"

She crossed her arms. "Fine." She nodded toward his friends splashing in the lake. "Why aren't you down there?"

"I don't like the water. You know that."

She did. She knew a lot about him. Brilliant but directionless, witty but humorless, and wasteful of precious time, he challenged authority rather than using his God-given talents to prepare for the real world.

"So how's student teaching?" he said.

"I start Monday. Third grade."

"Just what you hoped for."

Jennifer tightened her lips. "Dave, what do you want?"

His gaze rose from the ground, his eyes wrinkled in pain. "I just took my draft physical, Jen."

She caught her breath and reached out to touch his arm but thought better of it and withdrew.

"I'm going to be drafted in June. Right after graduation."

She clasped her hands together, blinked back the rising tears, and cleared her throat. "What are you going to do?"

"I don't know. I've tried everything. Navy and Air Force officer candidate schools are full. The National Guard is full. The Coast Guard is full. Even the enlisted ranks are all full. Everyone's trying to avoid the Army. And the jungle."

"Why don't you talk to your friends about it?"

He stared at Jennifer. "That *is* what I'm doing."

She shook her head. "We're two very different people now."

"Yeah," he said, staring at his shoes.

"Look," she said, "you'll just have to put your plans on hold for a while, that's all. It's only a speed bump."

"No, it's a head-on crash. Two hundred soldiers die each week." He ran his hands through his hair. "I don't want to end up like Eddie Thompson."

She shrugged.

"My buddy in high school who joined the Marines. He came home last summer, Jen. He left two arms and a leg in Viet Nam." His eyes moistened and he turned away. "Sorry."

She swallowed hard. She couldn't allow herself to be drawn in. He wasn't her responsibility. She had spent her years here preparing for her future and had made sacrifices. Yes, it wasn't fair to be drafted. But she was going it alone. Surely, he could find a way.

He took several deep breaths, his face hidden from her view. "They're going to draft me, Jen. I don't know what to do."

Damn him. She sighed. "David, I saw a Navy recruiter in the student union. They must want people."

He turned back toward her. "That's for naval aviation. Pilots."

"So?"

"A pilot? Are you kidding?"

"David, you can do anything you set your mind to." They watched each other in silence. "I have to go," she said, rising. "You should be with your friends."

He turned to leave, shaking his head. "Each of us is alone, Jennifer."

It was a shame he had gone off the deep end. She would never meet anyone like him again.

CHAPTER 7

The student union sang with conversation and laughter. The aroma of hamburgers sizzling on the canteen grill enticed the noontime crowd as students checked their mailboxes, browsed the small bookstore, or just relaxed between classes. On the new color television, Batman punished his foes with each "WHAM" and "POW." In TV-land, virtue still triumphed over evil.

Dave leaned against a column, watching the small table at the top of the stairs, strategically placed to greet arriving students. A lone Navy lieutenant sat erect in his dress blue uniform, smiling pleasantly, his hands folded on the table. Multi-colored ribbons decorated his chest, capped by a pair of golden naval aviator wings. Small piles of neatly organized brochures offered information, while the easel behind showcased a poster of an F-4 Phantom jet and a handsome young officer with his ultra-cool aviator sunglasses, a shard of white-hot light reflected by the dark lens. Two coeds stood near the table, giggling and playing with their hair. The young lieutenant laughed affably.

Dave took a deep breath and approached.

"Good afternoon," the lieutenant said, rising and offering his hand. "Lieutenant Grimes. May I offer you some information about the program?"

"No thanks," Dave said. "I'm just curious about something." He paused as a student passed nearby. "How come you guys are still hiring when no one else is?"

The lieutenant smiled. "Our standards are high. An applicant must pass a thorough physical exam. He must have perfect eyesight, excellent coordination and reflexes, and pass tests for flight aptitude and psychological fitness. Very few qualify." The officer seamlessly segued into his five-minute talk and finished with a practiced close.

"It's tough, but the benefits are well worth it." He glanced at the admiring coeds. "Here. Take a brochure. I'm here all week."

Dave did take a brochure and came back the next day for the lieutenant's masterful pitch.

"First, we send you up to Naval Air Station Grosse Ile, near Detroit, for your physical and psychological tests. If you qualify, you're sworn in for a six-year commitment. After graduation, you start Aviation Officer's Candidate School at NAS Pensacola. In eleven weeks, you are commissioned an ensign. After a year or more of flight training, you get your wings and first fleet assignment." He closed the pitch with a sweetener. "After your six-year hitch is up, you can get on with the airlines and fly 707 jets to London. The airlines are dying for Navy pilots. It's a sweet deal, and you know how those stewardesses are." The lieutenant was smooth. He could sell hair gel to a bald man. But the tricky part came when he asked, "Any questions?"

Dave had only one, but asking it was delicate. "If flight training is so hard, what happens if someone doesn't complete it?"

The lieutenant's brow furrowed. "He gets assigned some trivial post and usually an early release. The Navy needs pilots, not laundry and morale officers."

And so, that being the right answer, Dave found himself at NAS Grosse Ile, clad only in boxer shorts and socks.

"On the scale," the Navy nurse said. When he stepped up, she slid the counterweight along the bar. She pushed it again. And again. She peered at him over her glasses, cocked an eyebrow, and wrote on her clipboard. She strangled his bicep with a blood pressure cuff, openly displayed a huge needle about to draw his blood, and handed him a plastic cup with a curt, "You know the drill."

In a soundproof box, Dave donned headphones and pressed the button with each chirp and beep he heard. He read the lines on the eye chart, covering the right eye, then the left. "Want me to cover both?" he said. The bored technician's face didn't twitch. Dave opened the book of color blindness circles. "Forty-two, sixty-seven," he said, reading the numbers formed by pastel bubbles hidden within the gray.

"Deep breath," the doctor said. Dave shivered as the cold stethoscope moved across his back. The doctor thumped and listened, tapped Dave's knees for reflexes, and manipulated his limbs for flexibility. He shined a light into Dave's eyes, ears, and throat, inspecting every orifice. "Drop your shorts, please."

When the acceptance letter came, Dave headed for his swearing in. The décor of the small office shouted *military*—a metal desk, gray file cabinet, drab green walls. An American flag stood in the corner, gold fringe gilding the red, white, and blue. Sitting on a hard metal chair, he put his elbows on his knees, dropped his head into his hands, and expelled a long, slow breath. The door opened and a thirtyish lieutenant commander bounded in. Dave leaped to his feet.

"David Quinn?" the officer said with a smile, grabbing Dave's hand and pumping it with the vigor of a long-lost comrade. "You're a lucky man. I applied for aviation but failed the physical." He pointed to his glasses. "It's a hell of a program."

"Yes, I'm very excited." Dave fidgeted with his class ring. "My dad was Navy in the war."

"He must be very proud."

Dave turned his gaze to the floor. "He is." When he had called his father to break the news that he wouldn't be joining him at the insurance agency, the old man was thrilled.

"Son," he said, "don't worry about that. Your mother and I couldn't be prouder."

The officer put his hand on Dave's shoulder. "Shall we begin?"

Dave wrung his hands, cold despite the heated room.

The two men stood rigidly, facing each other, and raised their right hands.

The officer read from a notecard. "I, state your name."

"I, David L. Quinn . . ."

". . . do solemnly swear . . ."

Dave stammered, ". . . do solemnly swear . . ."

". . . that I will support and defend the Constitution of the United States against all enemies, foreign and domestic . . ."

Dave's mind raced as he repeated the oath. ". . . that I will bear true faith and allegiance to the same . . ." He saw his father, Chief Petty Officer Leonard Quinn, USN, in dress uniform on the deck of the USS Leon as she steamed into San Diego harbor in September 1945. ". . . and that I will obey the orders of the president of the United States . . ." He saw Jennifer leaning against the oak, arms crossed and slowly shaking her head. ". . . and the orders of the officers appointed over me . . ." He saw Eddie Thompson, imprisoned in his own body, his mother wheeling him down the sidewalk.

"So help me God," the officer said.

Dave swallowed hard. What other choice did he have?

"So help me God."

"Because I'm tired, Abbie. Tired of fighting everybody and everything." A fresh blanket of snow outside the bay window reflected the gray February sky into the parlor. "I just want to be left alone. I don't want to die in the jungle. I don't want to peddle life insurance. I don't want to be surrounded by the Thads and Chads and all the other benighted yahoos around here. I want to live on a small farm, to grow things, to live in nature. I want to be content. Aren't I entitled to that?"

"You mean like a commune?" Abbie said.

Dave nodded. "Only without the people."

"So that's why you signed up for Navy flight training?"

"Yes," he said, holding up his enlistment papers. "That gets me through the not-dying-in-the-jungle part."

"You? A naval aviator?"

"That's what I signed up for."

"But you can't be a Navy pilot. You hate the military." She thought for a moment. "And what about dropping Napalm on babies?"

"Don't worry, Abbie. I'll never see the inside of an airplane."

"But you just said—"

"I said I *signed up*."

"I don't understand. Did you join the Navy or not?"

"Look, naval aviation is the only program I could get into. So I go down to Pensacola for a few months and get commissioned an ensign. Then I wash out of flight training and spend a few years in some cushy stateside assignment. Then I get out and can resume my life."

"Oh." Her face contorted in confusion. "But you said we stand up for what we believe. What about the courage of our convictions?"

Dave's face grew hot. Why couldn't she understand? "Listen, Abbie, it's simple. I joined the Navy so there'd be no Army, no jungle, no body bag." He threw the papers on the table. "Problem solved."

She appeared near tears. "And the moral high ground?"

He shook his head and collapsed on the sofa. "That's easy to say if you can't be drafted."

They sat in silence for minutes. Finally, he sighed. "I'm sorry." He stood and offered his hand.

She didn't move. "I don't think so."

He stared at her.

"Find yourself another girlfriend." She looked up. "In ROTC."

His brow furrowed. "There are no girls in ROTC."

"I know."

CHAPTER 8

Julio Garcia leaned out the kitchen window, trying to catch the breeze. It was hot, as hot as San Antonio could be in July. His mama's two-bedroom, subsidized apartment had no air conditioning, or cross ventilation, or even screens. And a dip in the nearest public pool required a two-mile walk. His damp shirt clung to his torso.

From his third-floor perch, he watched the spot on the horizon grow into a Braniff Airways 727. The kitchen crockery rattled as the commercial jet roared overhead, clearing the building by several hundred feet on its approach to San Antonio International just across the highway. Julio grabbed his pack and kissed his mother splayed on the sofa.

"I'm off to work, Mama."

He'd worked at Whataburger part time after school since he'd turned fifteen, and full time in the summer since Mama lost her maid job at La Quinta. She seldom moved now, watching whatever the grainy black-and-white TV offered, too tired even to get up to change the channel.

"Julito, turn it to five for me. Gomer Pyle is on."

Though *Julio* everywhere else, in Mama's house he was *Julito.*

He spun the dial.

"Gracias, hijo." She smiled. "Papa would have liked this show."

"Papa was Army. He didn't like Marines."

She shrugged. "What's the difference?"

He shook his head. "It doesn't matter, Mama." He picked up his keys. "I have to get back to work." He always came home on his break to bring her dinner. The manager didn't mind. Everyone took free food home for their families.

Julio looked at her, unmoving on the sofa, her full figure straining against the huge house dress trying to contain it, and her ankles like water balloons about to burst. It broke his heart.

"Mama, are you taking your insulin?"

She nodded. "Si." Then shrugged. "Sometimes." She smacked her lips. "It's expensive."

"I don't want to lose you too, Mama."

"I'll be okay. I just need to drop some weight, that's all."

He couldn't bear to see her like this anymore. It was time to do it. He took a deep breath and sat beside her. "Mama, I'm going to quit school and work full time." He hurried to give the full pitch. "We need the money. For your medicine, for healthy food, and for a decent home." He tried to sound like he didn't require her permission.

"No." She left no room for negotiation. "You only have one year left. You're going to finish high school."

"But I can work full time year-round if I don't go back in the fall."

"If you quit, they'll draft you."

"I'm seventeen, Mama. They won't draft me until I'm eighteen. I don't even have a draft card yet." He took her hand. "Besides, *you* didn't finish school. And Papa didn't either."

"And he worked himself to death. I want more for you, Julito. You can be anything you choose. I want you to get an education. To make something of your life." She dropped her hand on her chest. "Not like me." She swept her arm across the room. "Not like this."

He knew he'd lost the battle.

She lifted his hand and kissed it. "My special angel, Julito. I wish you would believe in yourself like I do."

CHAPTER 9

Surrendering to the July heat of the gulf coast, the cab's rattling air conditioner blew a temperate, cigarette-reeking wind against Dave's face as they cruised past a landscape of gas stations, strip malls, and fast food joints.

"You're following in a great tradition, son," the cabbie said, looking at him in the mirror. "You must be very proud."

He sounded like Dave's father, who had been near tears with pride. Though not a hugger, he bear-hugged Dave at the departure gate. "Be safe," he said.

The memory brought a lump to Dave's throat as he watched the passing show—a tavern, a pawn shop, a rundown motel with a car pointing accusingly at each unit. He swallowed hard. This wasn't his fault. He had been trapped by an immoral system and just did what he had to do.

Fluttering red, white, and blue pennants lured the innocent into a buy-here-pay-here used car lot. Just beyond stood the guard gate beneath the sign *Pensacola Naval Air Station.* The cab slowed. Beside the road, a disheveled man held a placard demanding *End the War Now.*

"Hippie freak," the cabbie spit as he pulled up to the gate.

Though Dave's hair still touched his shoulders, he was clean shaven and wore loafers, slacks, and a collared sports shirt that smelled department-store fresh. He held up a copy of his orders for the Marine guard, who waved them through.

"NAS Pensacola," the cabbie sighed as though it were a lover. "The cradle of naval aviation." He nodded toward a stone monolith that supported a banked fighter jet, pointed heavenward as if in a celestial climb. Gold lettering spelled out *Blue Angels* on the aircraft's sky-blue fuselage. "That's the Tiger," he said. "The F11 Tiger. That's what the Blues fly. But I'm sure you know that."

Dave shrugged. The cabbie hadn't stopped talking since the airport.

"That was after my time," he said. "I worked on the Corsair. Quit school my senior year and signed up the day after Pearl Harbor."

The landscape transformed to a wide expanse of greenery. They passed stately brick buildings with white Grecian columns and manicured lawns, an Olympic-sized swimming pool, and a movie theater with *The Green Berets* on its marquee. A squad of uniformed men marched smartly on the parade grounds before an empty grandstand. A chapel, a barber shop, and a golf course glided by. The bachelor officers' quarters rested amid a banyan-tree-shaded garden and tennis courts. The tightness in Dave's shoulders began to abate.

Jet aircraft roared overhead, landing and taking off at Sherman Field to the west. A helicopter touched down on a concrete pad outside a huge hangar, where other aircraft sat in various states of disassembly as maintenance crews swarmed over them. As they passed the officers' club, a laughing couple emerged from the classic brick structure. A young ensign paused with his female companion at the top of the broad steps, his white uniform pristine, and slipped on his aviator shades. She took his arm and they hurried down the steps. Dave nodded his approval. This wouldn't be so bad.

Obsolete aircraft, cocooned in a sealant against the salt spray, lined the seawall, awaiting transport to their final resting place. Beyond the wall lay a vast expanse of sugar-white beach. In the brochure, attractive, tan young people frolicked in the surf and played volleyball in sand so fine it was said to squeak against each footfall. Not in the brochure was the squad of sweating men jogging in formation. These men didn't smile. They looked neither left nor right as they struggled through that soft, white sand. As the cab cruised by the obstacle course, Dave watched men drag themselves over plank walls, across log bridges, and under strands of barbed wire. One collapsed, and two others picked him up by the armpits and dragged him along.

Outside a structure marked *Survival Pool*, twenty men stood in line, suited up and awaiting their trials. They bore zombie-like glazed eyes and the slack expressions of defeated men. One pair of eyes met his. Dave stared into a face of hopelessness, and a shiver rippled through him.

As the cab turned onto a side road, activity abruptly subsided. Dave saw no marching, no traffic, and no aircraft, only vacant lots with wilting weeds and sand shadows of now-gone barracks. The cabbie pointed to a building standing alone. They drifted to a stop before the faded green, two-story wooden structure. Plank stairs led to the front door, where a lone soldier sat at a table.

Dave gawked at the curled shingle roof, warped steps, and unkempt sandlot. Encircle it with barbed wire and it could have been a POW barracks.

Dave shook his head. "This isn't it." He looked down at his orders. *Indoctrination Battalion, NAS Pensacola.* He held up the brochure showing a stately brick edifice with white columns. "I'm going to pilot training. For officers."

The cabbie threw an elbow over the seatback and glanced at the picture. "That's HQ, where the brass work." He turned his head. "And *that*," he said, nodding toward the sagging structure, "is INDOC."

Dave's temples throbbed as he stared at the claptrap dump. This might be worse than he thought. He handed the cabbie the fare, popped open the door, and stepped onto the pavement. The moist July heat enveloped him. He dragged out his suitcase and slung the guitar over his back.

"Chin up, son," the cab driver said through the window. "In a year and a half, you'll have your wings." He gave Dave a two-fingered salute from his forehead as he pulled away.

Dave turned, crossed the lot, and climbed the steps. The place looked even worse close up, and he could hear noise from inside. Great. No sound insulation. And though sweating before he reached the table, he decided not to make a fuss. Complaining to this soldier would be a waste of breath, like berating a store cashier about corporate policy.

"I'm David Quinn. Is this *officer* training? For pilots?"

"Yes, sir," the soldier said. He scribbled on the clipboard, peeled back a label, and handed it to Dave. The name tag read *Hello, My Name Is . . .* with *Quinn* inked in. Cheerful birthday balloons adorned one corner. Dave slapped it on his chest, smoothing it down to make sure his name was clear.

The soldier opened the metal box, rifled through it, removed a chain with two small medallions, and handed it to Dave. "Your dog tags, sir."

Dave read the inscription. *Quinn, David L. Serial No. 595923.* He looked up. "I'm supposed to wear this?"

"Oh, yes, sir. It's required," the soldier said. "To identify you in case anything should, you know, *happen.*" He closed the box, slid the pen onto the clipboard, and stood. "Plan to serenade the ladies?" He nodded toward Dave's guitar.

Was this guy playing with him? Dave may have just arrived, but he knew the military pecking order. An officer candidate must outrank an enlisted man.

"I do just fine with the ladies, *soldier.*"

"I see," the man said. "Well, shall we get started?"

Dave nodded his assent as they turned toward the door.

The man turned back. "Oh, and sir. I'm not a soldier. I'm a Marine." He pointed to the chevron on his sleeve. "Gunnery Sergeant Walker, United States Marine Corps. I'll be your DI, your drill instructor, for the next eleven weeks."

Dave blinked. Uh oh.

Walker reached for the doorknob. "Please, sir, after you."

Dave stepped toward the door.

"And, sir—"

Dave turned to face a wicked smile and a steely glare that bore into him.

"Welcome to the United States Navy."

CHAPTER 10

The door opened to a blast of locker-room pungent air and the sound of pandemonium. A young man as rigid as a post yelled, "Sir, this candidate did not eyeball the drill instructor, sir."

Another grunted out pushups on the floor. A third threw his back against the wall with a force that shook the building. His eyes bore the glaze Dave had seen earlier. Several dozen others with shaggy hair and sweaty civilian clothes flailed their bodies about and stammered incoherently to the barking of skin-headed, gun-barrel-thin, immaculately uniformed Marine drill instructors.

"You will stand at attention when you speak to me, candidate."

"The first word out of your mouth is 'sir,' candidate."

"You will not eyeball me, candidate."

Like a flock of terrified sheep under the nonstop commands of howling wolves, men raced about, or stood petrified at attention, or labored under physical punishment.

Dave gaped at the chaotic scene, then turned back to Walker. "Maybe I should just go to my room, Sergeant."

"You will address me as 'sir,' candidate," Walker said. "And you will stand at attention in my presence."

"What?"

Walker stepped forward, invading Dave's body space, his nose two inches from Dave's. "Stand at attention when you address me, candidate."

Dave stumbled back a step. What the blazes? He wasn't some seventeen-year-old high school dropout. He had graduated college and would soon be a naval officer. "I beg your pardon, Sergeant?"

"My pardon is the least of your worries, candidate. You will obey my orders, immediately and without question. Now stand at attention."

Dave involuntarily stiffened. He didn't take this kind of abuse from fraternity jocks, why should he take it from this guy?

"For the next eleven weeks, I own you, candidate."

The corners of Dave's mouth lifted into a smirk. So that's how it was. Psychology 101. This hillbilly thought he could play mind games with David Quinn? *Well, bring it on.*

Walker moved even closer. This time, Dave didn't yield an inch. He may have even tilted forward.

"And you will address me as 'sir' for the duration of your training."

Dave nodded. "Okay."

"WHAT?"

"Okay, *sir.*" The "sir" oozed contempt.

Walker's eyes widened. "The first word I want to hear out of your scummy sewer is 'sir.' Do you understand that, *can-di-date*?" He enunciated each syllable.

"Yes, sir?"

"WRONG! The first word is 'sir.' The proper response is 'sir, yes sir.' Can you manage that, maggot?"

"Sir, yes sir," Dave said in a monotone.

"Stand at attention when you address me, candidate," Walker shouted, his nose almost touching Dave's.

Dave straightened his spine as he watched the man's face furrow and redden. Maybe he'd stroke out.

"You will not eyeball me, candidate."

Dave looked away.

"And pull in that gut."

Dave glanced down, sucked in his stomach, and glanced back at the drill instructor.

"Why are you eyeballing me again?" he said. "Are you in love with me, candidate?"

"Sir, no sir. I am not in love with you." *What a jackass.*

"Ewe? Did you call me a ewe? Do you know what a ewe is, candidate?"

"Sir, yes sir. It's a pronoun."

"A ewe is a female sheep! Do I look like a ewe, candidate?"

"Sir, no sir, you don't." He looked like an angry squirrel.

"Ewe?" Walker shook his head. "Give me twenty."

Dave did not move.

"*Pushups*, candidate," Walker said slowly as though speaking to a child. "Get down on the deck and give me twenty pushups. Comprendo?"

Dave lowered himself to the floor.

"And count them off."

Dave rose onto his hands and toes, his buttocks high in the air. He lowered his chest to the floor.

"Jesus," Walker said. "Have you ever done a pushup, candidate?"

"Sir, yes sir." Dave counted. "One—"

"You will refer to me as 'the drill instructor.'"

". . . two . . ."

"And to yourself as 'this candidate.'"

". . . three . . ." Dave's arms started quivering.

"Do you understand, candidate?"

"Sir, yes sir." Halfway through his fourth pushup, Dave collapsed onto the floor with a grunt.

Walker stood over him, hands on his hips, shaking his head. "Get up."

Dave struggled to his feet. His heart pounded.

"Get over there." Walker dismissed him with a wave of the hand.

As Walker wandered off, Dave inserted himself into a row of candidates, their backs braced firmly against the wall. They stood silently with eyes forward. Dave looked left, then right, then across the room. Walker appeared in front of him. "Are you eyeballing me again, candidate?"

"Sir, no sir."

Walker glanced at the ballooned name tag of the next candidate, standing pressed against the wall and apparently several hours senior to Dave. "Did he eyeball me, candidate Titus?"

Staring in an unfocused gaze, Titus called out, "Sir, this candidate did not see that candidate eyeballing the drill instructor, sir."

Walker grunted and walked away, leaving the two unmoving men. A few seconds passed in silence.

"Thanks," Dave whispered.

"Shut up, asshole," Titus hissed through unmoving lips.

Walker reappeared in Titus's face. "Tell me, candidate, did I give you permission to speak?"

"Sir, no sir," Titus called out.

"I didn't think so. Give me twenty."

Dave smiled as Tight Ass dropped to the floor into pushup position in one fluid motion and called out. "One, two, three . . ." Dave stood mute and motionless, his back braced against the wall.

"What are you smirking about?" Walker said. "Get down there with him."

". . . nineteen, twenty." Tight Ass jumped up and resumed his position, his chest heaving.

Dave managed to grunt out six.

Dave's shoulders drooped under the nonstop assault. A deep ache permeated every muscle. His eyes unfocused, he could feel the heat of Walker's face hovering near his.

"Brace me, candidate," Walker yelled.

Dave threw his back against the wall with the little energy he could muster. A three-hour barrage of physical, emotional, and verbal abuse had left him exhausted. His physical resolve had abandoned him first. Hours of racing back and forth across the building, grunting out pushups, and slamming his back against the wall left him drained. His arms dangled at his sides. His neck muscles quivered as though supporting a bowling ball. His calves threatened to spasm into searing cramps at any moment, and his shoulder blades and lower back muscles weren't far behind. A throbbing headache pounded his temples. Had he not been so weakened physically, he might have been better able to ward off the psychological abuse for the hot air he knew it to be. But he no longer thought of Psych 101, or mind games, or Stockholm syndrome where hostages mentally ally with their captors. He thought only of the overwhelming fatigue that enveloped him.

Dave became aware of Tight Ass grunting out pushups. Walker's face came into focus.

"For Christ's sake, candidate, stand at attention. You're bent over like my grandmother. Keep your back straight, feet at a forty-five-degree angle, fingers curled like you're holding a roll of dimes."

When Dave forced his hunched shoulders to straighten, his neck knotted.

"Do not lock your legs, or you'll faint on a hot grinder." He looked down at Dave's feet. "Do you know what forty-five means?"

Dave struggled to maintain his sense of self. *The drill instructor's IQ*. And with that final thought, the spark of rebellion died. He just wanted to be swallowed up by some place cool and quiet and dark.

"Sir, yes sir," he said as Tight Ass leaped to his feet.

"See how it's done, candidate," Walker said. "If you can't hack it here, I think you might want to D-O-R right now and save yourself and everyone else a lot of trouble." He turned. "What do you think, Titus? Should candidate Quinn D-O-R?"

"Sir, this candidate has no opinion on whether candidate Quinn should D-O-R, sir."

"How about it, candidate?" Walker said to Dave. "Two of your classmates have already quit. One didn't last thirty minutes. Want to be third? Should I get the paperwork?"

Dave knew he could "drop on request" at any time. Aviation was a voluntary program. But to quit before commissioning would send him to the bottom of the enlisted ranks, and he would spend his Navy days chipping paint and swabbing the deck instead of relaxing in the officers' club. Not a barrel of laughs, but at least he would have avoided getting shot in the jungle. Maybe he *should* quit. After all, the recruiter had misled him. Sure, he had expected discipline and physical exercise. But he also expected respect, not insulting and physically abusive treatment. If this was how the Navy trains officers, he didn't want any part of it. Plus, exhausted after several hours, how could he suffer eleven weeks of this?

He remembered psych experiments that showed a subject could endure more pain if given a button to press that would end it. Up to now, knowing he could quit had made it tolerable, but he approached the breaking point. He could barely stand up. Anything to end this. His thumb hovered over the button. Yes, he would quit. As the words of surrender began to form, his eyes focused. Walker was smirking. A shudder coursed through Dave. He stiffened his spine and hardened his face.

"No."

Walker's nose moved to within an inch of Dave's face. "No?" he whispered. "No what?"

"No, you won't make me D-O-R."

Walker smiled. "Ewe?"

CHAPTER 11

Rays of sunlight filtered through billowing curtains into the bed chamber. White silk sheets lay tousled on the four-poster. A dozen pillows were scattered about, and a satin comforter cascaded from the bed. Dave's chest heaved as he lay gasping, his naked body entangled with Jennifer's. His skin glistened and his muscles ached. He would savor the long sleep that followed.

Her lips came to his ear. "I love you, David," she purred.

He gazed into her eyes. "And I love you."

Her loving eyes morphed into a venomous leer. Her sweet face contorted into a satanic fury. Her lips parted to the stench of hell. She shrieked.

"EWE?"

Dave whacked his head on the bunk above as he bolted upright to the blaring bugle.

"Reveille, reveille, reveille," a voice announced, "all hands hit the deck." Harsh lights blasted on, and men leaped from their bunks. It was zero five twenty. "Morning calisthenics begin on the grinder in two minutes," the loudspeaker commanded.

The building came alive with feet hitting the floor throughout the wooden structure. As Dave swung his legs off the bunk, the man above landed hard on the floor, his size-fourteen feet barely missing Dave.

"Hey, watch it, Sasquatch."

From the other bunkbed, Tight Ass descended as gracefully as an acrobat. The men jumped into their poopie suits—green one-piece coveralls—pulled on their boots, and raced into the hall like a tributary joining a river of green cockroaches fleeing the light. They poured out the back door into the darkness and onto the asphalt "grinder" behind the barracks. Weeds grew through the crumbling blacktop of the former parking lot.

Sergeant Walker appeared pristine, his Smokey-the-Bear cap tilted jauntily forward and a whistle between his lips. By contrast, the officer candidates of indoctrination battalion resembled the cast of a prisoner-of-war movie.

Dave's third roommate was the last man out the door. His sleeves covered his hands, and the legs of his poopie suit draped onto his boots. A chubby boy, Stump barely met the five-foot-two minimum height requirement. The ill-fitting garments had been issued their first evening in this hellhole, distributed with the same frenetic pace as the other activity around here, without great care as to precise fitting. Three sizes fit all. Small, medium, and large. Dave's naked wrists and ankles belied that claim and made his appearance as demeaning as his treatment.

"We will start with jumping jacks," Walker said. "Ready, begin." He called out the cadence.

Dave jumped up and down, flailing his arms. Despite exerting the minimum effort possible, he pulled a muscle in his shoulder and winced but continued flapping his arms like a bird with a broken wing.

"Next," Walker said, "pushups. Assume the position."

Dave dropped to the ground along with thirty-nine others. The warm, rough asphalt pressed into his tender palms. Yesterday's sun still radiated its heat from the black surface, bathing his face in its caustic fumes. Bottoming out overnight at eighty-two degrees, the temperature would soon rise with the dawn. Dave's head throbbed.

Walker called the pace for twenty pushups. "One . . . two . . . three. . ."

Dave collapsed at twelve.

The men jumped to their feet for squat thrusts, then back on the deck for sit ups, and again to their feet for more jumping jacks. If toddlers were six feet tall, this chaos could have been a pre-school recess. After fifteen minutes, they raced back into the building.

Dave ran toward the head, his bladder aching. He found the room packed and squeezed in. He recoiled as acrid fumes of urine engulfed him, his eyes tearing to ease the sting. Long metal troughs lined the walls as urinals. Men stood before them, squeezed together like piglets competing for a teat. Dave wiggled his way between two others.

He fumbled with the fly buttons. "Christ," he muttered, "not even a zipper."

A spray of urine splattered onto the green fabric. Dave grimaced and logged yet another indignity in the great tally book of his mind. But his revenge would be all the sweeter when he got his commission, then dropped out of flight school. They could feed him, clothe him, and train him, but they'd get no return on investment from David Quinn.

"Form up into four columns," Walker called out. "Squatty bodies forward, tall units aft."

Forty men shuffled about the grinder, arranging themselves by height into a four-by-ten rectangle.

"All right, ladies, we're going to chow. Let's see if we can get this gaggle to the mess hall in one piece," he said. "Battalion, forward, march. Left, right, left, right . . ."

The mob stumbled forward in a cascade of footfalls, more like the random popping of corn than the beat of a Sousa march. They moved along the asphalt road, already warmed by the rising morning sun. Dave's boots rubbed against his feet. At the chow hall, the men lined up single file.

"Close up ranks," Walker commanded. "Toe to heel."

As eighty feet shuffled forward, the line shortened by half.

"Not enough," Walker said. "Make that man in front of you smile."

Rapid-fire shuffling further compressed the line until boots touched toe to heel, leaving scant clearance for each man's body.

"Christ," Tight Ass muttered as Dave's beer belly pressed against his back.

Mercifully, Sasquatch stood behind Dave, his gargantuan feet keeping his torso at bay.

When Walker gave the order, the men hurried through the chow line, piling food on their metal trays. They sat at long tables and ate in silence.

After a few minutes, Walker called out, "Indoctrination battalion, form up."

Dave leaped up from his half-finished meal. From then on, he wolfed down his food like an animal in the wild. Everything in indoctrination battalion appeared designed to degrade and humiliate—the meals, the uniform, the haircut.

"In the chair, Jesus," Walker said as they stood heel to toe in yet another nondescript building, Dave's shoulder-length hair limp and damp in the July heat.

Dave got it. Jesus. Long hair. Quite the wit, this skin-headed hillbilly. Dave stepped up and popped into the chair. He'd be damned if Walker would win any mind games. The barber, a civilian about fifty, looked bored. This was Dave's opportunity to mess with Walker.

"I understand this might be non-regulation," Dave said, loud enough for Walker to hear, tousling his mane, "but leave it a little longer on top. I like to comb it back. Oh, and block the neck. I don't like it tapered."

Walker stood at parade rest near the door, watching.

His electric trimmers in midair and his face a stone wall, the barber paused. "Anything else?"

"Since you asked," Dave said, his eyes locked on Walker, "could you powder the back of my neck after you razor? I don't care for the alcohol-based aftershaves. I have sensitive skin."

"Yes, sir," the barber said as his thumb flipped the switch. When he placed the device against Dave's forehead, the loud buzz in Dave's ears became a vibration in his skull. With one sweeping motion, the barber ran the shears straight back, from forehead to nape of the neck, mowing a two-inch-wide swath through Dave's glorious mane. A thick tangle of hair fell to the floor. Dave watched his fellow candidates' eyes widen. Without pause, the barber cut a second swath from forehead to neck. More hair fell. Then another. And another. Within thirty seconds, the wall mirror reflected a bald Dave, his white scalp defined by a golden tan face.

"Next," the barber called out.

Dave ran his hand over the top of his prickly head. "Nice job," he said with a nod. "Thanks."

"Out of the chair, Jesus," Walker called, and the next man sat.

Dave watched fur fly as the old man wielded his clippers with the skill of a champion Scottish sheep shearer.

Twenty minutes later on the cross-country course, forty bouncing scalps marinated in the morning sun. Dave jogged near the end of the pack. With each step, the soft sand surrounded his boot and clutched it like clay. His calves ached and thighs burned. He gasped in the ninety-degree air. His sweat-drenched coveralls clung to his skin, pulling against every movement. Vessels throbbed in his head and a pain stabbed his side, but it didn't matter. That prick Walker wouldn't beat him.

Dave crossed the finish line, bent over, hands on thighs, and gulped the air. Stump staggered across the line dead last and collapsed onto his knees.

With a heaving chest and a scarlet complexion, he looked up at Dave. "Do you think we'll get a break after lunch?" He smiled. Gasping for breath, he actually smiled.

Dave shook his head. This man would never survive.

On the obstacle course, Dave's triceps quivered and heart pounded as he pulled the knotted rope, struggling to hoist himself over the wall. Tight Ass sailed to the top like a pole vaulter and stopped to pull Stump up while Sasquatch pushed from beneath. Dave struggled past them over the wall, bruising his chest and legs, and staggered on. He traversed a log crossing a shallow ravine, lost his balance, fell, and tried again. He danced through a field of tires, scraped his back slithering under barbed wire strung twelve inches from the ground, and struggled through the obstacle course in twenty minutes. Tight Ass finished in ten, Stump not at all.

The days dragged by and merged into an aching continuum. Each morning began with calisthenics, followed by the obstacle course, the cross-country course, and close-order drill. And marching, always marching in the burning Florida sun. They marched to chow to eat a five-minute meal, to the dispensary to be poked and prodded, fluids drawn and measurements taken, to the chapel on Sunday, banished to the balcony, where the wilted and malodorous troop sat, segregated from the scrubbed and crisply attired churchgoers. And when they had no other place to be, they marched up the sizzling grinder, turned around, and marched back down again.

Dave stood with a rifle on his shoulder, surrounded by a formation of sunburned, sweat-soaked, sand-encrusted candidates. Before them, the twenty-seven-year-old Marine gunnery sergeant towered like a recruiting poster. His snug uniform revealed not an ounce of body fat. Toned biceps and forearms protruded from his short-sleeved shirt. His tilted-forward hat shaded his sinewy neck and shoulders, and only a glint of moisture glistened from his skin.

"It is my Herculean task," Walker said, "to mold you forty swinging dicks into a military unit." He glared down and took a breath. "Shoulder . . . ARMS. Present . . . ARMS. Right shoulder . . . ARMS." Impotent rifles flailed about. "Battalion, forward . . . MARCH." They drilled on the blistering pavement under a cloudless sky. "Column to the right . . . MARCH," Walker sang. The troop turned right. "Right shoulder . . . ARMS." Dave's rifle jumped to his right shoulder. "Left shoulder . . . ARMS."

Dave transferred his rifle. A sharp pain seared the back of his head. "OW," he cried, his free hand reaching to massage the spot. He turned to see Stump fumbling with his rifle.

"Battalion, halt," Walker called out, his cadence interrupted. Everyone froze. He strolled through the ranks and stopped, his nose an inch from Dave's cheek. "Did I give you permission to speak, candidate?"

"Sir, no sir."

Dave's palms burned as he grunted out pushups on the hot asphalt.

A single overhead bulb illuminated the small room. Four men sat at a wooden table. Each wore a boot on one hand and a rag wrapped around two fingers of the other. The rags dipped into the black goo of a shoe polish tin and traced small circles onto the toe of each boot. Dave watched his zombie roommates dip and trace circles. Stump dipped and traced. Sasquatch, with his size-fourteen boots, dipped and traced. And even Tight Ass, the Douglas MacArthur of the battalion, dipped and traced. No one spoke, no one looked up, like fraternity pledges passively accepting any abuse to get into the club. Three months with these people? Dave exhaled a long sigh.

"Do you have a problem?" Tight Ass said, looking up from his circles.

"Yeah. Walker pisses on us every day, and you take it like sheep."

"He's just doing his job."

"So when he told Stump to either D-O-R or hoist his *gelatinous mass* over the O course wall, he was just doing his job?"

Stump and Sasquatch dipped and circled.

"He bears us no ill will," Tight Ass said.

"Maybe not, but he's a sadist."

Stump's mouth curled up into a smile.

Dave's eyes widened. "You think *you're* going to make it?" he said to Stump. "You can't march, you can't meet the physical requirements, you're barely taller than a dwarf."

Tight Ass stood. "Leave him alone."

Dave stood. "And *you* kiss Walker's ass every chance you get."

"Fuck you, Quinn."

Stump held up his hand to silence the combatants. He looked at Dave. "The battlefield isn't out there," he said with a wave of the hand. "It's in here." He pointed to his temple.

"So you're going to will your body over that wall?"

"No, but a positive attitude will get me there eventually."

"Then you don't hate Walker?"

"Why would I?"

"Because he tortures you every day?"

"It's not torture. It's training."

"Training on how to be abused?"

"No, training on how to deal with adversity. Everything is about something else. Marching is about precision, the C course, endurance, and the O course, team building."

Dave shook his head and flopped into his bunk. The others could submit to the humiliation, but he wasn't about to kowtow to Walker's demands. He would do just enough to get by and treat Walker like a non-person who had temporary power over his betters. Dave would put him into a compartment in his mind and close the door.

CHAPTER 12

At the desk in her upstairs bedroom, Jennifer turned the page of the workbook. The setting sun, which had bathed her room in its orange glow, now yielded to the blue-gray of twilight. She squinted in the fading light from the dormer window and flipped on the desk lamp, illuminating the only bedroom she had ever known. Decorated as though she were still a child, shelves housed her Barbie dolls, her Slinky, and her Magic 8 Ball. Mr. Potato Head looked down with one eye and Pat Boone with two. It could have been the room of one of her students.

The thought of the little ones brought a smile to her lips. When she saw the light in her children's eyes, the joy and wonder and pride on her third-graders' faces as they learned and grew, her heart swelled. She was truly blessed.

Finishing next week's lesson plan, she leaned back in the chair and looked up at her textbooks that lined the bookcase. On the top shelf, *Black's Law Dictionary* gathered dust. A graduation gift from Daddy.

Graduation. At commencement, David Brinkley advised her and three hundred others to "follow your heart." The school didn't need to pay him five thousand dollars to tell her that. She had known it since she was a child. She'd played "school" with her dolls, then with her friends, and then student taught in college. Who wouldn't follow her heart?

The street light flicked on.

She sighed. David, for one. Arranged alphabetically at the graduation ceremony, he was separated from his shaggy friends. Wedged between smug salutatorian Patricia Potts and closely cropped Roger Reams, Dave's shoulder-length hair cascaded in a tangle from beneath his mortarboard. Not hidden by his full beard, his bewildered eyes stared blankly.

It wasn't fair. She got to pursue her dream, while some of her friends had to fight a war. Because she was a woman, and they were men. If the war was essential to hold back the Communists, everyone should participate. Instead, she was safe and comfortable, living at home and teaching beautiful children at Shaker Heights Elementary.

Not that living at home didn't have its challenges. But what choice did she have? Aside from the one-thousand-dollar savings bond Daddy had given her for graduation, she had no money, and she vowed not to touch the bond. That was for her future, her financial security so she would have the independence to live her life as she saw fit.

"Supper is ready," her mother called up the stairs.

Jennifer wasn't hungry, but the family ritual demanded her presence, even though it was only the three of them. They always ate dinner by Daddy's schedule. As one of three name partners in the law firm, he loved his work, mostly as a rainmaker schmoozing clients, and was often late. Sometimes he missed the evening meal entirely, though she wasn't sure how he could play golf in the dark.

But this evening, he reclined in his BarcaLounger watching the war news on television and sipping his whiskey sour. Today's newspaper lay on the carpet next to him. He held up his glass and rattled the cubes. Mother hurried in with another, replacing the empty one in his hand.

"Dinner's ready," she said. It was almost a question.

"A moment. I want to see this," he said.

Jennifer stood in the archway to the dining room, watching the carnage.

The body of a young Marine lay in the mud. Jennifer had to look away.

"Daddy, turn it off."

He looked up at her.

"Please."

"I know it's unpleasant," he said, "but the cost of freedom is eternal vigilance. And each generation has to pay the price. Just as mine did in World War II." Jennifer bit her lip. Major John Pruitt, U.S. Army, had spent the war in a Judge Advocate General office in Cleveland and drove to work every day in a '37 Packard Roadster. All the girls had to compete for him, including Mother, then a secretary in his office. Now Daddy was all about making money while our boys were dying in the mud. She vowed never to subjugate her personality to his, like Mother had.

"Besides," he said, "Nixon has a secret plan to end the war. As soon as he's inaugurated, we'll be out of there."

"But why are we even there now?"

He blinked twice, as though no one had ever asked the question, and raised his palms. "We have to stop the Communists."

"Daddy, it's on the other side of the world."

"Where would *you* take a stand? Hawaii?"

She knew better than to talk politics with him. But she couldn't hold her tongue. "Wherever we do take a stand, if it's worth fighting for, shouldn't everyone participate? Shouldn't *I* participate?"

He clicked his tongue. "You're just a girl."

She glared at him.

"Okay," he said, "a *woman*," and rolled his eyes.

"Why do I get to pursue my dreams, while the boys have to put theirs on hold for two years? Or forever."

He pushed himself up from the chair. "That's the way it is. An accident of birth."

She followed him into the dining room. "But it's not right." And with that, she dropped it. He would never understand. So conversation around the table devolved to meaninglessness as sterile as the house, with sparse words sprinkled among the silence.

"How was your day?" Daddy asked.

"Fine. I prepared my lesson plans for next week."

More silence except the sounds of utensils on china.

When he rested his fork on his plate, Mother rose to clear the table.

"I still don't understand," he said. "You graduated third in your class. You could do anything. You could be a lawyer. And yet you choose to be just a teacher?"

His words ripped opened the old wound, but she stifled the hurt and anger.

Her answer came out a croak. "Yes, Daddy."

They sat in silence as Mother brought out the cherry pie.

Furious at her own cowardice, Jennifer swallowed back the bile and girded her loins.

"Daddy, as a teacher, I can do much more than a lawyer." Her voice trembled. She cleared her throat. "I can help other women get into the professions. Did you know that only nine percent of medical doctors are women? And only five percent of lawyers."

He rolled his eyes. "That's because they don't want to be doctors and lawyers. They want to be nurses." He carved three slices of pie and put them on dessert plates. "And teachers." He slid a plate in front of Jennifer. "And mothers. It's their nurturing nature."

Jennifer ignored her dessert. "Mother, don't you regret not pursuing your singing career?"

A far-away look briefly filled Mother's eyes. Then she smiled weakly, shrugged, and poured Daddy his coffee.

In the school she would open, Jennifer would give girls the confidence to . . . to . . .

Daddy dove into his pie as Mother shuffled back into the kitchen.

. . . to become doctors and lawyers. Yes. Her school would prepare girls to enter the professions. She dropped her fork onto the plate. Besides fostering independence and confidence, she'd teach math and science for medicine, communications and persuasion for law. Encouragement *and* academics.

She watched Daddy shovel in another mouthful.

But she'd never get there with Daddy's negativity. She needed to get out of this house.

"Listen, Sweetie," the matronly woman said, "when I was your age, I was married with two kids." She shoved an entire half of a PB&J sandwich into her waiting maw. "Enjoy it while you can." She wiped a dollop of peanut butter from the corner of her mouth with a thumb.

Crammed with bookcases, filing cabinets, and a copy machine, the teachers' lounge was not much bigger than the long table it contained.

"What I wouldn't give to be free, white, and twenty-one again."

Jennifer dipped her celery stick into the Tupperware cup of ranch dressing. "I love my parents," she said. "But I don't know how much longer I can live with them."

"They want you to leave?"

"Oh, no. They want me to stay. *I* want to leave." Her teeth crunched the cold fiber. She chewed slowly and swallowed. "My father supports the war, but I can't help thinking of all my friends who are being drafted." She dabbed her lip with a paper napkin. "I don't want to listen to it anymore." She sipped from a bottle of Coca-Cola. "But I can't afford an apartment. Housing is so expensive."

The older woman snorted. "Count your blessings, sweetie."

"Plus he's not supportive of my dreams."

"Join the Army. That would get you out of the house."

Jennifer smacked her lips. "That's silly. I love teaching too much. Besides, they need mechanics and engineers and pilots. Not elementary teachers."

The woman opened her purse, pulled out a compact, and examined her face in the small mirror. She ran a pinkie across each eyebrow, snapped the case shut, and dropped it into the purse. "Good enough for ten-year-olds," she said and headed out the door.

Jennifer dropped her chin into her hands.

At the far end of the table, Mr. Russell carefully folded the paper bag that had contained his lunch and slid it into his portfolio. One of only three male teachers in the school, he wore a pink short-sleeve shirt capped with a plaid bowtie.

"You don't have to be a serviceman to serve." He stood, pulled a brochure off the bulletin board, and slid it across the table.

Jennifer opened the wings of the tri-fold document. *Application for Teacher Position, 1969-70 School Year, Department of Defense.*

"Teach the children of servicemen," he said.

She smiled. "Thanks, Mr. Russell, but I don't have money for a move. Besides, I can't afford an apartment here. How could I manage one overseas?"

He turned the brochure over and pointed.

Her eyes widened.

Relocation expenses are included in the benefit package. Also, many assignments include on-base housing.

She picked up the paper, leaned back in the chair, and read. When finished, she looked at the ceiling. Teach children. Learn how small schools are run. And get out of the house.

She folded the brochure and slipped it into her purse.

CHAPTER 13

After eleven days of indoctrination battalion, the forty marched with a lively step toward Company A. They traded the ramshackle wooden barracks for a classic brick structure. Sweat-soaked overalls became short-sleeve khaki uniforms. And early morning eye-burning urine fumes became a well-ventilated head. Though not the Waldorf, the place had painted bulkheads, polished decks, and comfortable bunks. The four-man room even had two closets to house the occupants' meager possessions.

Dave shed his limp, damp coveralls for the last time. His new khaki uniform was so crisply starched, he had to peel the front of the shirt away from the back to pin on the hardware, and twist open the button holes so the buttons could penetrate. His flattened hand slid into each trouser leg, breaking open the starched seal. Pulling them on and squeezing into his spit-shined black shoes, he became a bald man in a large manila envelope.

The four men stiffened to attention beside their bunks. Walker entered the room, faced each candidate, and inspected him. "I see three Irish pennants," he said, standing before Dave. "Three demerits." A candidate officer following Walker wrote on a clipboard.

In preparation for each daily inspection, Dave had to insert his anchor insignia on each collar precisely three-eighths of an inch from the edges, meticulously center his nametag one-fourth of an inch over the left pocket, and spit shine his shoes to a blinding sheen. But most importantly, he had to microscopically inspect his shirt and trousers to remove any hint of a stray thread, the infamous Irish pennant.

He stowed his gear in the closet by the book. Toiletries were aligned and oriented, shirts and trousers placed correctly, and even underwear folded in precise six-by-six-inch squares. Arbitrary rules to be sure, but noncompliance attracted unwanted attention.

"Is this a static display?" Walker called from inside Dave's closet.

"Sir, no sir," Dave said.

Walker emerged. "Then why are your skivvies rigid?" he said, holding up a well-starched square of fabric.

Dave remained silent.

"Two demerits," Walker said to the man with the clipboard.

Dave wasn't about to iron his white boxer shorts into six-inch squares every day. So he ironed two pairs, put them out as a "static display," and hid away the underwear he actually wore.

"Attention to detail is essential for pilots," Walker said. "How will you fly an airplane if you can't follow simple instructions?" He dropped Dave's skivvies. They bounced once on an edge and settled on the deck, still a perfect square.

Attention to detail was the training mantra, but Dave could not see the connection between maneuvering combat aircraft and folding underpants. Despite Walker's phony sage advice, Dave would no more iron his shorts daily into precise six-inch squares than he would sleep on the floor.

Walker moved to Tight Ass's bunk. He pulled a quarter from his pocket and dropped it onto the sheet, precisely folded and stretched taut. The coin bounced. Achieving such bed-making perfection in the few seconds allotted each morning required creative solutions. Most men slept on top of the sheets so that only a slight smoothing was required. Tight Ass slept on the floor under his bunk to avoid even that small effort. Fresh linen arrived each Friday, so only on Thursday evening did the men crawl under the sheets for "hotel night."

Walker stepped to Dave's bunk. His face soured. The rumpled sheets sagged and the quarter fell flat. "Do you have a problem with authority, candidate?"

"Sir, no sir."

Walker assigned five demerits to the entire room for the offense and strode into the hall.

Tight Ass glared at Dave. "It's about the unit. We all pay. You can't sleep under your sheets every night."

Dave assumed his blank-slate face.

After weeks of rigorous exercise, Dave's strength and stamina soared. The once-grueling O course, C course, and calisthenics became routine. His chubby cheeks morphed into a chiseled jaw line, his white scalp grew tan and sprouted sun-bleached hair long enough to brush over, and his khaki shirt betrayed no hint of his former beer belly. And on the first cool evening of autumn, he dreamed of Jennifer and awoke aroused, a first since his arrival here.

As his body adapted, his mind remained resolute. During Walker's in-your-face rants about Dave's shortcomings, Dave queued the *Green Acres* theme and sang along in his head. Farm living is the life for me . . . When the shouting subsided, he called out, "Sir, yes sir." Sometimes, he even made his voice quaver.

But his immunity to indoctrination was not absolute. Each Sunday, he stepped lively as the troop marched to church to the stirring beat of the band playing "Anchors Aweigh." Inside, as the choir sang the Navy Hymn, a shudder moved up his spine. And in the classroom, he found the courses on aerodynamics and power plants to be interesting and naval history downright inspiring.

"The Battle of Midway marked the turning point in the war," the instructor said, "and Ensign Gay had a front row seat."

Dave gazed at the mural on the classroom wall. A sea battle raged. Ship and aircraft guns blazed, and smoke and fire rose from the sea. In the center of it all, a yellow speck floated.

In June of 1942, the sixth month of World War II, America desperately needed a naval victory. Much of the Pacific fleet had been damaged or sunk at Pearl Harbor. Admiral Nimitz searched for the Japanese fleet in a remote section of the Pacific near Midway Island, a dot of land at the edge of the Hawaiian Archipelago, thirteen hundred miles from Honolulu. When the Imperial aircraft carriers were spotted, Navy torpedo squadron VT-8 attacked first. They lost every aircraft and every pilot, save one. Although wounded, Ensign Gay survived crashing at sea amid the battle. For thirty hours, he bobbed in his life raft hidden under debris, watching the conflagration surrounding him. Torpedo planes, dive bombers, and fighters filled the sky and attacked the Japanese ships. The Battle of Midway turned the tide of the war in the Pacific.

"That's Ensign George Gay," the instructor said reverently, pointing at the yellow spot.

Dave's back contoured against the hard rubber side of the inflated raft. He rose and fell with the undulating swells of the mighty Pacific and shuddered with the thought of the black water churning to a depth of miles beneath him. He squinted against the flashes of light and flinched to the jarring blasts of sound. His sinuses were assaulted by air thick with the pungent smoke of explosives as he valiantly struggled to survive.

In that moment, he first glimpsed his father's patriotic fervor. Only a glimmer, it quickly passed. But he recognized it. Maybe the old man's sense of honor, duty, and love of country weren't that misguided after all.

Actually, Dave might enjoy being a naval officer for a while. Like that young officer he saw stepping out of the club with the pretty girl on his arm. That could be Dave in his cool white uniform, slipping on his shades as she wrapped her arms around his bicep and rested her head on his shoulder.

That's what he'd do. Once he dropped out of flight training, he'd get a cushy stateside billet and strut his stuff. Of course, he had to get his commission first. But he was now physically fit, the academics were a snap, and Walker's rants now blew by like the empty wind they were.

The rest would be easy.

BANG! WHIRRRR. SPLASH.

Dave braced as another wave of abdominal cramps rolled through his belly. He watched the Dilbert Dunker race down the track and plunge into the Olympic-sized swimming pool, its victim imprisoned inside. The contraption flipped over and came to rest with a thud, upside down and submerged. Dave awaited his turn in line.

Two rescue divers stood poised on each side of the apparatus. A head finally popped to the surface. The escapee swam to the edge of the pool and climbed out. The cable tightened, and the cage jerked over into an upright position, breaking the surface. Water cascaded out as the Dunker ascended the track to the top of the platform. The next victim climbed in, and the line shuffled forward.

"The Dilbert Dunker simulates a ditching at sea," the instructor had said. "Each candidate must extricate himself from the inverted and submerged aircraft."

Dave rehearsed the instructions for the zillionth time. You strap in. The cockpit is released. It slides down the track, hits the water, and flips over. You wait for the motion of the Dunker to stop. Give the bubbles a few seconds more to clear. Then reach to your lap and release the buckle. Your seatbelt and shoulder harness will fall away because you're upside down. Push away, that's down, from the seat. When clear of the cockpit, swim to the surface.

As the others gyrated, flexing and stretching, Dave counted the shiny scalps ahead of him. Fourteen. Fourteen to go and then him. His chest tightened. He became dizzy and grabbed Tight Ass's shoulder ahead.

"Jesus, Quinn, relax," Tight Ass said. "It'll be easy."

Dave took a deep breath. "Weren't you on the college swim team?"

"Yes, but you just unstrap and swim out. It's no sweat."

Dave snorted. Yeah, no sweat for a jock who never drowned. He remembered his childhood near-drowning incident, the choking horror of burning lungs and throbbing head as his breath ran out in the watery grave. He had become disoriented and couldn't find the entrance to the underwater cave as all turned black. When his eyes blinked open to the bright sunlight, he lay on his back on the bank, his friend crying. After his twelve-year-old bravado brought him to the precipice of death, he never again entered deep water.

"Look," Tight Ass said, "what's the worst that could happen?"

"I could drown."

"Nah." He shook his head. "That's the second worst. The worst is you could chicken out. You could D-O-R."

Another man strapped into the open cockpit. The line shuffled forward. The warning bell rang. *BANG. WHIRRRR. SPLASH.* Bubbles foamed as everyone waited in silence. A head popped to the surface, and the man swam to the edge of the pool. As the winch towed the Dunker back up the track, the next candidate climbed the stairs, and the line moved ahead.

When in the second position, the sting of bile invaded Dave's throat. He swallowed hard and shuddered as the bitter taste went down.

Tight Ass bounded to the top of the stairs. He shook his arms, rotated his head to relax his neck muscles, and leaped into his chariot.

He fastened the straps and saluted his readiness to the operator. He gave Dave a smile and a wink and gestured with a thumbs-up.

BANG. WHIRRRR. SPLASH. The Dunker flipped over and Tight Ass disappeared under a sea of white froth. Everyone watched and waited for him to appear at the surface in record time. Ten seconds passed. Then twenty. Then thirty. No Tight Ass. Two rescue divers sliced into the water from either side of the Dunker. Ten seconds later three heads popped to the surface. They pulled Tight Ass from the pool as he coughed and gasped for breath.

Dave's eyes grew huge as a cold, dark void enveloped him.

Without a pause, the cable tightened and the Dunker popped out of the water onto the track.

Dave climbed the stairs, struggling to keep his quivering leg muscles from betraying him. His foot slipped on a step. He grabbed the rail and caught himself.

The Dunker reached the top. Click. The locking mechanism engaged.

He stepped into the cockpit, sat in the seat, and pulled on his seatbelt and shoulder harness. Fingers shaking, he fumbled with the straps for a moment and then locked them into place with a click of the buckle. He looked out and saw Tight Ass sitting slumped on a bench, his head drooping between his legs.

The drumbeat of his heart throbbed in his temples. Although he hadn't been to church since junior high, he crossed himself and swallowed hard. Better dead than chicken out.

He saluted the operator, then clenched.

Nothing happened. Was it broken?

BANG!

His stomach rose to his throat as he shot down the track, a chlorine wind blowing in his face. The Dunker hit the water and flipped. Dave jerked forward in his harness, the straps digging into his torso as he hung upside down. He entered the black, airless cave. His eyes opened. Not black. White. An impenetrable white fog.

He couldn't see. Panic welled up. Wait, be calm. It was only bubbles, water clouded with bubbles. Wait for them to clear. Goosebumps popped up to shield him from the cold water. Okay, the bubbles were clearing. His mind raced through the instructions. The harness. Find the buckle. His hands groped at his lap. He felt the latch and yanked it. The straps fell away. Push down and swim. He pushed off and swam out of the cockpit. He took a large breaststroke. And another. And another. He hit an obstruction. The side of the pool? No, the bottom. Go the other way. He pushed off, raced toward the light, and broke the surface. A diver stood on the edge. Thumbs-up, Dave gestured. No sweat.

He reached the edge of the pool and held on for a moment. Everyone watched. With a single motion, he pulled himself out.

Tight Ass rose from the bench and headed back to the end of the line. "My belt got stuck," he said as Dave marched past toward the door.

Once in the locker room, Dave collapsed onto the bench.

Standing in his dress whites on the parade ground, Dave listened to the commanding officer presiding at the swearing in ceremony. "Long, proud tradition . . . privileges and responsibilities . . . United States Naval Officer . . ." And when Dave raised his hand and recited ". . . do solemnly swear to support and defend . . ." the lump in his throat surprised him, almost choking off the words "so help me, God."

He approached the platform and ascended the steps. The presiding officer bestowed upon him his commission and ensign epaulettes. Success. He would never see the jungles of Viet Nam. He would soon start flight training, find himself too frightened or uncoordinated or incompetent to continue, and be forced, reluctantly, to quit the program. He'd then get orders to some quiet billet to ride out his commitment. Or maybe they'd let him out early. After all, the Navy needed pilots, not untrained ensigns.

At the bottom of the steps stood Gunnery Sergeant William F. Walker, United States Marine Corps, the first to greet each newly commissioned officer. Tradition dictated that the new officer slip a five-dollar bill to his drill instructor, but Dave wasn't about to reward this prick. Walker snapped to attention in front of Dave and saluted smartly.

"Sir, congratulations," he said, holding his salute.

Dave stopped, stood at attention, and returned his most professional salute. He watched Walker offer his hand. Dave sighed. What the hell.

As they shook, a twenty exchanged palms.

CHAPTER 14

The cherry-red Corvette sparkled in the Florida sun. Its 300-horsepower V-8 engine rumbled as the convertible cruised down the two-lane road, scrub pines and palmetto trees gliding past. The '69 models had just arrived at Pensacola Buggy Works, the local Chevrolet dealer, when Dave appeared on the lot to get his wheels. Two other newly minted ensigns were already in the showroom picking out their Vettes to complete the uniform. And while Dave knew he wouldn't become a pilot, he would be an ensign for a few years.

Dave slowed as he approached the gate to the airbase. A nondescript sign read *Saufley Field.* The guard saluted him through, the blue bumper sticker identifying the driver as a United States Naval Officer. Dave swelled like a Macy's parade balloon as he returned the salute with a snap.

Ten miles northwest of Pensacola, Saufley Field was carved from the sandy soil and low brush of the Florida panhandle. It bordered the swamp-like Perdido Bay, and the Alabama wilderness beyond, and sat downwind of a paper mill that sent its sulfurous rotten-egg smoke wafting over the field.

Dave passed the flight line, its rows of T-34 Mentors waiting to train the next generation of naval aviators. He parked amid the other sports cars and hurried into the building. Young officers filled the classroom. Taking a back-row seat, he recognized most of his classmates from Aviation Officer Candidate School, but a few came from the Academy and ROTC programs, and a couple were Marine second lieutenants from Quantico.

"You men are the cream of the crop," the instructor said. "Very few make it to where you're sitting now, on the trek toward your Wings of Gold." A meteoric rise. Two weeks ago a maggot, now Dave was cream.

"This is the F-4 Phantom." The instructor held a model. "The workhorse of the fleet. She has dihedral wings and dual engines, each packing sixteen thousand pounds of thrust and a top speed of Mach 2.2. A great aircraft to fly. However"—he arced the model toward the deck—"lose an engine, and she glides like a Coke machine."

And with that, he launched into a harangue on basic aerodynamics. He drew an airfoil on the chalkboard. "This is a wing." Above it, he drew an upward-pointing arrow. "This is lift." He tapped the board with the chalk. "When lift exceeds weight, you fly." He explained laminar airflow, lift and drag vectors, and angle of attack. He droned on about aircraft movements of pitch, yaw and roll, and of the airfoil surfaces that enabled flight, the ailerons, elevators, and rudders.

Dave's eyes glazed. He hadn't expected a month of ground school before the first flight. This delayed his timetable. He had planned to demonstrate his flying ineptitude after a few training flights, maybe in a week, two tops. But now he had to suffer through courses on aeronautics, power plants, meteorology, flight physiology, and of course, the T-34 and its systems, flight characteristics, and procedures. So every day after class, he raced across the street to the bachelor officers' quarters and into the bar, a small but well-stocked refuge just steps from his room. He enjoyed his beer, surrounded by young officers in animated conversation, punctuated with hand gestures of aeronautical maneuvers. He'd have another bottle before heading back to his room, where he'd throw his training manuals on the coffee table, turn on the TV, pop another beer, and collapse onto the sofa.

The T-34 Mentor rolled down the runway. Like a convertible, the canopy remained open for takeoff, and the wind whooshed by with ever-increasing speed. In the tandem cockpit, the instructor sat in back, giving the front-seated student the sense of solitude.

Goosebumps popped from Dave's arms and neck. The aircraft's nose lifted to the horizon, and the bumping of the rolling tires ceased. They were airborne. The gear lever popped up, and the wheels folded into the wheel wells and slapped the bottom of the aircraft. The controls moved as if operated by a ghost, and the earth dropped away. Dave pulled his canopy closed, and the wind went silent. In his front row perch, he felt alone in the sky.

The flight instructor banked toward the west and climbed to two thousand feet. The intercom clicked. "That's Fairhope outlying field." The starboard wing dipped, and an airfield appeared beneath them. "We use it for touch-and-go practice."

Dave looked south at the Gulf of Mexico, west at the long strand of barrier islands that stretched to infinity, and up at the fading stars above.

"That's Mobile Bay ahead, and that's Dolphin Island, and that's . . ."

The words faded as Dave's spirit soared.

"Ensign." The stick shook between Dave's legs. "Ensign!"

"Uh . . . yes, sir?" Dave said.

"Want to take her for a bit?"

"Yes, sir," he said without hesitation, surprising himself.

"It's your aircraft."

Dave tapped his helmet in acknowledgment, grasped the stick with his right hand, and squeezed.

"Gently," he heard on the intercom.

He loosened his grip and made small movements—to the right and the aircraft banked right, to the left and it banked left. He pulled back, and the nose lifted and airspeed bled off. He pushed the stick forward, and the nose dropped and airspeed increased. Overwhelmed by the freedom, the solitude, and the beauty, he now understood the poetry of those who had preceded him.

I have slipped the surly bonds of earth.

Up half the night studying, Dave leaped from bed in the early-morning darkness and hurried to the flight line for his second hop. At 0600 he met his instructor in the ready room. Lieutenant Junior Grade Galt, not much older than Dave, had only recently earned his wings and had not yet had a fleet assignment. They briefed today's flight.

Yesterday had been a "familiarization" hop—really a sightseeing joyride for the front-seated student pilot. Today, the work would begin.

They walked outside to the dark flight line, carrying their flight bags and helmets. Dave followed Galt around the aircraft through a preflight inspection, circling the plane to evaluate its airworthiness.

Galt checked the engine, fuselage, and landing gear for any obvious discrepancy. He examined hydraulic lines, gas caps, and a dozen other things. He removed the lock on the elevator and tested the control surface for freedom of movement. Dave remembered the vivid film of an aircraft taking off with its elevator lock still in place, immobilizing that control. The aircraft lifted off the runway and the nose pointed higher and higher until she stalled and crashed in a fireball. The lesson seared into him the importance of the preflight.

Dave climbed into the front seat, strapped in, and slid on his helmet. Galt strapped in aft.

"I'll talk you through startup and taxi," Galt said. "And I'll assist on takeoff."

"You want *me* to take off?" Dave said. "Today?"

"That's why we're here, Ensign."

Dave pulled out the prestart checklist and read each item aloud as he performed it. He finished by pushing his mixture and RPM levers full forward and setting his throttle position.

"Permission to start, sir," he called over his shoulder.

"Granted," Galt said.

Dave twirled his finger at the lineman holding the fire extinguisher, and received a thumbs-up. He cranked the engine. The propeller turned in hesitant jerks. When the pistons fired, the propeller raced, sending a warm wind past the open cockpit. Dave reduced the throttle to 1200 RPM and pressed the intercom button.

"Engine instruments normal," he said.

A double click indicated Galt's acknowledgment.

The lineman guided Dave onto the taxiway and released him with a salute. At the run-up area, Galt took the aircraft, turned it into the wind, and ran the engine through its checks, explaining in detail each move. Dave watched as his throttle and control stick responded to invisible hands in the dual-controlled cockpit.

"Engine checks complete, controls free," Galt said on the intercom.

Crossing the double yellow line, the aircraft rolled onto the runway. Dave looked down the five thousand feet of concrete at the eastern sky, becoming pink in anticipation of the dawn.

"You have the aircraft," Galt said.

Dave took the controls and shuddered as he pushed the throttle to its forward stop.

As the weeks passed, Dave drank no beer, studied each night, and excelled in the air. On their ninth flight, Galt certified him as ready to solo. The next morning, Dave signed out his aircraft, pre-flighted, started, taxied, and took the runway. He pushed the throttle full open. With the roar of its engine, the T-34 shook and began its roll. Dave worked the rudder pedals to stay on the runway centerline. At rotation speed, he eased back the stick, lifted off into the blue, sun-drenched sky, and soared alone toward heaven.

A dozen student pilots and their instructors stood about the officers' club bar. Dave and Galt sat at a table, each sipping a beer, awaiting the ceremony to recognize first solo flights.

Dave took a swig. "Are you career Navy, Lieutenant?"

Galt shook his head. "If this war ever ends, I plan to get a job with the airlines."

Dave perked up. "I thought that was just a recruiting pitch."

"It is. But it's also true. The airlines love military pilots." Galt raised his glass. "Who else gets this kind of training and flying experience?"

"Ensign David Quinn," a voice said.

They both jumped up and made their way to the podium. Handing Dave a framed certificate, the squadron commander turned toward the camera and smiled.

"Congratulations, Ensign," he said as a bulb flashed.

Galt unsheathed a survival knife from his belt. He took the end of Dave's tie, pulled it straight out, and, completing the age-old ritual, sliced it in two.

He shook Dave's hand and winked. "Navy flying is fun," he said, "but the real payoff is an airline career."

Dave saw himself in a Pan Am captain's uniform, piloting a Boeing 747 across the Atlantic, sipping coffee from a china cup served by a beautiful and doting stewardess. He nodded at the thought. This could be a career that suited him.

But first, he must complete flight training, and the biggest challenge still lay ahead.

The sea calm, the sky blue and cloudless, and the sun glimmering off the Gulf of Mexico, Dave looked down at the USS Lexington steaming a thousand feet below. Its foamy wake cut a white line in the dark water. Alone in the T-28 Trojan, Dave gawked at the smallness of the object he had to land on. Eight months had passed, and payment for club admission came due today.

When abeam the carrier, Dave banked into his approach turn and retarded the throttle.

"I have the ball," he announced into the mic.

Crossing the ship's wake, he rolled wings level onto the final glide slope. His perspiration-soaked flight suit clung to his back. He looked toward the deck and saw the mirror, the visual system that guided the pilot. The meatball, a small orange light shining in the center of the mirror, showed him to be on glide slope.

After a month of practicing simulated carrier landings on a painted square on a runway, he could hit the numbers every time. But here, the target moved, and water surrounded the touchdown point. Miss the landing spot now, and you don't end up in high grass beside the runway. You topple into the sea.

"Roger, ball," the voice of the landing safety officer crackled back into his headset. Dave could see him on the stern of the ship next to the mirror, the tiny flight deck beside him.

Barreling down the glideslope, the half mile between final rollout and touchdown on the ship's deck took only seconds. Things happened fast, with little room for error. Everything had to be on the mark—airspeed, altitude, alignment. Only fine control adjustments could be made close in.

"You're high," the LSO said.

Dave's mouth and throat were dry as talc. When he squeezed the throttle aft just a hair, he could hear it in the sound of the engine. The nose inched down, and the orange meatball returned to the center of the mirror as he dropped back on glide slope.

How did it come to this? Enraptured by dreams of a Pan Am captainship and doting stewardesses, he now was barreling down on a postage-stamp-sized flight deck. One misstep, and he'd sink deep into the ocean's black void, dead at twenty-two. He'd been caught in a whirlpool. The current, at first gentle, now spun out of control. But he'd never quit. Better dead than look bad.

His breath quickened as he approached. The angled deck grew until it filled his windscreen. As the ship's fantail blurred past a few feet beneath him, he yanked the throttle closed. He slapped hard onto the deck and lurched forward in his harness as his hook caught the wire, spooling him to a stop.

He raised his head. He had survived. The lineman signaled, hook up. No time to think. No time to rejoice in his first carrier landing. He raised the lever. As the hook rose, the cable dropped to the deck, and the lineman directed him to the centerline of the launch deck. The yellow-shirted launch officer clenched his left fist in front of his face and twirled his right index finger over his head. The T-28 needed no catapult. Standing on the brakes, Dave pushed the throttle full forward. The engine roared, and Dave saluted.

Yellow Shirt unclenched his fist, kneeled forward toward the bow, and with the grace of a ballet dancer, gently touched the deck with his index finger. Dave released his brakes and shot forward, the thrust of the 1500-horsepower radial piston engine pressing him back against the seat. The ship's bow disappeared beneath him, replaced by the sun shimmering on the open sea. He climbed back into the landing pattern with the other student aircraft, and turned downwind for the next of his five required landings.

Six months later, in an aircraft hangar in Corpus Christi, Texas, Wings of Gold were pinned onto the chest of Lieutenant Junior Grade David L. Quinn.

CHAPTER 15

When Julio stepped onto the platform to receive his high school diploma, he looked into the audience and saw Mama seated in the third row. She had walked seven blocks in the heat to be there, a monumental effort for her. He would repay her love and take care of her forever.

On the walk home, she perspired profusely. "I need to rest." She plopped down on a bus stop bench, drew a tissue from her bra, and sopped her brow.

He sat next to her.

Her face flushed and breathing heavy, she wrapped her large arms around him and kissed him sloppily on the cheek. "I'm so proud of you, Julito. I love you very much."

He returned the hug and swallowed hard. There would never be a good time to break the news. "Mama, I have to tell you something."

She released him and drew back, her face questioning.

He cast his eyes toward the sidewalk. "I enlisted in the Army."

Her eyes widened, her mouth dropped open, and she crossed herself. "Dios mio."

"I want to serve my country like Papa did."

"Your Papa got shot in Korea, and for the rest of his life, he limped around with a bullet in his rump." She began to weep. "Julito, there's a war. I don't want you in a war."

"All my friends are enlisting."

"You're not like them, Julito. You couldn't take a life."

"I know, Mama. That's why I signed up for medic training." The official title was *Combat Medic Training*, but he left off the "combat" part. "I'll be helping people, Mama. I won't be shooting at them."

She swallowed and wiped her nose. "But they'll be shooting at *you.*"

"No, I'll probably be in a field hospital. Not on the front lines."

"There are no front lines in that war. The bad guys are all around."

"Mama, the alternative is for me to wait to get drafted. Then they'll give me a rifle and teach me to kill. And when I got out of the Army, all there would be for me here was flipping burgers at $1.60 an hour. What's the future in that? Earning $1.85 an hour?"

A bus stopped and the door hissed open. She looked up, shook her head at the driver, and waved him on.

"But if I get into the medic training program, I serve my time, then get out and get a good job in health care, maybe as an EMT. I could take care of you. We could move into a nice place."

"If? You said *if*."

"I already took the tests, Mama. I'm just waiting to hear."

"I don't want you to leave me."

"I'll be back after eight weeks of basic training. Medic training is at Fort Sam Houston, so I'll be nearby. For sixteen weeks."

Her shoulders drooped with a long exhale. She traced a cross on his forehead. "May Jesus watch over you, Julito." She kissed his cheek, pushed herself up from the bench, and struggled forward.

CHAPTER 16

Lt. Ron Nelson wiped his face with the sleeve of his flight suit. As perspiration trickled from his forehead, the sting of the salt burned his eyes. The scar on his chin chafed in the heat. But after two years here, he had grown used to it. Standing on the tarmac in the shade of his aircraft, he awaited the arrival of the squadron's newest pilot. Though surrounded by activity on the busy Air Force base, he remained deep in his own thoughts.

"Go easy on the new guy," the Old Man had said.

Nelson snorted. For a commanding officer, how could he be so naïve? Nelson had been dealing with student pilots and hotshot, newly winged officers for a long time. After three years in the training command as a flight instructor and two years here as a safety and training officer, he knew the tiller needed a strong hand. "Going easy" was a recipe for death. Why would this new pilot be any different?

"For Christ's sake, Ron," the CO had said, "at least keep an open mind. Don't be so quick to judge."

Orders were orders, so by God, he'd try. But every experience he'd ever had told him what to expect—a cocky son of a bitch whose arrogance and confidence exceeded his piloting skill. But the student couldn't be blamed. The training command encouraged it. He was the cream of the crop. A stud. A double entendre literally meaning student but suggesting a magnificent creature sought for breeding. Fed a steady diet of that pap, each emerged believing it.

Some of these hotshots acted like they had climbed Mount Everest, like they'd overcome life's most challenging obstacle. Try growing up in foster care because your mother didn't want you. Try enlisting in the Navy at seventeen when you were still a child because you had nowhere else to go. Work like a slave, get in a ROTC program, get a commission and into flight training. Then almost throw it all away because you're a stupid kid. A shrink would have a field day with you. He'd say you're lonely and scared and overwhelmed by abandonment issues and feelings of inferiority. But you don't tell the shrink he's right because he would kick you out of the program. You hide it deep. Everything is fine. Even when your wife leaves and you weep, you swallow the pain.

"Give him the benefit of the doubt," the Old Man had said. "Don't assume he's reckless just because . . ."

Nelson watched the CO searching for words. Because *I* was?

"Getting the job done doesn't require you to be a hard-ass."

He heard that a lot. From the Old Man, from his previous CO, from his ex-wife and subsequent girlfriends. A hard-ass. But *he* called it having standards. And demanding others meet them, especially in aviation where one foolish move could ruin lives. Coddling prima donnas didn't work, but being a hard-ass did.

Nelson wiped his face again. Even in the shade of the wing, the perspiration poured from him.

"Damn, it's hot," a voice said. "I could use a beer. Want to get a beer, Lieutenant?"

His copilot, Ensign Roger Maximilian, sat on the concrete, his back resting against the starboard tire. Perspiration freckled his forehead and soaked dark half-moons under the armpits of his baggy green flight suit. Matted hair marked a recently removed flight helmet, which sat beside him.

The shadow of their aircraft formed a tranquil island in a sea of turmoil. All around them, the airfield bustled with activity under the morning sky. Ground vehicles scurried about a vast expanse of concrete. Fighter jets prepared for takeoff. A lumbering C-130, its silver fuselage gleaming, taxied under the pull of four whirring turboprops. Line crews loaded ordinance beneath a B-52 bomber as waves of shimmering heat rose from the tarmac. A jetliner landed, smoke swirling from each tire as it squeaked on touchdown. It turned off the runway, taxied past a dozen gleaming Air Force Phantoms aligned in a perfect row, and parked at the white terminal building. Royal palms with white-painted trunks framed the structure. The sign on the control tower read *Clark Air Force Base—Welcome to the Philippines.*

"What do you say, Lieutenant? A beer?"

Nelson couldn't hold back the exasperated sigh. "We don't drink on duty, Max."

"I know, but it sure is hot."

Nelson sopped his brow. Max had it right. The mid-morning solar furnace baked the tarmac. Puddles of last night's rain steamed upward like a sauna. Even this shady spot provided little relief for the already-ninety-degree temperature and 100 percent humidity. Of course, it was hot. That was how nature responded when lush, sun-absorbing, tropical greenery was hacked down and entombed in a wide swath of foot-thick concrete.

BOOM!

A flash of silver glinted above as two Air Force F-4 Phantom fighter jets roared over the airbase in tight formation, their wingtips only feet apart.

Nelson watched the lead jet break left over the airfield, followed seconds later by his wingman.

"You sure?" Max said, mopping his brow with his sleeve. "A cool one would taste great right about now." He raised his hand in a pledge. "I won't tell Mamasan."

Nelson scowled. No one even knew whether she really existed. The conjecture sprang from the popularity of the arrangement, and the place he kept in town, despite having a BOQ room.

He looked at Max, with his deep tan, sun-bleached hair, and long sideburns. Though a beer-swilling, hedonist-playboy horn dog, the ensign was also a damn good pilot who had learned from his screw-ups, unlike some of these young training command prima donnas who made the same mistakes over and over until disaster struck.

"Look, Max, *you* know we're not having a beer, and *I* know we're not having a beer, so cut the crap, okay?"

Max shrugged. His attention turned to the red fluid dripping onto the tarmac next to him. He dipped a finger into the small pool and smelled the liquid. "Well, I'm going to have one when we get back." He sopped his forehead again. "Man, it's hot." He looked skyward. "Where *is* he?"

The two Air Force fighter jets touched down twenty seconds apart and taxied to the line of parked F-4s. Line crewmen hurried a ladder to each plane as the canopies swung upward. As the pilots exited the aircraft, the line crews saluted smartly. An Air Force major and a captain crossed the tarmac toward the terminal, carrying their helmets. Both wore fitted Air Force blue flight suits and had perfect haircuts and well-trimmed mustaches. They spotted the Navy pilots and veered toward them.

"Great," Max said, leaping up as they approached, "Eddie Rickenbacker and his faithful companion."

"Good morning, gentlemen," the major said, "you girls lost?"

"Morning, Frank," Nelson said.

"Nice sideburns, Elvis," the young captain said, reaching toward Max's temple. "Did the Navy rescind its grooming regulations?"

Max swatted his arm away. "Did the Air Force issue you that 'stache in flight school?"

The captain looked over the naval aircraft with her faded gray paint and gigantic propellers, squatting apart from her sleek neighbors. Like a giant donut on either wing, each radial engine sported nine beer-keg-sized cylinders mounted in a circle and drove a huge, tri-blade propeller. From the bulbous cockpit in the nose of the aircraft, convex windows bulged out like the eyes of a giant bug. And the mammoth tail sported a faded checkerboard pattern of orange and yellow. This awkward contraption appeared on no Navy recruiting posters. She was not called Phantom or Skyhawk or Crusader. Officially designated the S-2F Tracker, this U.S. Naval aircraft was known throughout the fleet simply as *the stoof.*

As he examined the aircraft, the captain put his hands on his hips. "Major, I thought the Dodo bird went extinct."

Max glowered.

"Her beauty lies within," Nelson said. "The stoof is like an aging matron—sturdy, reliable, and forgiving."

"Ha, stoof," the captain guffawed. "Even the name is goofy."

"And she doesn't need ten thousand feet of runway to land," Max said, his pitch rising. "A few hundred feet of deck and a cable is all we need. On a carrier. At Yankee Station. In the war zone."

"The war's five hundred miles that way, Elvis," the captain said with a head nod. "I don't see any Viet Cong around here."

Max clenched his teeth.

The major smoothed down his mustache. "So what's the Navy doing in our neck of the woods?"

Nelson raised his chin toward the horizon. "We're meeting a new pilot."

The major nodded. "Train him well, Ron."

"I'll do my best, Frank."

As the Air Force pilots turned and strutted toward the terminal, Nelson swelled with pride. His Max had learned respect for the mission, the aircraft, and the Navy. And a humility for the awesome responsibility when one assumes control of an aircraft. Nelson's greatest achievement, Max shone as proof positive that being a hard-ass worked.

As the Air Force pilots marched away, Max pointed at the horizon. "There he is."

A speck in the distant sky grew into a shimmering DC-8 jetliner. She touched down on the runway, rolled out, and turned onto a taxiway. A lineman guided the pilot into a slot a mere hundred feet away. He crossed his flashlight wands, and her nose dipped as she came to a stop. Linemen hurried to chock the wheels while others rolled stairs into position. The airliner towered over the stoof.

Nelson and Max emerged from their shady spot and approached the stairs under the hellish heat lamp. The forward hatch opened and a stewardess appeared.

"Damn," Max said. "I wonder what lucky Air Force puke she's dating tonight."

She stepped aside and young men in uniform emerged from the air-conditioned cabin. Each registered dismay as the damp heat slapped him.

Nelson watched the line of men step from the hatch. Maybe the new officer would be different. Nelson silently renewed his vow to the CO to withhold judgment.

A young naval officer swaggered through the hatch and paused at the top of the stairs, causing the line behind to stumble to a stop. His hat was cocked forward and his khaki uniform pristine. The single silver bar of a Lieutenant Junior Grade adorned his hat and each collar. Golden wings glistened on his chest. Squinting, he dropped his bag and reached into his pocket. He pulled out a sunglass case, popped it open, and removed his aviator shades. With delicate finesse, he slipped them on. A glint of the white-hot sun flashed off the gray mirrored lenses.

Bile rose in Nelson's throat. From the shades and the swagger, he already knew. This one would be trouble.

CHAPTER 17

From his perch, Dave surveyed his new domain and nodded. This was perfect. An expansive base bustling with activity would be the ideal place to get the experience he needed to become a Pan Am pilot. And his glorious future would begin in a tropical paradise.

Two rumpled men stood at the bottom of the stairs—one frowning, one smiling.

Dave puffed out his chest. Naval aviators were the best-trained pilots in the world. A year and a half of flight training cost the Navy $250,000—a huge investment that represented his value. As he strutted down the stairs, the older man's frown became a scowl.

"Lt. Quinn?" he said as Dave stepped onto the tarmac. "Ron Nelson. Welcome to the P.I."

A jagged scar defined his chin.

Dave dropped his bag and saluted smartly just as Nelson offered his hand. Dave's salute bobbled into a handshake.

The smiling younger officer thrust out his hand. "Roger Maximilian." He grabbed Dave's and pumped it enthusiastically. "Call me Max."

That name sounded familiar. Dave's eyes widened. "Not *the* Ensign Maximilian. *Ensign Max*. You're a legend in the training command."

Max beamed. He made a pistol with each hand and pointed at Dave, who raised his arms in mock surrender.

"Don't shoot," Dave said.

They both laughed. Nelson rubbed his forehead.

Ensign Roger Maximilian had achieved a distinction as rare as the Navy Cross—he was a permanent ensign, having been passed over for promotion to lieutenant junior grade. An ensign routinely advanced in rank after twelve months. But for three years now, Max had not been promoted. It was like flunking first grade several times.

The Navy cut pilots a lot of slack for their behavior, especially during wartime, so Max's achievement was particularly noteworthy.

Dave beamed as he looked around at the dazzling array of aircraft and activity. "This is outstanding." He picked up his bag and turned toward passengers headed for the terminal.

"This way," Nelson said, tilting his head in the opposite direction. "This is Clark Air Force Base. The Navy is forty miles that way."

Dave turned. A shining C-130, its four turbo props spinning, filled his field of vision. His eyes widened and grin broadened. The aircraft taxied forward, revealing a gray, faded stoof behind. Dave looked to the left, then the right. His heart sank. Slipping from his fingers, the flight bag dropped onto the tarmac.

Max grabbed the bag, carried it to the plane, and threw it through the narrow hatch.

"It's a short hop to Cubi Point," Nelson said.

"Come on," Max said. "I'll walk you through the preflight."

Dave tagged behind. He pointed to the oil stains on the concrete beneath the engine and the puddle of red fluid beneath the wheel.

Max nodded. "We'll write up those gripes when we get back."

Dave paused. "Isn't that hydraulic fluid?"

"Yeah," Max said.

"Don't we need that for brakes? And to lower the landing gear?"

"Yeah."

Dave removed his hat and wiped his forehead. "Shouldn't it be fixed now?"

Max guffawed. "This isn't TWA. Here the mission comes first."

"But a leaking hydraulic line?"

Max shrugged. "Minor gripes can wait. Besides, Air Force techs don't know a stoof from a hole in the ground. I wouldn't let them touch her. No, we'll wait until we get home."

"Lieutenant, why don't you ride shotgun," Nelson said. "It's never too soon to start. Max can sit in back."

Dave followed Nelson through the hatch, along the narrow aisle past two crewman seats, and into the cockpit. He took the copilot seat on the right. They strapped on their parachutes and buckled into their harnesses. Dave inspected the scarred gray interior. Scratches marred the control panel. Duct tape covered the hole of a missing instrument. "INOP" was marked on the autopilot, its joystick tilting listlessly to starboard. Dave spotted a smudge of black grease on his khaki shirt. He took out a white handkerchief and rubbed the spot, spreading it out.

Nelson quickly read the startup check list, flicking switches and turning levers. Max, still outside, pointed a fire extinguisher at the engine and twirled his finger.

Nelson called out to Max through the window, "CLEAR."

Max gave him a thumbs-up.

Nelson turned the switch. The engine cranked for a few seconds. *BANG*! A cloud of white smoke billowed from the cowling as the port engine popped to life. The spinning propeller quickly dissipated the smoke.

That didn't look good. "Is that normal?" Dave said.

"What?"

"All that smoke."

Nelson looked away and started the second engine with the same result. "Yeah, it's normal."

Dave tightened his harness with an extra tug.

Max climbed aboard and strapped into the empty radio operator's seat.

Nelson keyed his mic. "Clark ground control, Checkertail two four ready for taxi."

"Roger two four. Cleared to runway two zero."

The aircraft bounced along the taxiway.

"Ground maintenance," the radio blared, "we need a clean-up on aisle four."

Dave watched a truck race past them to their just-vacated parking space. Men jumped out, poured sawdust onto the puddles of red and black goo, and swept it up.

"This is a top-flight facility," he said.

"Yeah, the Air Force glory boys," Max said on the intercom. "They get the sexy planes, top-notch maintenance, nice facilities, respectful line crews, sleep at home every night, and no carrier landings." He snorted. "A bunch of pampered pansies."

Engines sputtering and popping, the aircraft stopped at the double yellow lines marking the runway boundary. A flash of silver filled the windscreen, and they rocked in the turbulence of the landing jetliner.

When the larger aircraft completed its landing roll and turned onto a taxiway, their headsets again crackled. "Checkertail two four, you're cleared for takeoff."

They rolled onto the runway. Nelson pushed the dual overhead throttles full open. The airframe shook as the mighty engines thrust them forward. Dave's eyelids still fluttered to the thrill of acceleration as they rattled and rolled. The sound of rapid-fire banjos blasted Dave's headset with "Foggy Mountain Breakdown." He looked back at Max, grinning broadly. A cassette player was jacked into the aircraft intercom. Max turned up the volume.

At eighty-five knots, Nelson eased back the yoke. The nose rose, and the aircraft lifted off using less than a third of the runway. Nelson slapped up the landing gear lever and the wheels thumped into the wheel wells. Ascending from the airbase, they leveled off at three thousand feet over a wide valley. The temperature had fallen, and Dave's perspiration-soaked uniform began to dry. They bounced along as thermal updrafts buffeted the aircraft.

"We'll be at Cubi in twenty minutes," Nelson said. "No need to climb higher." He made his final control adjustments for level flight. "And knock off the hillbilly music, Max."

The aircraft flew southwest, down the central valley of Luzon toward Subic Bay, over cultivated farms that crisscrossed the valley and lush emerald jungle that climbed the mountain ridges to the west. Dave gazed at the landscape. He'd never been in the tropics.

Nelson pointed left toward the south. "That's the Bataan peninsula."

"Sounds familiar," Dave said, grinning, "They have hot women over there, Ron?"

Max coughed.

"No, Lieutenant," Nelson said. "They have cold men over there. The Bataan Death March in 1942. Thousands of Americans and Filipinos died for their country."

Oops. He'd better watch what he said to this guy.

Silence fell over the cabin as the scenery drifted by. At the southern end of the valley, they flew over a ridge and a large bay appeared.

"Subic Bay Naval Base," Nelson said. An aircraft carrier and several smaller vessels hugged the piers. A small city squatted adjacent to the port.

"Manila?" Dave said.

"Nah, that's Olongapo," Max said. "Great town. You'll see."

The stoof overflew the base. As they followed the shoreline south, thick tropical growth encroached to the water's edge. In the distance, a spit of land jutted into the bay. Carved from the jungle, a runway appeared, then a hangar, several aircraft, and a road snaking back into the overgrowth.

"Cubi Point Naval Air Station," Nelson said.

They flew over the runway and received clearance to land. They broke to downwind, rolled onto final approach, and smoothly touched down on the numbers. The aircraft rolled out and turned off the runway.

They taxied past a P-3 Orion. Its silver fuselage, broad wingspan, and four turboprops dwarfed the smaller aircraft. Now *that* was an airplane. Dave stared out the bulbous window.

Nelson noticed. "They're just passing through. Headed to Guam. Stopped to refuel."

The P-3 had replaced the stoof as the backbone of the Navy's antisubmarine warfare. Dave had asked for a P-3 squadron but had got orders here instead. The newer, larger, glitzier aircraft was land-based and capable of patrolling for over twelve hours. So the stoof had been consigned to backwater missions such as towing targets for allied navies and ferrying men and mail to the decks of aircraft carriers.

They taxied to a line of four stoofs. One was on blocks, like a stripped car, missing an engine, wheel assembly, and horizontal stabilizer.

"That's the fleet," Max said. "Helen Keller there is our hangar queen."

Nelson parked in the line. The engines popped and wheezed to a stop. The three men climbed out, crossed the tarmac, and entered the hangar. At the maintenance desk, a chief petty officer eyed Dave as Nelson wrote up the gripes.

"Anyplace to get a beer around here?" Dave said, leaning against the counter.

"Damn straight," Max said. "The Cubi O Club is the best in WestPac, maybe in the whole fleet."

They exited through a back door onto the asphalt parking lot. A silver Jaguar XKE convertible with flecked finish sparkled in the bright sunlight. Max threw his flight bag into the back seat and hopped behind the wheel.

"Nice," Dave said, dropping his bag next to Max's. "I have a Vette. She should be here in three weeks."

"Over here," Nelson said, standing next to a Plymouth Valiant.

Dave eyed the faded paint and metallic tape that patched rusted-out holes in the body. The asphalt below was visible through gaps in the floor, and twisted wire secured the muffler to the back bumper. Much like the stoof. Nelson was a strange bird. Why would a naval officer drive such a wreck?

"The heat and humidity devour metal in the PI," Nelson said. "We cover the holes with metallic tape."

"The Vette's body is fiberglass, not metal," Dave said.

Nelson opened the trunk. Dave retrieved his bag and threw it in.

Max started the Jag with a low rumble. "Got a date. Ciao." He raced off with a squeak of the tires.

As Dave opened the Valiant's passenger door, the hinges screeched in protest. The car appeared to be in critical condition, bandaged with shiny tape. He could feel the seat springs as he sat. "The Vette cost me five grand, but she's cherry. What'd this ride cost?"

Nelson climbed in and turned the key. "Two hundred." The starter whined for ten seconds before the engine caught.

"I call her *Red*," Dave said. "She'll do zero to seventy in 5.9 seconds."

Nelson engaged the clutch, and they shuddered into motion amid a swirl of blue exhaust. "The speed limit here is thirty."

They followed a winding road through dense foliage and a gauntlet of unseen creatures whose shrill cries protested the intrusion; past machete-wielding Filipinos who hacked at roadside growth; and between small clearings carved from nature to accommodate man's structures—a Quonset hut dispensary, wooden WWII-vintage enlisted barracks, and the officers' club.

"How about we check out the O Club for a brew?" Dave said.

Nelson looked at his watch. "It's eleven hundred. Let's get you settled in." He slowed at a curve in the road. "That's married officers' housing." A side road looped through a clearing with six identical one-story block houses, unadorned save flower beds lining the walks. He pointed at a seventh, larger house. "That's the Old Man's place. He and Margaret are having a Hail and Farewell there tonight at nineteen hundred. You'll meet all the officers. The wives too."

Another building appeared. A sign over the door read *Bachelor Officers' Quarters*. Brakes squealed, and the Valiant bounced to a stop.

Dave gaped. "This is the BOQ?" Thick vegetation overwhelmed the white-washed concrete two-story structure.

Nelson sighed as his car door screeched open. Inside, he took a key from the Filipino desk clerk and led Dave down a drab, green hall. "We've got all the comforts here. Pool table, bar and mess hall down below, swimming pool out back. And Mamasan does your laundry for fifteen bucks a month." They arrived at a door with a small plaque which read *LTJG QUINN, USNR*. Nelson unlocked the door and pushed it open. Dave stared at the bare block walls and dangling light fixture, at the spartan bed, dresser, and black rotary phone, and at the plastic sheets covering the jalousie windows, punctured by a groaning air conditioner.

"These are temporary quarters, right?"

"Yeah," Nelson said. "For eighteen months."

Great. His entire tour.

"Make yourself at home. I'll see you tonight." Nelson handed him the key and hurried off.

Dave's shoulders slumped. He picked up his bag and shuffled into the prison cell.

CHAPTER 18

Cars lined the loop at married officers' housing. Dave strode down the street in his dress whites—white trousers, white shoes, white hat, white gloves, and white choker cinched tightly about his neck with gold buttons. Black and gold LTJG epaulettes adorned his shoulders. The wings of gold upon his chest attested to his accomplishment, and the lone National Defense ribbon to his inexperience. Aviator shades hid his eyes and reflected the fading light in the western sky. You only had one chance to make a good first impression, and boy, did he look good.

Under the growing gray shadows of dusk, he stumbled against the curb. He removed his sunglasses and marched up the flower-lined walk. At the door, he put them back on and knocked.

The door opened to an evening dress of tropical flowers and exotic birds. The woman smiled warmly. "You must be Dave." She extended her hand. "I'm Margaret." She took his hand and covered it with her other. "Welcome to our home."

He removed his hat and shades, stepped into the party, and froze. Everyone else was wearing civilian clothes—the men in slacks with colorful, open-collared shirts, and the women in bright dresses.

"I . . . I thought it was dress whites."

Margaret smiled, patted his hand, and led him to the only bald man in the room. "Doug," she said, "may I present Lieutenant Quinn."

The squadron commanding officer flashed a genuine smile and shook Dave's hand. "Welcome aboard," he said. He tapped his glass, *tink*, *tink*. The din abated. "Welcome, everyone." He stood between Dave and another man. "We're here tonight to hail aboard Lieutenant Dave Quinn and to bid farewell to Lieutenant Bob Mosher. Please introduce yourselves or say goodbye, as appropriate."

Everyone laughed with the heartiness due a senior officer's witticism.

Max tottered toward Dave, a beer in his hand. "Hey, buddy, like your new digs?"

Thank God. A familiar face.

Suddenly, a hand landed on his shoulder. He turned to see a Hawaiian shirt splashed in color. "At the last one of these," the man wearing it said, "Max brought a hooker."

"Not a hooker, Seymour. My date. I didn't pay a cent."

Seymour's smile glowed with good cheer. "She got drunk and propositioned the Old Man. Right in front of Margaret. It was a hoot."

Max's face reddened. "Seymour's such a spaz in the air, it took him a year to get his aircraft commander designation."

"Max has been with so many hookers, he's a walking petri dish."

"Oh, yeah? Well, Seymour is so whipped, Carol keeps his balls in a box and only lets him have them on the weekend."

"Even Sally Mattressback won't have anything to do with Max."

"That's not a real person," Max said.

Appearing satisfied with the outcome of the exchange, Seymour put out his hand to Dave. "Ken Sawyer. Welcome aboard." He slapped Dave on the back, and wandered off.

Dave looked at Max. "Did he say *Ken*?"

"Yeah."

"Then why did you call him Seymour?"

"Because he doesn't like it."

Max spotted a couple and dragged Dave over. A man, thirtyish and hair closely cropped, without the regulation-busting two-inch sideburns worn by the younger men, stood close to a pregnant woman. "Lieutenant Commander Holt, Brenda," Max said, "may I present Dave Quinn."

Holt thrust out a hand. "Welcome aboard, Lieutenant."

Brenda smiled broadly. "Hello, Dave."

Dave lost his struggle with eye control and looked at her belly.

She laughed. "Yes, I'm pregnant."

"Congratulations," he said. "What are you hoping for?"

Simultaneously, Holt said, "a boy," and Brenda said, "a girl."

Everyone chuckled.

Brenda took her husband's arm. "We already have a girl. Phil wants another man in the house."

Max slapped Dave's shoulder. "Commander Holt's the other training officer. Besides Nelson, he'll fly some hops with you. Then I get to show you how things are really done around here." Max's head suddenly spun to the side as though radar-controlled. "Ooh," he said like he just spotted a cinnamon pastry. He put his hand on Dave's shoulder and guided him away.

"Great to meet you," Dave managed to say over his shoulder to the couple.

"DOD school teachers from Subic," Max said, nodding toward three women surrounded by hovering, bronze young officers with short, sun-bleached hair. Everyone held a drink. "Seymour and Carol are, um, engaged. She's the queen bee, the Cleopatra." Seymour's arm was drunkenly draped over the dark-haired woman. "And Lieutenant Too-Tall Ted over there drives an Avanti." A man stood erect, his hand on the waist of a slender woman.

When Dave's eyes met hers, a thunderbolt whacked his chest.

As they approached, Max donned his broadest grin. "Good evening, ladies. May I present the squadron's newest pilot, Lieutenant David Quinn."

Carol's hand jutted out. "Glad to meet you."

"Welcome, Lieutenant," Ted said.

"Hello, David," the slender woman said. "I heard you were coming."

Heat rushed to Dave's cheeks as he stared at the striking woman with auburn hair cascading over her shoulders. In makeup and heels, she was no longer a ponytailed schoolgirl, but had the same penetrating eyes.

Ted raised an eyebrow. "You know each other?"

Jennifer nodded. "We went to college together."

"I didn't know. . . ." Dave said. He finally offered his hand. "Hello, Jennifer." Their fingers touched.

Ted tightened his grip around her waist.

"Hi, ladies," Max said, shouldering his way through to the only unattached woman. "I was hoping you'd be here, Gina."

The women exchanged glances. Carol rolled her eyes.

"Welcome to *Peyton Place*," Seymour slurred at Dave.

"More like *Lord of the Flies*," Carol said.

Dave furrowed his brow.

She winked at him. “Adolescent boys on an island.”

CHAPTER 19

Jennifer didn't normally shop on Saturday morning. After each wonderful but exhausting week with eight-year-olds, she usually slept in. But today she had a yen to head over to Cubi Point to pick up a few things and see what new merchandise might be available, so she summoned one of the fleet of Blalock cabs that swarmed over the base.

Last night had been a shock. She barely recognized Dave, even knowing he would be there. In their four years of college, he had devolved from a clean-cut teenager, full of wonder and questions, into a scraggily bearded, shaggy-haired, slovenly hippie wannabe, bloated from beer and devoted to disruption and self-indulgence. But last night, he looked fantastic in his dress white uniform with his wings and LTJG epaulets. He was clean-shaven with neat, short hair, a tan face, and a chiseled jawline.

The taxi stopped at a large Quonset hut nestled amid tropical foliage, marked only by the small sign, *Cubi Point Navy Exchange*. As she pulled open the store's glass door, the humid smell of the primitive jungle yielded to the crisp breeze of humming air conditioners. A few steps transported her from the land of dinosaurs to electronics. Shelves overflowed with merchandise for the young man. She meandered through displays of stereo equipment, wood carvings, and uniforms, glancing down each aisle as she passed. Military insignia, sunglasses, black-velvet paintings. She nodded at several familiar faces but did not see the one she sought. Posters of airplanes, women, and movie stars. She sighed as she reached the back of the store. In the small section of housewares, she dropped several items into her basket and started back toward the cashier.

Suddenly, Max marched in waving his arms, with Dave two steps behind.

"The Japs make great stereo equipment," Max said. "And this monkeypod wood is very cool. The Filipinos carve everything from it—bowls, figurines, even navy stuff." He reached onto a shelf. "Here. This is a must-have item." He handed Dave a three-foot pair of naval aviator wings carved from the golden-brown hardwood.

With Max as tour guide, Dave glowed with the innocent childlike wonder that she remembered. And he looked as good as he had last night, his short-sleeved khaki shirt accentuating his muscular arms and flat stomach. But it was just like the old Dave to latch onto someone like Max, a hard-drinking, womanizing, party boy, instead of someone like Ted. Ted. She stopped behind a wall of television boxes. He wouldn't like her being here.

"You need an amp, turntable, tape deck, speakers." Max pointed and loaded items onto the flatbed cart Dave was pushing until piled with boxes. When Max spotted a Filipina cashier, he slapped Dave on the back.

"That should do you for starters," he said and toddled off to make her acquaintance.

Jennifer watched Dave as he leaned heavily against the flatbed to start it moving toward checkout. It was now or never. She swallowed and emerged from behind an aisle.

"Your shirt won't support that."

He turned.

She pointed at the wooden wings atop his cart.

"This?" He picked it up. "I'll have Mamasan add extra starch to my uniform. It should work."

She surveyed him from crown to foot. "I barely recognized you last night."

"Thanks." He blushed. "I think."

"Yes, it's a compliment."

They stood in silence inspecting each other.

"How do you like it here so far?" she asked.

"I'm buying things for my room." He nodded toward the cart. "And I've met a lot of people." He pointed toward Max, chatting to the young cashier as she rang up customers. "I understand he's dating Gina."

Jennifer snorted involuntarily, then covered it with a cough. Dating? More like stalking.

"Ted seems nice." He tilted his head.

"Yes, he's quite the gentleman." She looked down. "We're just friends."

Dave nodded and cleared his throat. "How long will you be here?"

She smiled. "Not long." She twirled a finger about a strand of hair. "I'm just getting a few things." Lunch might be nice. She wouldn't mind catching up with this new Dave.

"No, I mean in the Philippines."

"Oh," she said. "My DOD teacher contract is year to year. So, at least until the end of the school year." She looked directly into his eyes. "Longer if I renew."

Dave wobbled. A thigh-high toddler tugged at his trousers.

"What's that?" the little girl said, pointing toward the wings Dave held.

"Melissa," a woman called. Commander Holt's wife Brenda hurried over with an exasperated smile and a cart filled with Pampers. "Lieutenant Quinn is busy."

"I'm three," Melissa said, holding up three fingers.

Dave crouched to her level. "Hi, Melissa. I'm"—he looked at his fingers—"twenty-three."

"You only have ten." She again pointed at the monkeypod carving. "What's that?"

"My wings. It means I'm a pilot. I'm going to hang it on my wall."

She looked up at Brenda. "Mommy, can we get one for Daddy?" She turned to Dave. "Daddy's a pilot, too."

"Maybe later, sweetie," Brenda said. "Let's leave Mr. Quinn and Miss Pruitt to their shopping." She smiled at Jennifer. "These are murder to find around here." She pointed at the pile of disposable diapers. "I'm stocking up."

They watched the woman waddle off, struggling with a cart, a baby-distended belly, and the energetic child in tow.

Jennifer took a breath. Should she ask him? It'd be easy. She could just say, let's have lunch and catch up. He seemed so different now.

"Brenda's such a trooper," she said.

"Why is that?"

"Look at her."

Dave looked at Brenda, then back at Jennifer, and shrugged. His intelligent man-boy eyes shone with his old clueless insensitivity, not like a partner who would support her dreams.

Her shoulders sagged as she sighed deeply. “I have to run.” She waved politely and hurried off.

CHAPTER 20

Dave watched the first hint of dawn appear above the jungle foliage as he and Nelson toted their helmets and flight bags across the tarmac toward the line of stoofs. He wasn't looking forward to flying with this guy.

"We have five aircraft in this squadron," Nelson said. "Helen is always down. We use her for parts. That leaves four available, including the Old Man's plane, Double Naughts. We'll be taking her out today." Nelson rubbed his hand across the "00" on the nose of the stoof.

"Hah! *Double Nuts*," Dave guffawed. "A plane with balls." Maybe Nelson did have a sense of humor.

"Not *Double Nuts*, *Double* Naughts—two zeros."

Dave sighed, and his smile evaporated as he followed Nelson around the aircraft on his pre-flight inspection.

Nelson's hand slid along the fuselage. "These radial engines pack a punch," he said. "Eighteen hundred horses each, thirty-six hundred total. That's ten of your Corvettes."

Printed under the pilot's window was the commanding officer's name, *CDR DOUG JENSON*, and under the copilot's window, *LT BOB MOSHER*, the outgoing pilot Dave had replaced. Nelson pointed.

"Your name will eventually go there," he said. "Maybe."

Dave followed Nelson through the hatch. Hunched over, they moved along the low, narrow corridor. Control cables and electrical wires threaded their way through the fuselage spars that encircled them along the gray bulkhead. They passed the two crew seats and abandoned racks where anti-submarine equipment once sat and through another hatch into the cockpit.

Nelson took the copilot seat on the right. Dave strapped into the pilot's seat, buckled his parachute harness, and ran through the prestart checklist. A lineman on the tarmac pointed the fire extinguisher nozzle toward the cowling, and Dave cranked the port engine. It popped, then billowed white smoke, then roared. The huge spinning propeller quickly dissipated the smoke. He then reached down and started the starboard engine.

Dave keyed his mic. "Cubi ground, Checkertail Zero Zero, ready for taxi."

"Roger, Zero Zero," the radio crackled, "cleared to Runway 36, altimeter two niner niner zero, wind zero one zero at ten."

Dave taxied forward past the P-3 parked nearby. She was beautiful, her glistening fuselage and four massive turboprops towering above them. When they reached the approach end of the runway, Nelson reported.

"Takeoff checklist complete," he said. "Ready?"

Dave nodded, and broadcast, "Cubi tower, Zero Zero ready to go."

"Roger, *Double Nuts*, you're cleared for takeoff."

They rolled onto the runway and stopped. Dave advanced the throttles to full open and scanned his gauges.

"Temperatures and pressures normal," he said and released his brakes.

The stoof accelerated rapidly. At eighty-five knots, Dave eased back on the yoke, and they lifted off in the first quarter of the runway.

Nelson nodded. "She can take off in twelve hundred feet if you ask her to."

They turned south, passing the field, and climbed over the bay. A second stoof rose from the runway and veered westward over the open sea. Several ships dotted the horizon.

Nelson nodded toward them. "The Aussie navy is in the neighborhood. We're towing targets for them today." He pointed at the second stoof.

Dave swallowed. Getting shot at didn't sound like much fun.

They continued south along the coastline toward the mouth of Manila Bay. An island appeared at the bay's entrance.

"Corregidor," Nelson said.

Dave looked down at the small rock.

"In 1942, our troops held out for five months before the Japs overran them."

They crossed the bay and circled the city of Manila. From the international airport below, a Pan Am 747 lifted off the runway.

Dave lit up. "That's what I'm going to fly," he said, "after I do my time here."

"Do your time?"

"Yeah, get the training I need for Pan Am."

Nelson turned toward Dave. "You're getting way ahead of yourself, Lieutenant. You need to focus on now. This airplane. This flight. Now."

"Well, sure, but that's my plan." This guy was a real downer.

Nelson sighed. "You know, when this war ends, there'll be thousands of pilots who'd like your precious Pan Am job. Guys with more hours, with fifty combat missions, and with squeaky-clean fitness reports. If you want to have a prayer of getting an airline job out of here, you'd better focus on right now. Learn your procedures. Get your aircraft commander designation. Fly at least fifteen hundred hours. Show us what you're made of. Then, if you're lucky, get into a P-3 squadron for your next assignment and rack up another two thousand hours. And then, maybe, just maybe, the airlines will talk to you."

Dave didn't need a rebuke. He would do whatever it took.

Nelson gestured to the north, and Dave banked the aircraft toward the interior. They flew in silence.

"Mount Pinatubo," Nelson finally said, nodding.

Dave headed directly toward the smoking volcano. He circled the rim and looked at Nelson for approval. Nothing. He flew directly over the gaping maw—a moon crater with yellow and white sand and steaming vents. Updrafts buffeted the aircraft. Acrid sulfur fumes penetrated Dave's sinuses. He gagged and his eyes watered.

"Any danger here?" Dave said.

"If it erupts. Or even blows a little vent. But that hasn't happened in months."

"Sounds dangerous." Dave banked away from the inferno.

"Then why did you fly over it?"

Max snickered. "Nelson loves to do that. He lets you screw up any way you can think of." He rattled the dice in the cup, spilled them onto the acey-deucy table, and moved his checkers, counting out the roll.

The game table was as much a part of the ready room as the flight scheduling board. The Quonset hut served as the operations center of the squadron, with scheduling, training, briefing, and debriefing. The rear housed the game table, coffee mess, and back door to the flight line.

"Why would he?" Dave said, rising from the table and taking the three steps to the coffee machine. He reached up to the wall-mounted rack, a five-foot-wide plywood squadron insignia of a red star on a checkerboard background, varnished to a high gloss. From wooden pegs hung the officers' mugs sporting decals of squadron insignia, wings of gold, and scantily clad women, with inscriptions such as *Mighty Max*, *Stoof Jockey*, and *Tiger Lil's Men's Club*. He took down his recently purchased mug adorned simply with *LT QUINN* and aviator wings, filled it with the dark coffee, and returned to the table.

Max rolled again. "You learn more by screwing up. If it doesn't kill you."

"Well, he strikes me as bitter and seems to have me in his sights."

"He's a gung-ho lifer."

"I'll bet it's that scar," Dave said, touching his chin.

Max fell silent.

"I tried to orbit down below the rim," said a voice behind Dave. "But he drew the line there. I guess he does value his own skin."

Dave looked up to see a mass of muscle that barely met the Navy's five-foot-two height requirement, but with arms and a neck as wide as the head bulging from a size-too-small khaki shirt.

"You haven't met Norm." Max smacked his lips. "He had the duty the other night."

"Hello," Dave said, standing and offering his hand. "I'll bet you've played some football."

Norm grabbed Dave's hand with a beefy mitt and shook vigorously. Dave's knuckles collapsed within the sinewy grip, but he managed to suppress the yelp of pain before it escaped his throat.

"I have," Norm said. "I played ball with Roger Staubach."

Max snorted.

Dave extracted his hand and massaged it. "*The* Roger Staubach? Of the Dallas Cowboys?"

"Yep. He's a great guy."

"You played pro ball?"

"Ah, no, in the Navy."

"You played with Staubach at the Academy?" Dave looked for Norm's Naval Academy ring. He had met very few "ring knockers," so known for tapping their rings to remind others that they were Annapolis men.

"For Christ's sake," Max said. "He met him once at a scrimmage at the Pensacola BOQ." Max's face flushed. "Nobody buys your horseshit, Flex."

Norm smiled and raised his eyebrows.

"Gina does."

Max bared his teeth, but rank and heft worked against him. He turned to Dave. "And Zero Zero *is* called *Double Nuts*. Nelson just doesn't like it. But you want to stay on his good side. He's tight with the Old Man."

Squadron officers filed through the front door of the Quonset hut, past a wall-mounted scheduling board hanging above Petty Officer Second Class Cox's desk. They filled their coffee mugs and reclined in the rows of vinyl upholstered armchairs.

"How often do we have these things?" Dave said.

Max shrugged. "Whenever the Old Man gets the urge."

The door opened and Cox jumped to his feet. "Attention on deck!"

Everyone rose as the CO strode to the podium.

"Be seated, gentlemen. The smoking lamp is lit." Zippo lighters clicked open, and flames curled into glowing cigarette tips. "Let me first say to Max, thanks for waxing my airplane on Saturday. It was a real surprise."

"Brown nose," someone called out with muffled clarity. The officers laughed.

"But jeez, Max, you only waxed the starboard side. Now it flies sideways. The yaw is pronounced."

"Sorry, Captain," Max said. "I ran out of steam. And beer." More laughter. "Just crank in some right rudder trim. She flies great."

The CO shook his head. "Okay, let's get on with it." He congratulated the men on successful ongoing flight operations, on the great maintenance that kept four of the five squadron aircraft flying, and on the excellent safety record. Finishing the ten-minute speech, he paused.

"There's something else I want to say." He took a breath and looked at his officers. "Being a naval officer and a naval aviator is a privilege. Yes, you worked for it. And you deserve credit. But it's a privilege to be chosen for that opportunity and an honor to serve. Naval aviation has a long and proud history of service. To God. To country. And to our fellow servicemen." He scanned each face. "It's not a trade school." He looked directly at Dave. "Every day we risk our lives in service to our country. Why do we do that? To get a better job?" He shook his head. "No, we do it because work needs to be done, and we have been chosen and trained to do it."

The room was silent.

"People rely on our skills. They put their lives in our hands. When we deliver a human being to the deck of an aircraft carrier, that's one hell of a responsibility. And I, for one, thank God for the privilege to serve." His hand rose from the podium. "There's a war on. Let's get out there and win it." He flashed a thumbs-up. "Carry on, gentlemen."

Cox jumped up. "Attention on deck." Everyone rose as the CO walked out.

Dave wiped sweat from his neck and whispered to Max. "I never said it was a trade school."

"It's just the usual pep talk," Max said as Nelson walked by. "Lieutenant Nelson. One moment please." Max grinned. "A little bird told me it's your fortieth birthday." A crowd gathered. Max produced a black balloon and a card. "Happy birthday," he said.

Applause and catcalls filled the Quonset hut.

Nelson eyed Max. He opened the card and read aloud. "This certificate entitles Lieutenant Ronald L. Nelson to a *Round the World* at Tiger Lil's Premier Massage Emporium." He looked up at a beaming Max. "You got me a gift certificate to a whorehouse?"

"A massage parlor," Max said, his grin fading. "Sort of."

Nelson sighed. "Thanks, Max," he said and walked out the door.

Max stood holding the balloon. "He didn't love it." He let the balloon float away. "Of course, Nelson's an old guy. Maybe his equipment is on the fritz."

CHAPTER 21

"Trust me," Max said, leaping from the convertible. "I've done this before."

Dave sighed and hoisted himself out of Max's XKE. As they approached the guardhouse, Dave looked at the arch over the gate and forced a weak smile. "Abandon all hope, ye who enter here."

"More like abandon all *rules*," Max said with a wink.

"Sir," the guard said with a nod and smile but no salute to the civilian-attired officers.

"Hey, Sully," Max said as they strode past. "How's it hanging?"

Dave held his breath as they passed through the gate and crossed into the bright security lights illuminating the bridge. When he finally breathed, he could taste the stink of sewage wafting up from the dark canal below. The quiet, fifty-yard bridge transformed into the busy, litter-strewn main street of Olongapo. Shop owners beckoned them. Children followed with their palms cupped. A street vendor sweated over an open grill. Dave recoiled at the offer of a stick of meat. His eyes darted about. A gang of pre-teen boys loitered nearby.

"Stealy boys," Max said, nodding. "They find a drunk sailor separated from his shipmates and pick him clean."

Max abruptly turned off the main drag onto a dark side street. Dave stuck close as they navigated the twists and turns of back alleys.

"This is a great town," Max said. "The place was colonized by Spain."

Dave nodded. After the natives killed Magellan.

The pilot's mantra .was *situational awareness*—always know where you are and be aware of the events happening around you—but Dave had become irretrievably lost.

Max rounded a corner and hurried through an open door. Dave followed. Inside, he squinted against the smoke cloud that hung like fog. Two sailors hunched over the bar. A couple moved furtively in a dark booth. Max chose a small round table. Dave swatted his handkerchief on his chair seat before sitting. A bargirl appeared with two bottles of beer.

"Hi, baby," she said to Max. "You want company?" She plopped down on his knee without awaiting an answer. "I no see you long time." She pushed out her lower lip in an exaggerated pout.

"I've been busy, Maria," Max said, "keeping America safe for democracy."

Another bargirl, about twice Maria's age, alighted on a chair next to Dave. His spine stiffened, and he leaned away.

"Your friend shy," Maria said to Max.

"He's new. I'm showing him the ropes."

Maria's young face scrunched. "You show ropes?"

"I do," Max said, his hand on her hip, "but not enough to hang himself."

"Why he want to hang himself?" Maria said. "Consuela make him happy."

Consuela smiled at Dave through her heavy makeup, batted her thick lashes, and rested her hand on his forearm. "You buy me drink, sugar?" Her heavy breasts pushed up from the low-cut dress, and her perfume enveloped him.

He lifted his beer and took a long draught. Bitter on the back of his tongue, it constricted his throat as it went down.

She slid closer, her thigh touching his.

Perspiration ran down his temples. "Maybe we should leave, Max."

"No way, amigo. We just got here." Max waved at the waiter.

Dave leaned toward Max. "I thought you liked Gina," he whispered. "Jennifer's friend?"

"I do. So?"

"Please, Max, let's go."

"Go ahead. Be a killjoy."

"I don't know the way back."

Max waved a hand. "Out the front door, then left, right, left, and follow the main drag."

Dave's head swam. He leaned back in his chair and took another swig. Consuela rested her hand on his knee. Dave clenched the rim of the table and looked pleadingly at Max. She drew her long red fingernails from Dave's knee to his inner thigh.

Dave jerked his chair back and jumped up. "I'm sorry, Max. I have to go."

"Fine," Max said, looking away.

"Nice to meet you, ladies." Dave threw a five on the table and raced toward the door.

Max shook his head. "It's okay, Consuela." He patted his thigh. "I have another knee."

Dave pushed open the heavy metal door. Max called out, "the *front* door," as the back door slammed shut behind Dave.

Finding himself in a dark alley, unfamiliar except for the smell of garbage, Dave spun around. He pulled on the locked door behind him, then looked down the alley, one way, then the other. *Left right left.* He turned left and raced off, then right, then left. He saw nothing familiar. There were no street lights, only dimly lit windows. He slowed and wandered deeper into the city. A skinny dog scavenged for food. A baby cried from a shanty's open window. Three teenaged boys huddled against a wall, smoke rising from the small circle. One noticed him and elbowed another. Heads turned and they watched him hurry past.

Hopelessly lost in a dark labyrinth, Dave jogged back and forth, passing the same window, the same baby, the same dog. Exhausted, he leaned against an alley wall and got a whiff of something foul but familiar. Before him, only feet away, was the canal, and beyond, the quiet naval base. Fifty yards of putrid water separated Dave from freedom. He looked down the waterway and saw the glow in the sky of the bridge lights in the distance. He picked his way along the shoreline to the last building and peered around the corner of a stucco wall. A one-hundred-yard no-man's land separated his hiding place from the foot of the bridge.

Dave's mind raced. Should he run? Or be cool, walk confidently. He put his hands in his pockets and his head down, took a deep breath, and stepped out of the shadow. As inconspicuous as a fishing boat was to seagulls, he strode briskly toward the bridge.

A presence brushed his side.

"Dolla mista?" a small boy said with his palm up.

Dave pulled his wallet from his hip pocket, stuffed it into his front pocket, and sped up his pace. Others appeared, calling to him, hands reaching and touching, grabbing at his pockets. He spun in circles to face his tormentors, but they surrounded and pawed at him. When he saw the older boys approaching, he broke into a full gallop, the swarm in pursuit, yelling and laughing. He gasped for breath as he charged across the open area. He hit the bridge at top speed and raced across.

CHAPTER 22

The ship carrying his Corvette had docked at Subic about the same time Dave had been wandering the back alleys of Olongapo. The next morning, Max took him to the port. Dave beamed as he signed the paperwork and got the keys, but his spirits sagged when he saw the grit-covered Vette. He wiped the handle on the door with his handkerchief before opening it and saw a hole in the dash where his radio had been.

"Bummer," Max said.

Dave turned the key. Silence. Not even a click. Opening the hood revealed cables dangling where a battery used to be. They attached jumper cables from the Jag. After three unsuccessful attempts to start her, Dave looked at the gas gauge. It read *E*. Bone dry.

"Christ," he said. "They even stole the gas."

They borrowed a five-gallon gas can and trudged over to the gas pump. The second time, she started like a champ. Driving to the gas station to top her off, Dave watched the engine temperature gauge rise into the red zone. He pulled over, raised the hood, and removed the radiator cap. He jumped back as scorching fumes billowed out. The hot metal popped and groaned. He looked in. Max pulled up and stood next to Dave inspecting the steaming engine.

"They drained the antifreeze," Dave said. "A few more miles and I would have burned her up."

That afternoon, Dave sat in his purring Corvette outside the Subic base school. Radio replaced, top down, and washed and waxed, she sparkled. Squinting in the bright sunlight as the teachers filed out, he reached for the case, popped it open, and removed his shades. He slipped them on and practiced a couple of quick smiles in the mirror.

He looked cool and he resolved to *be* cool. But when Jennifer came out with Carol, talking and laughing, that old jolt hit him.

"Good afternoon, ladies," he said, hearing the quaver in his own voice. "Buy you dinner?"

"Not me, Dave," Carol said. "I'm meeting Ken." She smiled impishly. "But you go ahead, Jen."

Jennifer's eyes flashed at her friend. "I really can't, David. But thanks."

He raised his eyebrows. "They have fresh lobster at the O Club."

"Your favorite." Carol elbow-nudged her friend.

Jennifer shook her head. "I don't think—"

"It's just dinner," Dave said. "You'll be home before dark. I promise."

Carol pushed Jennifer and mouthed, "Go."

Jennifer sighed. "Well, okay. Thanks." She climbed into the passenger seat.

Carol winked and flashed a quick finger wave.

"Nice wheels, huh?" Dave smiled as he engaged the clutch.

Jennifer hesitated. "Your car is, um, career appropriate."

"Yes, I know, I used to mock cars. But it's part of the uniform." He turned, cupped a hand between his mouth and her ear, and whispered, "I'm playing a role to reach my target."

"Which is?"

He smiled. "Pan Am."

She looked at Carol as the Vette lurched from the curb.

He negotiated the winding road with skill, his shades remaining in place under the dark jungle canopy. "When are Carol and Seymour—uh, Ken—getting married?" he said.

"Married? They're not getting married."

"But I thought—"

"Carol just enjoys, you know, his company. She wouldn't marry him."

"Why not? Is there something wrong with him?"

"Yes. He's a pilot."

"That's not a plus?"

"Not in the husband category. Carol doesn't need to answer her door one day and see two grim naval officers staring back at her."

On the screened patio outside the officers' club, they sat beneath ceiling fans stirring the warm air. The navy-gray concrete floor extended beyond the screens, where thick fauna dripped with moisture. Dave helped Jennifer with her bib as the waiter placed two lobster dinners on the linen-covered table. In a tank nearby, oblivious crustaceans undulated slowly. Dave refilled the wine glasses, sipped the five-year-old French chardonnay, and regaled his dinner companion with his thorough knowledge of the grape.

"I love this variety," he said, "with its delicious vanilla notes, and only the lightest touch of fruit and oak." He took another sip. "It goes great with lobster."

Jennifer shrugged. "What doesn't?"

They both laughed.

Dave told her of his adventures in the two years since college—Officer Candidate School and flight training—with the requisite airplane hand gestures.

"I taught elementary school and lived at home," Jennifer said. "Daddy wanted me to go to law school." She looked at her hands. "I disappointed him. He said anyone can be a teacher. Go for the gold." She looked back at Dave. "But I love what I do." She said she planned to start her own school. She'd teach for five years, maybe ten, get experience teaching, save her money, and learn how schools are run. "My school will build confidence and independence in girls, prepare them to enter the professions. And not just nurses and teachers. I mean doctors and lawyers and architects. We won't teach home economics or origami."

"My dad wants me to come into the family business," Dave said. "But I *am* going for the gold. I've decided my next Navy assignment will be P-3s, to get some quality hours for the airlines. Then, in five years I'll be a copilot for Pan Am, and in fifteen I'll be captain of a 747."

She looked him over. "I have to say, I'm quite impressed by the determination and work it took to get where you are. Very few could do it."

He couldn't hold back the smile.

"It's quite a transformation," she said. "You used to be so . . ."

"Shaggy?" he said.

"No . . ."

"Plump?"

"No, David, I don't mean your appearance." She struggled for the words. "You're . . . different now. Your goals have changed. Dramatically."

"The Navy was *your* idea. Remember?"

"Yes, but as a temporary escape hatch, not a career. In college, you wanted to grow grapes and make wine."

He smiled. "Yeah. When I was fourteen, my neighbor had a grape arbor. I made wine every year. I really loved it. Making it, that is. The wine tasted awful." He sighed with an unfocused gaze.

"You see? You light up when you talk about that. But when you talk about flying, it's like . . . bragging rights." She looked into his eyes. "But there's only one critic who's important, and he's in there." She pointed to his heart. "Do what you love, David."

"I love flying."

She eyed him thoughtfully. "Then I wish you the best. Go with your dream. And maybe the war will be over soon."

"God, I hope not."

She looked startled.

That didn't come out right. "No, what I mean is . . . if the war ends before I get out, the Navy and Air Force will dump a lot of pilots, and they'll all be competing for airline jobs."

Her jaw became set. "People are dying, Dave. *Children* are dying. You've seen the pictures."

"Yeah, war is terrible."

She reached for her purse. "I'm ready to go home."

He pushed back his chair. "Okay, but I'm on call. Mind if I check messages at my place before I take you back to Subic?"

"I don't think so, David. I can take a cab."

"No, I'll drive you back. Come on. It'll only take a second. You can see the evil one's lair."

CHAPTER 23

Jennifer regretted coming as the Corvette pulled to the curb at the BOQ and parked amid the taxies. She didn't want to see his room. She was still numb over his indifference to the suffering of war because it served his purpose. Like Daddy during World War II, who played the Lothario of Shaker Heights while the blood of their boys drained into the sands of Iwo Jima.

Dave jumped out, opened her door, and offered his hand. She took it and stood, then withdrew from his touch. At his room, he pushed open the door and she stepped in. Her fingers touched her parted lips as she absorbed the décor.

An entire wall was covered with stereo equipment—an amplifier, turntable, two reel-to-reel tape decks, and waist-high speakers in mahogany cases. Tapes and records filled bookcase shelves. A Papasan chair dominated a corner of the room. The five-foot-diameter bamboo bowl tilted on a pedestal with a huge flowered cushion and wicker footstool. One didn't sit down, he got in. A small bamboo bar and two bar stools occupied another wall. Posters looked down from above—a Pan Am 747, Marlon Brando, a Playboy centerfold, a P-3 Orion.

"Maybe I should wait outside."

"No, no, I'll just be a second." He fiddled with the phone answering machine.

She set her purse on the bar.

"Care for a drink?" he said, still playing with the recorder.

"No, thanks." Atop the bar stood a beautifully carved monkey pod sculpture of an eight-inch-tall man surrounded by a removable barrel.

"What's this?" She pointed at the figurine.

Dave turned and his mouth dropped open. "That's, um, Woody," he stammered.

"Woody? Why do you call it Woody?" She reached for it.

He bolted across the room just as she lifted the barrel from around the man.

TWANGGGG.

Jennifer emitted a startled squeak, jumped back, and dropped the barrel.

A naked man stood with a six-inch erection vibrating on a spring.

She looked at Dave, then back at the wooden appendage, still oscillating. "Really?" She grabbed her purse. "I have to go," she said and scurried out the door.

CHAPTER 24

Dave couldn't wait to finish training and start flying hops with Max and the other pilots. Every training flight with Nelson was torture.

"You're landing too long," Nelson said on their fifth flight in as many days. "You must land on the numbers."

Dave chopped power late and floated hundreds of feet beyond the "07" painted on the approach end before settling onto the runway.

"If you can't hit the numbers," Nelson said, "how are you going to catch the three-wire when you get to the fleet?"

Dave pushed the dual throttles full forward and lifted off, completing another touch-and-go, and climbed back into the Cubi Point landing pattern. At a thousand feet, he turned downwind. As they passed abeam the numbers and turned toward final approach, Nelson pulled back one throttle.

"You just lost your starboard engine," he said, simulating an emergency.

Dave fumbled the procedures and overcompensated by holding too much power on the good engine. He managed to find the runway but landed long again.

Nelson shook his head. "You have to know these procedures by rote," he said. "There's no time to think in an emergency. You must react instinctively."

"I got her down on one engine," Dave said.

"Excuses don't cut it around here. They'll be your epitaph."

Dave applied full power and took off again.

"Engine fire," Nelson said. "What do you do?"

"Shut it down."

"The steps, Lieutenant, what are the steps? One, two, three."

"Uh . . . turn off the fuel."

Nelson raised his visor. His eyes squinted. "Lieutenant, your heart doesn't seem to be in this. If you expect me to certify you're ready, you'll have to show me more. A lot more."

After each training flight, Dave collapsed in the ready room, drenched in sweat, hair matted and skin prickly, as Nelson enumerated each of Dave's aeronautical shortcomings.

What a pain. Why couldn't he be more like Commander Holt? Soft spoken and polite, Holt taught as though he were talking to his daughter, Melissa. Landing a little long? Let's reduce power another inch of manifold pressure at the one eighty. Strong crosswind? Drop the wing into the wind and apply top rudder for directional control. He even made being shot at seem peaceful when showing Dave how to tow targets for allied navies.

"You'll like target towing," Holt said from the copilot's seat. "Straight and level hours. No trips in country. No carrier landings."

Dave looked down at the South Korean destroyer as it tracked due west in the South China Sea, its guns trained on the sky. The stoof approached from the north, flying straight and level and perpendicular to the ship's course. From her tail extended a two-thousand-foot-long cable, dragging a red sleeve like a large windsock. Dave sat in the pilot's seat, his tense fingers gripping the yoke.

As they passed overhead, Holt keyed his radio mic. "Clear to fire," he transmitted.

A silent puff of smoke billowed from the ship's guns, and a black burst of flack appeared near the target. A moment later, the sound of the guns and the distant exploding shells reached them.

"Once we're overhead," Holt said, "we clear them to fire. Their guns don't swing to the vertical, so we're safe."

The Koreans ceased firing. Dave turned 180 degrees and approached the ship from the opposite side.

"Cleared to fire," Holt broadcast again when overhead.

Dave saw the smoke from the guns below. A silent burst of shrapnel shredded the target, sending evidence of its violence running up the long cable and into the airframe. By the time it reached Dave, it was just a shudder. Only then did the sound of the explosion reach his ears as a low distant rumble, not as bad as he had feared.

"They got it, sir," Cox said on the intercom.

"Roger," Holt said. "Reel out another target."

After his final training flights, they released Dave to fly with other squadron pilots. Nelson offered a grunt and a scowl, while Holt offered his hand.

"Now you start earning your pay," Holt said. "You'll be flying with Max a lot. I'm sure he'll have some things to show you."

On the tarmac of Taipei International Airport, Max handed a box of books and vinyl records to crewman Cox through the stoof hatch.

Dave leaned against the fuselage. "So I need another hundred flight hours, then gotta pass my flight check, get my aircraft commander designation, and start racking up those pilot-in-command hours."

Max lifted another box through the hatch. Half-moons of sweat darkened his armpits.

Dave wiped his forehead. "In fifteen months, I'll leave here with fifteen hundred hours, get another two thousand in a P-3 squadron, and be in the catbird seat for that Pan Am job after my six-year hitch." Dave noticed an open box on the tarmac, reached in, and pulled out a book the heft of a brick. Gold leaf on the heavy cover read *War and Peace,* Leo Tolstoy. He looked into the box. *Crime and Punishment. Valley of the Dolls. How to Avoid Probate.* "Are you going to read all these?"

"It's for the chicks," Max said.

"Your dates read Dostoyevsky?"

"No, man. The books go on my bookcase. They give the place class." Max shoved another box through the hatch. "Plus, they're cheap. Books are only ten New Taiwanese dollars. Records too."

"Because they're all pirated," Dave said. "Taiwan never signed the international copyright treaty." He opened a book and pointed. "They even copy the copyright symbol."

Max shrugged.

Dave tilted his head. "So on your thousand-dollar wall of stereo equipment, you're going to play scratchy twenty-five-cent bootlegged records?"

"This isn't for me," Max said, his hand on his chest. "It's for you, part of your training."

"To get to Pan Am, I need training in *flight*, not in shopping."

"This *is* flight training—how to load the stoof. For example, do you know how many passengers you can carry?"

"There are only two seats in the back, Max."

"Okay, bad example." He looked at the ground. "Okay, let's say you see a motorcycle in Okinawa, a Honda 350cc, and the price is half what it is in the PI. What are you going to do?"

"You can't fit a motorcycle through this hatch."

"We do it all the time. You just have to disassemble it."

Cox nodded. "I brought several back for shipmates," he said through the hatch as Max handed him the last box.

The fuselage dropped slightly, startling Dave, who had been leaning against it. The wheel struts compressed half an inch under the added weight. Dave eyed the two remaining objects on the tarmac. "Are you sure we can haul all this?"

"Don't worry," Max said as he turned to the pair of hundred-pound, two-feet-tall porcelain elephants. "End tables," he said before Dave asked. "Give me a hand."

They strained to lift one and push it through the hatch. With a jerk, the main struts settled a full inch.

"Jesus, Max, we can't carry all this weight."

Max sighed. "Look," he said as they lifted the second elephant, "the stoof weighs eighteen thousand pounds empty. Full fuel tanks are another four thousand. Plus three guys, say two hundred apiece with gear. That puts us at 22,600 pounds. Our max gross is 25,500. That leaves almost three thousand pounds for cargo. We could stick twelve fat guys in here and still be good." They pushed in the second elephant. "Plus, if you can see four inches of the wheel strut piston, the weight's okay." Dave could see at least six.

The stoof groaned. Dave jumped as she pivoted back on her main gear like a seesaw, her nose slowly rising and her tail settling gently on the tarmac.

Max grinned sheepishly. "Balance. Now that's another matter."

Max stuck his head through the hatch. "Push it forward. It's too far aft."

"I know, sir," Cox said. "But we're running out of room forward."

Cox grunted as he pushed the elephant up the aisle, sliding the weight forward along the teeter totter until the nose settled again as the tail rose.

Max turned to Dave and opened his palms. "Ta-da," he said, just as a truck squealed to a stop.

Three men leaped out and unloaded a large mahogany desk, disassembled into four pieces, each protected by torn cardboard and each barely smaller than the three-by-two-foot stoof hatch. Max avoided Dave's stare. The wheel struts compressed another inch as the men loaded the desk. The stoof groaned again and settled back onto her tail.

"We should be okay," Max said.

"Max, we're out of balance. We're sitting on our tail."

"We're not finished loading," Max said as he squeezed through the hatch. Dave followed him up the narrow aisle, the cargo strapped all around. As they moved forward, their added weight settled the nose wheel to the ground. Max flashed a grin at Dave. They entered the cockpit, strapped in, and started up. As they taxied toward the runway, Dave looked out his window and watched the wheel strut bounce sluggishly with the bumps. He cinched tight his chute.

On the runway, Max pushed the throttles full forward. The stoof began to roll and bumped along like a heavily loaded gravel truck. Dave gripped his harness. The stoof rolled. And rolled. And rolled. At rotation speed, Max eased back the yoke. The nose came up, but the wheels remained affixed to the runway. Dave looked at Max's placid face as the aircraft continued to accelerate. Finally, the bumping of the wheels stopped and the stoof lifted off into the Chinese sky.

Two weeks later, off the northern Philippine coast, an American destroyer fired its final volleys. The stoof crew reeled in the cable and turned toward home, crossing into the interior. Below, a mist-enshrouded resort town peeked through the clouds from high in the mountains of Luzon.

"Ever land at Baguio?" Max said. They circled a short landing strip perched atop a mountain crest, punctuated at each end by cliff drop-offs. "Short field landing. Gear down, half flaps, eighty-five knots." They wobbled in, Max at the controls, mountain peaks above them on all sides. "Not as short as a carrier landing. But then, there's no wire to catch you."

"We're awfully close to stall speed." Dave squeezed the clamps on his parachute harness.

"It's a skill you can use, Dave. You never know when you'll need to get into a tight spot." They rolled onto final approach. "What do you do if you're short of the runway?"

"Add power."

Max reduced power. "Suppose you can't? Suppose you've lost an engine."

"Um, land short, in the grass."

"You see any grass here?"

Dave didn't. The approach end of the runway dropped off a cliff with rocks and jungle below.

As the aircraft descended and the runway approached, Dave's pitch rose. "Bend over and kiss my sweet ass goodbye?"

"Let's do something more useful. What did Ted say?"

Dave had suffered through Ted's training class two days earlier as the immaculately coifed pretty boy expounded on basic aerodynamics. "Flaps change the camber of the wing and give you more lift," Ted had said. "But also more drag." His wooden pointer tapped the lift and drag vectors drawn on the board. "So when you lower your flaps, you pop up, but you also slow down." He peppered the board with a crescendo of taps. "This is why we never, repeat, NEVER, use flaps to gain altitude." He knocked his academy ring twice on the table as an exclamation point. "Oh, you'll pop up all right, but then you'll stall and leave a very sad widow. Or girlfriend." He smiled at Dave. "If you have one."

Max reduced the power further. The aircraft descended to runway altitude but several hundred yards short. The cliff face loomed.

"Max!" Dave squeaked. "We aren't going to make it!"

Max slapped down the flaps lever to full. Valves turned, hydraulic fluid applied force, and the flap on each wing lowered, changing the camber of the airfoil. Ted's imaginary upward lift vector grew longer, more powerful. The increased lift popped the aircraft up as the airspeed rapidly bled off toward stall speed. The stoof shuttered from the approaching stall just as the numbers appeared beneath her, and she dropped firmly onto the runway. With full flaps and a slight headwind, they landed at a ground speed so slow that Max stopped in a few hundred yards.

"Ta-da," he said.

Dave's white-knuckled death grip on his harness loosened. "We didn't need to land here. Ted said never do this. NEVER."

"Being told isn't enough. To understand, you need to experience it." Max taxied to the tarmac. "Plus, they have great bamboo furniture here."

They entered the back door of the ready room, Max carrying a bamboo hanging chair. Nelson stood before the seated pilots, today's lesson on the chalkboard next to him:

ENGINE FIRE

1. M—MIXTURE

2. F—FEATHER

3. E—EMERGENCY SWITCHES

"You're not a hotshot pilot just because you have good hand-eye coordination and motor skills. Anyone can sail calm seas." He waived the wooden pointer across the assemblage. "You have to know your emergency procedures, what to do when something unusual happens, something that might *never* happen. And you must know them by rote. There's no time to reflect. You're not taking a civics test. When your engine is on fire, it's chaos. You must react instantly, automatically, and correctly." He tapped the board. "M-F-E—mixture, feather, emergency."

Dave and Max plopped down in the back row.

"What do you do if you have an engine fire?" Nelson said. A mock-up of the stoof control panel was mounted on a stand. "One, mixture lever—pull closed." He grasped the mixture control lever with raised fist and jerked it back. "This shuts off the fuel." He put his palm on a large red button. "Two, feather button—press." He pressed the button. "This feathers the prop, reduces drag, and lets you fly further."

Dave whispered to Max, "So you can reach the crash site."

"Three," Nelson said, glaring at Dave, "emergency switch—flip the switch and a fire extinguisher under the cowling goes off, dousing the fire."

Dave whispered, "Why's he always angry?"

Max shrugged. "Maybe he's not getting any from Mamasan."

"Does he even have a mamasan?"

"No one knows."

"In an emergency," Nelson said, "you must react automatically. Like taking a crap. Do you have to think through the steps? Let's see . . ." He held up one finger. "Step One: drop drawers." Then a second finger. "Step Two: mount commode." And a third. "Step Three: Release sphincter?" He looked around with a scowl. "No. You just do it—one-two-three—without thinking."

Dave elbowed Max and scribbled on his kneepad: "D-M-R. Drop. Mount. Release."

That night mighty stoof engines idled in a low growl as Dave watched Max go through the pre-taxi checklist. "Are you sure this is okay?" Dave said.

Max turned dials and flipped switches. "Sure. I just need a warm body for the right seat."

A red light illuminated on the console. Dave pointed. "Starboard electrical generator failure light."

Max looked. "It'll be okay. The port generator is fine. It's a short hop. We'll be back in two shakes."

"But procedures require—"

"Look, Norm is trying to move in on my girl. I need these brownie points with Gina. And you agreed to go."

Dave opened his mouth but said nothing.

"Okay then," Max said. "Let's get this furball to Manila."

A cat carrier on the deck between them emitted a plaintive cry.

The blue sky yielded to the advancing twilight as the stoof crossed Manila Bay and landed at the international airport. Max exited the hatch with the cat carrier and trotted across the tarmac to a baggage handler loading a Pan Am jetliner. Dave admired the gleaming new aircraft.

"Gina owes me now," Max said, strapping back in. "We saved her precious cat several extra days in a crate. It should be in the States by morning."

They took off into the dark sky and settled in for the short cruise across the bay.

"Uh-oh," Max said. He pointed at the illuminated port generator failure light. "The other generator. The good one."

A shot of adrenaline blasted through Dave. He stared down into the blackness of Manila Bay. A familiar panic filled his mind with visions of drowning in a black, breathless sea. He grew dizzy and grabbed the yoke to steady himself.

"Hey!" Max said.

Dave's hands flew off the yoke. He gripped his harness and forced himself to breathe slowly and deeply.

"Take it easy, buddy," Max said.

With both electrical generators out, the instrument lights grew dim as the batteries discharged. Soon, all went dark and the radios fell silent. Dave shined his flashlight onto the flight instruments as Max picked his way between the dark coastline and the moonlit bay.

With the lights of the runway in sight, Max slowed the aircraft and slapped down the gear lever. Valves turned and the motor-driven pumps diverted pressurized hydraulic fluid to the landing gear. The nacelles opened and the wheels lowered with a thud. Dave visually checked the over-center lock.

"Starboard gear down," he said. He shined the light out Max's window. "Port gear down."

"Check the nose gear," Max said.

Dave didn't move.

"Remember how?"

"Of course." Dave sat motionless. "Not really."

"That panel on the deck."

Dave tried to reach down, but his shoulder harness and parachute kept him in place.

"You'll have to unstrap."

"Take my chute off?"

Max just stared.

Dave unstrapped and got down on his knees. He opened the panel to the whoosh of the airstream below. He contorted his body in the cramped space and pointed the flashlight through the hole. "Nose gear is locked down."

As he strapped back in, they entered the landing pattern. With no radio, no lights, and no electrical power, the dark stoof landed unannounced at Cubi Point Naval Air Station.

CHAPTER 25

Nelson stared out the window of the CO's office, steam rising from the coffee mug in his hand. The morning sun streamed in.

The commanding officer rose from his chair. "Back to your old ways, Max?" He sat on the corner of his metal desk, inches from the two junior officers standing at parade rest.

Nelson sipped his coffee. He knew this was coming. Quinn was a bad influence. Maybe the Old Man would finally see things his way.

"You know, Ensign, I can get past you doing your girlfriend a favor." The CO walked behind the men. "And I can even get past using a naval aircraft to transport a cat." He came around into the men's faces. "But what I cannot comprehend is your phenomenally bad judgment in taking an aircraft, *my* aircraft with a failed generator for such a horseshit reason." He sighed and shook his head. "What the hell were you thinking?"

"Well, sir," Max said, "Gina needed to ship her cat back, and the other generator was okay, so—"

"Shut up and listen! I don't want to have this conversation again. Ever." He took a breath. "Look," he said, running his fingers across his scalp. "I appreciate your skill at the controls and command of procedures. They're important. But good judgment is critical. And you're not showing me much of that. Didn't you learn anything from that training command stunt of yours, *Ensign*?" He eyed Dave. "And *you*, Lieutenant. Why in God's name did you go along with this?" He assumed a look of disgust and waved his hand. "You're dismissed."

After the men scampered out, Nelson sat down opposite the captain. "Sir, Lt. Quinn isn't ready for his aircraft commander designation. And, frankly, I wonder if he ever will be." The Old Man pulled out a cigar and put his feet on the desk. Nelson leaned forward. "He hasn't learned his procedures, he doesn't accept instruction, and he mistakes mediocrity for excellence." Nelson tapped the desk twice with his finger. "He's a cocky know-it-all."

The CO held the cigar box toward Nelson. "Weren't we all?"

Nelson declined the offer with a wave. "Captain, he could hurt someone. And damage one of your aircraft."

The Old Man raised his palms. "There's a war on, Ron. The Navy needs pilots, and we can't pump them through the training command fast enough. Besides, he wouldn't have got his wings if he couldn't fly."

"He *can* fly. It's not his *skill*, it's his *attitude*."

"Give it time. He'll come around."

"And if he doesn't?"

The CO took a long drag on the cigar and sent a plume of smoke skyward. "It's your job to make sure he does."

Nelson respected Commander Jensen. But he had that part wrong. Nelson's job was to make sure this arrogant kid didn't kill someone. Nelson knew. He too had been caught up in the glamour of naval aviation. The status, the respect, the girls. And it almost cost him everything. But he had his wakeup call early. Flying was serious business—as was serving your country. But these young hotshots still couldn't see past the glory, the prestige, the fun.

"Captain, I really have a bad feeling about this one." He didn't want to prostrate himself before the commanding officer, but what choice did he have? He swallowed hard. "He reminds me of myself."

His fingers touched the scar on his chin, protruding and badly healed. Whenever he met someone, their eyes didn't meet his; they went to his chin. He could have had the scar removed. In fact, several flight surgeons had encouraged him to do just that. But it was his hair shirt, an act of penance, and whenever he looked in a mirror, a reminder of his sin. His gut roiled as he thought of that terrible day.

In the training command, Nelson's friend Crockett had been a strapping young man—tall, blond, and with a smile that attracted the girls like an Elvis hip gyration. Even his name made them swoon. So being Crockett's wingman in the Pensacola bars had its advantages, and Nelson gladly accepted the benefits. His time in the training command had been magnificent. The flying, the cars, the parties. And the girls. Especially the girls.

"Let's give them a show," Crockett said one afternoon.

Two young women waited in a red '55 Ford convertible beside a country road. At Saufley Field, Nelson and Crockett mounted the tandem-seated trainer.

"You take the front seat," Crockett said as he climbed in aft.

After six months as student pilots, they were hot stuff. A few low passes just feet above the girls began the performance, followed by aerobatics. Of course, for the girls to clearly see their magnificence, the studs had to fly low, much lower than the rules of aerobatic safety demanded. A loop, a barrel roll, an Immelmann. But what really set the ladies' shorts afire was the Cuban Eight, a maneuver of a loop, a roll, and a loop in the other direction, forming a figure eight in the sky.

Descending inverted after the first loop, Nelson failed to apply forward stick to hold the forty-five-degree angle or to reduce his throttle. As a result, when he did rotate, he found himself in a vertical, high-speed dive. He yanked closed the throttle and pulled hard on the stick as the ground raced toward them. His vision became gray as the G-forces sucked the blood from his head. He had almost made it when he clipped a treetop and pancaked hard into an open field. Nelson gashed his chin and blood flowed onto his flight suit. He unstrapped and turned around. Crockett wasn't moving.

Three months after the crash, the Board of Inquiry allowed Nelson to resume flight training after formally chastising him. But their letter of reprimand paled against his self-recrimination.

For fifteen years now, as Nelson pursued his career, Crockett sat in a wheelchair, urinating into a catheter that filled a bag tied to his leg while an attendant cleaned up his bowel movements. A severed C-1 vertebrae left him a quadriplegic in a Pensacola nursing home, with no movement or feeling below his neck.

On Nelson's last visit, Crockett appeared to be shrinking. When not strapped down, his head lolled about while atrophied muscles left his arms withered and hands curled forward. Now forty, the same age as Nelson, he looked sixty. He could move his head only a few degrees left or right and speak with difficulty, though hard to understand. But he was completely present. A brain without a body. Nelson saw a man who would never know love, or intimacy, or children, or the cool breeze through his hair on an Alpine slope. Just the humming of the respirator that kept him alive.

The CO stood, came around the desk, and put his hand on Nelson's shoulder. "I understand your passion, Ron. And I appreciate it." His friend-voice morphed to command-authority. "But we have a mission to carry out, and we can't afford to be down any pilots." He picked up Nelson's coffee mug and held it out. "Push him through."

The petite woman slid the plate of adobo in front of Nelson, seated at the small kitchen table.

He picked up his fork and speared a piece of braised chicken. "Push him through. That's what the Old Man said." He pointed his fork at her, the marinade of garlic, vinegar, and soy sauce dripping onto his plate. "Sure. Let him kill himself." He fed the morsel into his mouth. "Or someone else."

He chewed, savored the taste, and swallowed. He looked at the food on his plate and shoveled in another mouthful. Thank God for Nenita. Not only was she a great cook, she washed his clothes, kept the small apartment clean, and provided other wifely services without wifely demands. She never accused him of spending too much time at work, or of being emotionally unavailable, or of not buying her the gold T-bird with red leather upholstery.

"I can't disobey an order, but how could I possibly do what he asks? It would betray everything I stand for. I'm the safety and training officer. It's my job to whip these new hot shots into shape and knock some sense into them before there's a disaster. Quinn isn't going to make the same mistakes I did. Not on my watch."

Her eyebrows lifted sympathetically at his plight. She poured him a beer, stood behind him, and kneaded her thumbs into his shoulder blades. His neck twisted in pleasure. She was also a great listener.

After a year together, he still didn't even know her age. She could have been thirty or fifty. Her bronze skin and demure nature defied time. But she had the serenity of an experienced woman, tempered by a hard life and appreciative of a kind man. Plus, she didn't treat him like the enemy, someone to be feared and avoided, as did everyone else around here.

"But if I disobey a direct order, I'd be sure to get another dead-end assignment, would never make lieutenant commander, and my career would be over." He exhaled a long sigh. "I don't know what to do."

She moved her hands up and massaged his temples, her gentle touch matched by her soft voice. "You tell Commanding Officer this pilot not safe."

"I have, Nenita. He doesn't believe me."

"Then you *show* him, Ron."

He closed his eyes as her delicate fingers traced small circles on his forehead, then applied gentle pressure to his closed eyelids. As his stress melted away, her words lingered. *Show him.*

He clasped her hands and brought them to his chest. "Yes. The next time Quinn wants to do something stupid, I let him, and the Old Man will see that I'm right."

She leaned forward, tickled his nipples through his shirt, and whispered in his ear, "Be careful, Ron." She kissed his neck. "I no want to see you hurt."

CHAPTER 26

Perched atop barstools at the officers' club, Dave and Max sipped beers and contemplated their reflections in the mirror.

"Just get yourself a mamasan," Max said, caressing his bottle. "Problem solved."

"I don't want a mamasan," Dave said. "I want Jennifer."

Max shrugged, his gaze glued to a tight-skirted waitress wiggling away. "How long have you known her?"

"Six years. I met her the first day of college."

Max smiled. "Did you ever . . ." He punched the air twice. "You know."

"No, Max! We just dated a few times, okay?"

"So what happened? Weren't you cool in college?"

Dave snorted. "*Cool* doesn't impress Jennifer."

"Well, you're not a college student anymore. You're a naval aviator."

"And she still isn't interested."

"Why not?"

"She met Woody."

"So? She not into art?"

"Not that kind."

Max expelled an exasperated sigh. "Dave, you're going about it all wrong. Getting chicks is simple. All you have to do is follow"—he paused for effect—"*The Procedure.*" He raised his eyebrows in prologue to the wisdom about to be dispensed. "Three steps. First, demonstrate excellence in her presence. It's a genetic thing. They're drawn to the alpha male. Of course, *we* get a pass on that one, being pilots, fighting the war, facing danger every day. On any flight, we may take off and never come back."

"I tried that. She's not impressed by what we do."

"Really? Okay, then show her something else she values. If maturity is important to her, be mature. If sensitivity is important, be sensitive. The point is, show excellence, whatever *she* thinks that is."

"Should I be writing this down?"

"Second, you have to keep your lust in check. If you're drooling all over her like a rutting pig, she's in control. Wait for her to make the first move. And third, when she does—now get this—you withdraw." Max leaned back with a satisfied smile. "Get it? They can't resist when you play hard to get."

Dave sipped his beer.

"Okay," Max said. "I can understand your reluctance. You like her. Then go with Plan B, Seymour's preferred method." He held up a forefinger on each hand. "All you need to do is get her talking about what she finds interesting. I don't know, window coverings or some such silliness. Then let her talk. She'll think you're fascinating." He belched and took another swig of beer. "Personally, I'm not crazy about that method," he said with a shrug, "because then you have to listen to her prattle on."

Dave nodded. "She does love kids. And teaching."

Max raised his bottle. "There you go."

Dave stared into the mirror. "I don't know. It sounds . . . manipulative."

"It *is* manipulative. So what? You control circumstances to get a favorable outcome. You manipulate the controls of an airplane to get where you want to go, don't you? You don't let her fly herself. What's the difference?

"The difference is it's lying."

"Not lying. *Selling*. And they *want* to be sold."

Dave shook his head. "She's not like that."

Max snorted. "They're all like that."

The door opened, bathing the officers' club in an orange glow as the last rays of the evening sun angled in. Heads turned in the crowded bar as the foursome paraded through. Ted guided Jennifer across the room, his fingertips gently on her waist. A clinging evening dress fell across her slender frame. Seymour followed, and Carol trailed two steps behind him. Ted glanced at Dave and Max caressing their bottles of San Miguel at the bar.

In the mirror over the bar, Dave watched the two couples. Ted steered the small party past and into the nearby dining area. He held out a chair for Jennifer at the linen-covered table. She sat delicately as Seymour plopped down across from her. He looked up at Carol, still standing and staring at him. Ted stepped in and held out Carol's chair. He sat and lifted his linen napkin. With a practiced shake, he unfurled it onto his lap, then led the party in animated conversation. Dave watched Jennifer listen in silence and regularly glance in his direction.

Max waved a finger toward the mirror. "Why should they be the only ones with round-eyed girlfriends?" He spun around. "Let's pay our respects."

Dave groaned. "Not again, Max. Leave it alone."

Max stood and tugged at Dave's arm. "Come on, buddy. Back me up here."

Dave sighed, hoisted himself from the barstool, and followed as Max wobbled toward the table.

"Ladies," Max said with a small bow. "And gentlemen." He pulled up a chair and plopped down without invitation. Dave remained standing. His eyes met Jennifer's.

"Did the kitty make it back to the States?" Max asked.

"He's on the way," Carol said. "Gina is very grateful."

"Then why won't she take my calls?"

Carol shrugged, Ted snorted, and Seymour sipped his beer.

"Put in a good word for me," Max said.

"I don't think so."

"Come on, Carol. She'll go out with me if you'll help."

"No, Max."

"Why not?"

"Because you're not right for each other."

"Sure we are."

"Let it go, Max," she said.

He crossed his arms. "I'm not leaving until you tell me why you won't help me with Gina."

Ted rose, his hulking frame dominating the gathering. He stepped forward. "Ensign—"

Carol stretched out her arm and blocked him. She sighed and leaned forward toward Max. "Why? *Why?*" Her eyes pierced into his. "I'll tell you why, Max. Because you're an egotistical, alcoholic, whore-mongering reprobate." Her placid smile, head tilt, and raised eyebrows punctuated the observation.

Max blinked twice. Several moments passed as his beer-soaked gray matter processed the insult. "I'm not egotistical," he finally said.

"Oh, brother." She rolled her eyes.

"I have *confidence*," he said. "I'm the cream of the crop."

"Dave?" Carol said.

"Nice to see you again, Carol," Dave said. "Let's go, Max." He nodded at the group and met Jennifer's eyes again. Ted found her hand on the table, gave it a squeeze, and smirked. Dave put his hand on Max's shoulder. "Come on, buddy."

Dave could see Jennifer in the bar mirror watching him shepherd his friend away.

CHAPTER 27

Dear Mama, Viet Nam is a beautiful country. My company is on a hilltop called Firebase Easy. It's hot here, like home, but the afternoon rain cools the air. I am completely safe, so try not to worry. I am learning the skills of a medic so that when I come home and get a good job, we can move to a nice house.

Julio sat on an empty ammo crate, writing the letter on his knees. The denuded hilltop was a blighted island carved from an emerald jungle, the land pocked with scars and littered with tents, military equipment, and a latrine just upwind of his hooch. But the soldiers passed the day in idleness within the wire perimeter, as though the war had ended and all that remained were the wounded earth and the silent plumes of smoke in the distance. Where was the action? Where were the casualties?

Julio had been accepted into Combat Medic Training a week after graduation. He went on active duty a month later, spent eight weeks in boot camp, two weeks on leave with Mama, and then sixteen weeks at Fort Sam Houston. His medical training had been more comprehensive than he had expected. It started with basic health and hygiene, then CPR, and how to treat shock and burns and dislocated shoulders. They practiced giving shots to each other, drawing blood, and starting IVs. They sutured bananas, splinted arms and legs, and performed a tracheotomy on a dummy. They moved into head trauma, gunshot wounds, and amputations.

He often felt queasy, and it worried him. How would he react to a real amputation if training on a dummy made him sick? But it was natural. He'd get over it. He had to.

His hard work paid off. Finishing first in his class of forty earned the reward of his choice of assignment. The other thirty-nine would go to Viet Nam.

"Wiesbaden," a classmate said. "No question. Those frauleins are hot."

But how much experience would he get at a hospital in Germany, cleaning bedpans and inserting catheters? He didn't join up to meet hot girls. He wanted experience to become an EMT and save Mama from her miserable circumstances. Plus, the extra $50-a-month combat pay he could send Mama would be a godsend for her. The decision was easy.

"I'm going to Viet Nam, Mama." He didn't tell her he had a choice.

When the Flying Tiger charter airliner lifted off Travis Air Force Base outside San Francisco, Julio felt the anxiety and thrill of his first airplane ride. He watched the Golden Gate Bridge pass beneath them as they headed across the vast Pacific. They stopped in Anchorage, then Okinawa, and finally Cam Rahn. On the hot tarmac, he boarded a Huey. Again, the thrill and anxiety of flight energized him. But this was gritty, loud, and close to the earth, nothing like the high-flying commercial jetliner. The humid, pungent breeze of the jungle peppered him through the open-doored contraption as the chopper whop-whopped across the treetops and deposited him on a hilltop fire base.

Yes, he worried for his own safety and for leaving Mama alone. But he was excited, too, for the opportunity for terrific medical experience. When he got home, he would get a job and take care of Mama and become the greatest EMT San Antonio had ever known. He'd reassure a woman injured in an auto accident that she was in good hands as he bandaged her leg. He'd stretcher the heart-attack victim into the ambulance and monitor his vital signs as they raced to the hospital, siren blaring. He'd splint the child's broken arm and comfort him with a soothing bedside manner.

Julio squinted against the rising yellow sun and scribbled on the paper.

I wish I could be nearer to you, Mama, but the professional opportunities for me are here. I am learning important medical skills for my job when I get home, tending to the injuries of my fellow soldiers, and perhaps even saving lives.

"Hey, doc. Got any more of that pecker cream?" Sergeant Franco's muscular frame cast a wide shadow across Mama's letter. "I'm kind of inflamed here."

Julio folded the stationery and slipped it into the plastic bag with Mama's picture and the other writing paper. He opened his medical kit, pulled out a small tube, and handed it to the sergeant. He looked away as Franco dropped his drawers and slathered the ointment on his genitals.

CHAPTER 28

His hand a visor, Dave shielded his eyes against the tropical sun that baked the brown bodies on the narrow beach. Squeezed between the runway and the bay, the strip of sand sprouted coconut palms, with picnic tables in the scant shade beneath. Several bohios—open four-post huts with palm-frond-thatched rooves—provided the only relief from the sun. Waves lapped the shore.

Carol and Seymour lounged on beach chairs. Commander Holt and Brenda talked quietly in the shade of a bohio.

Al Ross, the squadron personnel and morale officer, strode the beach. On duty and in uniform, he held his hands loosely behind his back and meandered among oil-slathered bodies as though casually conducting an inspection. His pale skin, slicked-back black hair, and pencil-thin mustache suggested a sunless existence.

His wife Trudy remained fully covered by a muumuu and a large straw hat, only her hands exposed to the sunlight. She wandered the assemblage, surprising partygoers with a sudden appearance in her flowing garment.

"We're having Bible study this evening," she said to each reveler she encountered. "Would you care to join us?"

But it was the group a few steps away that held Dave's shaded gaze.

Naked from the waist up, Norm flexed his pecs, lats, biceps, and a half dozen other muscles. "So Staubach said to me, 'Norm, I really admire you pilots. I could never master that.'"

Several women surrounded him, including Gina, Jennifer, and some of the wives. Ted stood close to Jennifer, smiling casually. He could have been a model in his swim trunks and open pullover. Tan, blond, white teeth. A bronze cross nestled in his blond chest hair. His golden Avanti not far away, gleaming in the sun.

Dave and Max stood next to the reclining Seymour and Carol, Dave watching Jennifer as Max pulled another beer from the ice chest.

"I'm telling you," Max slurred, "if you want to attract a woman, just follow the procedure."

Carol opened one eye.

"Sure, Norm can flex," Max said. "But that isn't excellence. And he wouldn't withdraw if she advanced. He's got no finesse. He doesn't follow the procedure."

Carol groaned and rolled over.

"Go ahead. Go over there and do something excellent."

"Like what, Max?"

"I don't know. Dazzle her with your wit."

That wasn't going to work. The last time he spoke to Jennifer, Woody's appendage still twanged on the spring as she scooted out of Dave's room. The recollection sent a mini-shudder rippling across his shoulders.

Max polished off his beer, tossed the empty can into the barrel, and grabbed another. "Come on." He tugged Dave's arm and pulled him into the circle.

Dave took a deep breath and stepped forward as though continuing an ongoing conversation with Max.

"I dreamed you and I and Norm augured in."

"Augured in?" a woman nearby said.

"Yeah," Max said, "augured in, dumped one, screwed the pooch."

She shrugged.

"CRASHED," Max said.

Dave nodded. "So you get to heaven and St. Peter says the only rule is 'don't kick the ducks.'"

Norm looked annoyed. "Is this a joke?"

The women donned wary expressions.

Dave continued, "Within a minute Max trips over a duck, and he's immediately paired for eternity with a disgusting, hideous skank."

Jennifer's face soured.

Max waved his beer. "No way."

"Then Norm's told the same thing—don't kick the ducks. Well, sure enough, he trips over a duck too, and is immediately paired forever with another gross sk—"

Jennifer crossed her arms.

"—uh, unattractive woman. For eternity."

"Why do I get a skank?" Norm said.

Seymour lifted his head from the beach chair. "Cause you kicked a duck, for Christ's sake. Let him finish."

"So then *I* get to heaven," Dave said, "and I'm immediately paired with a gorgeous, sexy, loving woman. So I say to her, 'How did we get here?' and she says, 'I don't know about *you*, but *I* kicked a duck.'"

Carol snorted, and the other ladies exploded in laughter. But Jennifer's face remained frozen.

"Why do *you* get the babe?" Norm said.

"Great story, buddy," Max slurred, his head sagging and eyelids drooping. "I need a nap."

Dave watched his wingman abandon him as Max stumbled down the beach toward a one-man survival raft that had drifted in and now bobbed in the small waves against the shore. He climbed in and lay down, the inflated side cradling his head like a giant pillow. As the waves lapped against the raft, the undulating swells rocked Max like a baby in a cradle, and his eyes fluttered closed.

Dave's joke had impressed Jennifer like an F-4 Phantom with a dual flameout. But he remained in the group to be near her, while the other men showcased their physical attributes and glib manner.

Thirty minutes later, partygoers stood at water's edge, peering at a yellow speck on the horizon.

"Ha!" Seymour said. "Lost at sea. Classic Max."

"I'll bet he didn't even take his beer," Norm said.

Dave paced about, squinting toward his friend. "We need to help him."

Low storm clouds crossed the mountain ridge beyond and darkened the bay. A bolt of lightning struck the water.

"Looks like rain," Seymour said. "So much for my tan."

"Where's Search and Rescue?" Dave said.

Norm pointed. "Over at Subic."

"We have to call them."

Seymour threw his head back and polished off his beer. "There's no phone here." He tossed the empty into a barrel for two points.

As the distant sky darkened and the surf roiled, Dave ran his hands across his closely cropped hair. His eyes darted between the yellow raft and the blackening sky. Lightning flashed and thunder cracked. Dave's jaw dropped. When a bolt struck near the raft, his agitated movements became purposeful. He turned, raced to his car, and leaped in. The engine roared. He yanked it into gear and floored it. Sand rooster-tailed into the air. He fishtailed across the beach and hit the "Playa Paraiso" sign, flattening and rolling over it. He was stuck.

The boys looked on with bemusement, Jennifer with dismay.

"Stay clear," Dave yelled. He shifted into reverse and rocked back and forth. He floored it again, leaping off the sign as the metal shredded the fiberglass and pulled off half the rear bumper. Tires squealed as he hit the asphalt and raced down the narrow road, his bumper dragging.

An hour later, Dave rattled back up the road and parked in the now Avanti-less lot. Shutting down the engine, he scanned the beach. No Ted. No Jennifer.

A Subic Search and Rescue launch roared to within twenty feet of the water's edge. Max jumped off the deck and waded ashore dragging the life raft.

"Thanks, Leonard," he called.

The coxswain goosed the throttle, the bow rose, and the launch roared away.

"Hit me," Max said. A cold beer flew his way. "That was spooky."

"Dave saved your bacon," Seymour said.

"Thanks, buddy," Max called, waving. The gang encircled the car in ghoulish fascination. "Aw, man, look at your Vette," Max said. "What happened?"

"What happened," Seymour said, "is he blasted out of here like the Chinese Communists were coming ashore."

Dave climbed out and examined the broken bumper wired to the chassis and the shredded fiberglass.

"I'm real sorry, Dave," Max said.

"It's okay, buddy." Dave ran his hand over his damaged baby. "I'm going home now."

"No," Max said. "Stay."

He gave him a beer, put a hand on his shoulder and led him to the beach chairs. They reclined in the bright sun, the afternoon squalls having passed as quickly as they had appeared.

Seymour, Max, and Dave lay on the beach chairs in silence.

"You should go talk to her," Max said.

"Who?" Dave said.

Max snorted.

"She's with Ted," Dave said.

"No, she's not. She's right over there." His head tilted toward the bohio. "Out of the sun."

Through his dark shades, Dave turned to see Jennifer reading a paperback at a wooden picnic table under the bohio. Beside her, Carol rested in a beach chair. He watched Jennifer for several minutes. She wouldn't look his way.

"She's not interested."

"You never know," Max said, with a head nod directing him to move. "She must have sent Ted packing."

Dave didn't move.

"Give it a shot."

Dave shrugged, rose, and lumbered over to the shady hut. "Afternoon, ladies. Had enough sun?"

Jennifer nodded, her gaze not leaving her book.

"The last time I saw you in a bathing suit, we were at a pond in Ohio, and you told me to join the Navy. Remember?"

"Yes," she said, "before you became a connoisseur of native art carvings."

Carol looked at Jennifer and then back at Dave. "I'm going to get a Coke," she said.

Jennifer grabbed her wrist, but Carol twisted gently and broke loose. Her departure left behind a long silence.

Dave finally spoke. "We just got back from Taipei."

Jennifer turned the page of her book.

"And Bagio," he said. "It's a really short field." Jennifer forced a perfunctory smile. "And we're headed for Okinawa next week."

Her attention returned to her book and he stared into the distance. After a few moments, he sighed and turned to leave.

"I'm sorry about your car," she said. "You're a good friend to Max."

He stopped and turned toward her. "Thanks."

"Can you fix it?"

He shook his head. "Not here. It'll have to wait until I get back home."

"That's too bad. I know you love that car."

He shrugged. "Happiness resides not in possessions or in gold. Happiness dwells in the soul."

She looked at him with a head tilt.

"Democritus."

She snorted. "Like I know who that is."

"Things aren't important. People are."

She smiled and put down the book. "I always loved our philosophical talks."

"Of all possessions, a friend is the most precious." He bobbed his eyebrows. "Herodotus."

"Now you're just showing off."

"Nyuk, nyuk. Curly Howard."

"That one I know."

The grunts and shouts of the others playing volleyball filled the air. Dave turned toward the game. "So where's Ted?"

He could feel her staring at his profile.

"Look, Dave," she finally said, "Ted is fun and kind and considerate, a real gentleman."

A volleyball flew by with Max stumbling after it in hot pursuit.

"But?" Dave said, turning back toward her.

"Ted likes pretty things. Like his car."

"The Avanti?"

She shrugged. "Is that what it's called?"

Dave nodded.

"But we don't have much in common. Nothing to talk about that matters." She gazed at the mountain ridge across the bay. "You've always been interested in ideas. They say that small minds speak only of people and average minds of events. But great minds talk of ideas."

"I have a great mind?"

"Don't let it go to your head." She donned an unconvincing scowl. "But I had expected you to pursue an intellectual career."

He snorted. "Like insurance? You're lucky, Jen. You knew what you loved early on. I never had that."

"Yes, you did. Your winery."

Dave could see the rows of grape vines on rolling hills, nurtured by a warm sun, as the sweet smell of mash fermenting in oak barrels wafted from a wooden barn. A tasting room just off the highway welcomed visitors. And a country house stood on the knoll overlooking it all.

He sighed. "That's no career."

"Choose a job you love, and you'll never have to work a day in your life," she said. "Confucius."

He smiled. "So how is it—teaching here?"

"Very busy. And draining. And wonderful." Her face lit up. "Career Day is coming up. And we're working on the Christmas pageant. The children really get into it. My class is working on the stage sets . . ."

Dave smiled as Jennifer's words tumbled out. Talk about what she loves.

After a few minutes, she stopped suddenly and blushed. "Your work is important too, Dave."

"Thanks," he said, but his face must have said he didn't believe her.

"I mean it," she said. "Being a pilot is a fine career. I'm sure military flying skills are transferable to the civilian world back home. Use it to help people. Besides, it's not like you're killing anyone."

CHAPTER 29

Dave sat opposite the highchair. A baby examined him, gurgling with a stalactite of drool dangling from her chin. Her arms undulated and her hands grasped at unseen objects.

Brenda smiled warmly. "We're so glad you could come. We don't entertain much anymore." She nodded toward the children as Commander Holt lifted the wine bottle and refilled Dave's and Jennifer's glasses.

The six seated around the dining room table may have been eight thousand miles away and amid lush jungle fauna, but this was as much a home as any Dave had ever seen—the smell of a home-cooked meal, the sounds of children, and above all, love filled the room.

"Sophie is beautiful," Dave said. "I can't believe she's already five months old." He smiled at the other child. "Melissa, do you like having a sister to play with?"

"Yes, Mr. Kin," the little girl said, "I share my toys with her." Everyone smiled. "And I will share my room with her too when the new baby comes."

A pregnant pause engulfed the table.

"Oops," Brenda said.

Dave rose. "Congratulations." He embraced Brenda, then shook Holt's hand.

"Thanks," Holt said, "but it's not all fun." He stood and carried plates into the kitchen.

"So," Brenda whispered to her guests when her husband was out of earshot, "how are you two doing?"

"Brenda!" Holt called from the kitchen.

"Just making conversation, Phil." She shook her head at Jennifer.

Melissa tugged on Dave's pant leg and raised her arms. He looked to Brenda, who nodded. He lifted Melissa onto his lap.

"When you have a baby," Melissa said, "can she come over and play with us?"

Jennifer smiled.

"We can't have a baby, Melissa," Dave said, glancing at Jennifer. "We're not married."

"Okay." She smacked her lips as if irritated at having to clarify. "*After* you get married."

Dave blushed. "Well . . ."

"Please." Her huge blue eyes could win any staring contest.

"Okay."

"Thank you, Mr. Kin. You're the bestest."

He looked at the ceiling, put a finger on his chin, and pursed his lips. "Maybe I'm second. Your daddy's the bestest."

Melissa considered this, nodded in agreement, and kissed him on the cheek.

Jennifer sipped her wine. "You don't seem to have any trouble with *her*. Maybe it's just my eight-year-olds that are beyond your ability."

When Jennifer had asked him to speak to her class for career day, he had said yes without hesitation. How better to win her favor than to participate in the work she loved?

When he first stood before the class, he had whispered from the side of his mouth, "I'm not comfortable with this."

"They're eight years old," Jennifer whispered back. She switched to her teacher voice. "Class, this is Lieutenant Quinn. He works at Cubi Point Naval Air Station. Lieutenant Quinn is a naval aviator. He flies airplanes. The ones you see taking off and landing at the airfield across the bay."

Dave's golden wings glimmered on his tropical white uniform. He peered out at eighteen expectant faces.

"Good morning students." He cleared his throat. "Flying is not magical. It's science." He turned and drew the cross section of an airfoil on the blackboard. "The laminar airflow of the wind stream crosses the cambered airfoil of the wing, and that dynamic interaction creates lift." He drew an arrow on the board signifying a lift vector. "And drag." He drew a drag vector. "Control these dynamic forces with the flight controls—ailerons, elevator, and rudder—and you have controlled flight."

He paused and smiled. The eighteen stared, their hands folded.

"The ailerons, the tiny airfoils on the back of the wings, they control roll, lateral rotation about the longitudinal axis. And the rudder pedals, yaw, longitudinal rotation about the vertical axis. And the elevator—"

"Mr. Quinn," Jennifer said, "why don't you tell the class about landing on an aircraft carrier?"

The children perked up.

"Oh, sure. Well, I haven't landed on a carrier since the training command. That's where you go to school to become a pilot after you graduate from college." He glanced at Jennifer. "So stay in school." He smiled and punched the air for emphasis.

A battalion of blank faces stared back. His smile evaporated.

"Anyway, I'm land-based now, so no more carrier landings. But here's how it works. The optical landing system sends a beam of light that tells the pilot if he's on glide slope—whether he's positioned properly to make a successful landing and catch a wire."

A hand rose.

Dave pointed. "Yes?"

"Can you fly upside down?"

Dave blinked. "Well, yes, I did in the training command, during aerobatics training—you know, loops, barrel rolls, immelmanns. But we're not allowed to fly upside down in the stoof."

The boy smiled broadly. "Cooooool."

Another hand rose. "Is the stoop a bomber?"

"No. The *stoof* does onboard carrier antisubmarine work. It flies off a carrier in the middle of the ocean and looks for Russian subs."

Wide eyes stared back. "Do you drop bombs on them?"

"Uh, no. Someone else does that. I mean, no, we're not at war with the Russians. We just find their subs. Well, I *personally* don't find them, but that's what the plane was designed for. Our mission is different."

"You ever shoot down a Jap?"

"No," Dave stammered. "The Japs, I mean the Japanese, are our allies now. Our friends."

"Do you shoot at the Viet Cong?"

"No, but I get to wear wings." He pointed to his chest. "And these cool aviator shades."

"The Japs killed my Uncle Bill. My daddy said they're sneaky, you know, Pearl Harbor."

Dave lifted his wineglass and shuddered in recollection of the whole disaster. "I bombed."

Jennifer swatted his shoulder. "No, you were wonderful." She giggled. "'Stay in school.' Like my third-graders are about to drop out and get jobs."

After dessert, Dave and Holt retired to the screened porch to smoke cigars. The sounds of unseen jungle creatures filled the air.

"I see you're scheduled for your aircraft commander check ride on Monday," Holt said. "Good luck."

"Thanks. I just passed five hundred hours." Dave looked down. "I'm a little concerned. Nelson keeps harping on my procedures. I don't know why he's doing this to me."

"He's not doing anything *to* you, Dave, he's doing it *for* you." He rested his hand on Dave's shoulder. "He wants you to be ready when you have a serious emergency. Or in combat, when someone's shooting at you."

"Combat? That's not going to happen. It's a stoof, for crying out loud."

Holt chuckled. "You're right. That's very unlikely."

"No, it's more than that," Dave said. "Nelson has something against me. I think he resents my ambition."

"It's great to have a goal, Dave. But right now, it's not about us. It's about duty to others. First and foremost, we're here to serve."

"Begging your pardon, Phil, but I'm here to fly, not to serve."

Holt blew a column of smoke upward. The ceiling fan quickly dissipated it.

"Maybe that's what's bothering Nelson."

Dave and Max stood on the tarmac beneath the nose of *Double Nuts*. Cox, perched atop a ladder, peeled off a tape stencil from below the copilot's window. *LTJG DAVID QUINN* appeared in bright yellow lettering.

"I *am* the greatest," Dave said in his most Champ-like impersonation. He raised his clenched fists as the shutter clicked.

That night, Dave hung the framed photo and S-2 aircraft commander certificate on his now-cluttered vanity wall. The Pan Am poster and monkeypod wings were surrounded by pictures and plaques celebrating his commission, first solo flight, first carrier landing, and Navy wings.

The room packed, people sat at the small bar, or on the bed, or stood. Max canoodled with a dark-skinned beauty in the large papasan chair. The three-foot speakers converted the magnetic impulses on the five-inch reel tape into a booming beat, while a small black and white television broadcast static. A battery-powered model airliner hung on a string from the ceiling fan, making wide circles, inches above the heads of the celebrants.

Dave stood next to Jennifer, seated on a barstool.

"Congratulations," she said, raising her wine glass.

"Thanks, Jen, but it's just an award. Nothing to get excited about."

She laughed. "That picture tells a different story." She pointed at the photo of Dave, his arms raised in triumph.

He held up his hands in surrender. "You got me."

She smiled and rested her fingertips on his arm.

Seated next to Jennifer, Carol raised her glass. "To Dave," she said.

Amid hoots and applause and clinking glasses, "To Dave," everyone sang.

"If you ever don't make it back," Seymour said, eying Dave's stereo equipment, booze collection, and black velvet art, "can I have your stuff?"

The ancient black telephone jangled, barely audible above the celebration. Carol dragged it over to Dave. He nodded, took it into the bathroom, and shut the door. The walls vibrated with the bass beat. He sat on the toilet, the five-pound device on his lap.

"Lieutenant Quinn," he answered into the huge mouthpiece.

"Hello?" said a voice. "David?"

"Dad? Is that you?"

"Hello, son," the voice said.

"Is everything okay?" Dave's mouth was suddenly dry and his palm on the receiver wet with sweat.

"Fine," his father said, "Everything's fine. How's it going over there?"

"Great, Dad," he said, still concerned. "How's Mom?"

"She's asleep. It's 6:00 a.m. here. I wanted to call at a time convenient for you."

"It's evening here." Dave awaited a response. The phone was silent. "Dad?"

"Son, I need to talk to you about something."

Dave tensed again. "What is it?"

"I wrote you that we might sell the business and retire."

"Yes, Dad, I remember."

"Well, your mother and I have decided to sell. And we've bought a condo on the Gulf Coast."

"You're moving to Florida?"

"Yes. And retiring."

"That's great, Dad."

"I know we talked about you coming into the business, but . . ." He stumbled.

"Dad, my career is going great. I'm going to fly for Pan Am. I'm no longer interested in insurance."

"Yes, I thought you felt that way. That factored into our decision. But we have a buyer, and we're set to close the deal tomorrow. I wanted to let you know before we did anything final. You know, just in case you—"

"I appreciate it, Dad, I really do, but I've found my career."

"Are you sure, son? It can still be undone. But after today, there'll be no turning back."

"Yes, Dad, I'm sure. Give Mom my love."

Jennifer had been bewildered by Brenda's response. As she watched Dave disappear into the bathroom dragging the huge telephone, she remembered dinner the other evening. The aroma of the men's cigar smoke wafted in from the screened porch as she and Brenda sat on the rattan living room furniture. The girls had been put to bed, the dining room and kitchen cleaned, and the low voices of the men in conversation blended in a bass harmony with the music from the jungle. Jennifer sipped her coffee. She set the cup and saucer on the end table, leaned forward, and put her hands on her knees.

"Aren't you afraid?"

Brenda nodded. "Sometimes. But he's doing what he loves."

"But the danger . . ."

Brenda sighed. "Life is uncertain. I can't stress over what might be." She smiled. "But right now, I'm happy, and the girls are happy." She patted Jennifer's hand. "Phil is a good man, Jennifer. He deserves to be happy as well."

Jennifer leaned back against the cushioned barstool and wondered if *she* might be the selfish one, thinking of her own career while these men risked their lives. David was a good man too. Loyal to a fault. When a drunken Max had dragged him to the table at the O Club, Dave looked mortified. But he stood by his friend. Then, at the beach, he had destroyed his beloved car in a panic over Max's safety. Plus, he was so cute in her classroom. A naval aviator intimidated by eight-year-olds. She smiled at the recollection. No wonder three-year-old Melissa was in love with him. And he had seemed genuinely interested in her career, so much so that she had invited him to speak to her class. Maybe he had turned the corner and could be a supportive partner for her dream. Perhaps it was time to step forward and make it work.

At midnight, the last partygoers stumbled out of Dave's room. Seymour's arm draped over Carol as they wobbled into the hall. Carol looked back.

Jennifer slung her purse over her shoulder. "Give me a moment." She pushed the door closed, turned, and rested her palms on Dave's chest.

"Congratulations, Mr. Kin." Her arms slid around his neck and his hands found the small of her back. "You're the bestest."

CHAPTER 30

The moment the Huey medivac chopper touched down, Julio and the crew chief leaped into the chest-high elephant grass. Julio tended each of the wounded men, applying splints, injecting morphine, or pressing gauze to staunch the bleeding. Braving enemy sniper fire, they loaded the injured, and Dustoff-One-Zero ascended and whop-whopped just over the jungle canopy toward the field hospital at Long Binh.

A kid, not much older than Julio, gripped his hand. "Thanks, doc," he said. "You saved my life. I'll never forget."

Julio's headset crackled. "Incoming." The chopper banked sharply and the bright sun flashed in. Julio felt a whack on his shoulder. He was hit.

The empty beer can bounced off him and fell harmlessly into the mud. "Garcia, what the hell are you going to do?"

Julio squinted against the blinding spotlight in the sky.

He shaded his eyes with a pair of deuces. "I fold," he said, throwing in his hand.

The poker games lasted hours every day, sometimes with as many as seven players at a time on the makeshift outdoor table. Julio hated the game, but as the new guy, he wanted to fit in. Besides, what else was there to do? There a month, he hadn't yet treated a single wound beyond putting a Band-Aid on a scratch. Sure, he'd seen fungal infections, bacterial infections, viral infections, VD, parasitic diseases inducing fever and diarrhea from tics and spiders and even poisonous centipedes. But how would experience in treating jungle diseases help an EMT in Texas?

"When are we going to see some action?" he said.

All heads turned toward him.

Franco's face scrunched up. "What the fuck, Garcia?"

"Yeah," said Sol. "We're the luckiest platoon in this godforsaken hellhole."

"Damn straight," Spider said. "I ain't getting blowed apart so you can practice on me. I got ninety-seven days and a wake-up left."

Julio's face flushed. He just wanted to be a good medic but hadn't even been on patrol yet and had no more experience treating traumatic injury than when he left the States. Stuck on this desolate hilltop, he watched a flight of choppers headed north.

He stood.

"Hey, it's your deal, Garcia."

Julio turned. "I got first watch. Need to get some shut-eye." He went inside his hooch and lay on his cot.

"He's got to write another letter to Mama," Sol said, followed by kissing sounds.

"Hey, Sarge," Spider said, "shoot me in the leg so Garcia can patch me up."

Julio listened to them guffaw. He stared upward as the smell of marijuana wafted by. Maybe they were right. Fifty years from now, when his grandchildren asked him what he did during the war, he would tell them he passed out pecker cream.

CHAPTER 31

Dave stared ahead trance-like as they droned through the sky. Max read a magazine. The aircraft jerked, followed by the sound of a distant explosion. Dave keyed his intercom mic.

"Did they get it, Cox?"

"Yes, sir," crewman Cox said from aft. The shredded banner fell away from the end of the cable and fluttered toward the sea.

"Okay, reel out another." Dave turned to Max. "Don't get me wrong. I'm happy to be getting all these hours. But I've done twenty of these. It's getting tedious." It'd been a month of drilling holes in the sky over allied destroyers to provide target practice for sailors from Taiwan and Korea and Australia.

"Relax," Max said. "Enjoy the moment." He turned the magazine ninety degrees and examined the contents.

"When I got my aircraft commander designation, I expected, I don't know, more. But we're just working stiffs."

"Dave, we're naval aviators. That's as good as it gets."

"We're stoof drivers, towing targets for nineteen-year-olds to shoot at. We're not astronauts."

"Speak for yourself, Lieutenant. *I'm* an astronaut." Max tapped his temple. "In here."

"Target reeled out," Cox said.

The engines droned on and distant explosions resumed. Dave returned to his catatonic pose and Max to his literature.

But Dave's boredom evaporated after they walked across the tarmac with helmets and flight bags, entered the back door of the ready room, and heard the CO announce a deployment to Da Nang.

Dave's jaw fell open. "Da Nang? They have real targets in Viet Nam. Why do they need us?"

"Carrier on-board delivery," Max said. "When they get busy, we help the COD boys with their hops between Da Nang and Yankee Station."

Dave expelled a long breath and sank deep into the upholstery of the ready room chair.

In the early morning darkness, Dave ran through the pre-start checklist and fired her up. As Nelson looked on from the copilot's seat, Dave could still taste the bile and mouthwash from his earlier retching. They took off and climbed out over Subic Bay. The second stoof with Max and Seymour joined them in loose formation as the mouth of the bay opened to the vast South China Sea. Dave leveled off and set a course due west toward Viet Nam. After two hours of droning vibrations, a thin white strand of beach appeared, separating the blue water below from the emerald jungle ahead. As they approached, Dave gazed down at the beauty and tranquility. This didn't look like a war zone. More like Eden.

The city of Da Nang appeared, followed by the airbase beyond. Nelson keyed his mic.

"Da Nang Tower, Checkertail Zero Zero inbound for landing."

"Roger, *Double Nuts*," the radio responded. "Report final."

"I'll take her," Nelson said to Dave. He gripped the yoke and put his feet on the rudder pedals. He retarded the throttle, lowered the flaps, slapped down the landing gear, and put the nose into a dive.

Dave grimaced. "Aren't we a little steep?" He dug his fingers into his harness straps.

The altimeter unwound as the aircraft dropped rapidly.

"Zero Zero on final," Nelson broadcast.

Dave looked over. "Final? We're at a thousand feet. We're not on final."

"Roger, *Double Nuts*, you're cleared to land."

Nelson pulled the throttle full aft. "We want to be as small a target as possible."

Dave's eyes widened, and he scanned the jungle below. The aircraft dove for the runway. At the last instant, Nelson pulled back the yoke and flared, stopping the descent a few feet above the concrete. Tires squeaked on landing. They rolled out and taxied to a metal line shack. *Da Nang COD* was painted over the door, and an upside-down mop sprouted from a bucket of sand. A placard read *simulated palm*. They shut down the engines and exited the hatch, their hair matted and faces sweating. As Max and Seymour taxied up, Nelson walked around *Double Nuts*. He pointed to the horizontal stabilizer.

Dave looked up at a penny-sized hole. "A bullet?" His jaw dropped. "We got shot at?"

Nelson nodded. "But it's only small caliber, and she's a sturdy old gal."

As Dave gaped at the hole, Nelson pointed toward a stark wooden building behind the line shack. "The BOQ," he said. "Let's get some rest."

Early the next morning, Dave stood beside the stoof hatch and watched Nelson address two young sailors with duffel bags.

"Men, when we get to the carrier, there's a lot of activity. Things happen fast, so you need to know the drill."

The teenage sailors hung on every word.

"When we land, and you open the hatch and exit the aircraft, be sure to turn toward the tail. If you turn the other way, a spinning propeller is waiting for you."

The sailors' eyes grew huge.

"And take off your hat, or the propwash will do it for you. If it gets sucked into a jet intake and blows the engine, you'll be up shit creek."

The stoof approached the fleet, overflew a carrier, and broke left toward the downwind leg. Gripping the yoke, Dave looked down at the carrier below. His wet flight suit clung to his clammy skin.

"It's just like training," Nelson said. "As you pass the ninety, you should pick up the ball. When you see it, call it."

When abeam the ship, Dave banked left. Halfway through the turn, an orange dot appeared on the carrier's stern to guide him toward the postage-stamp-sized flight deck where he had to land this thing.

"I have the ball," Dave broadcast.

"Roger, ball," the LSO replied.

He crossed the ship's wake and rolled the wings level onto final. With the ship dead ahead, he aligned himself with the center line of the angled deck and focused on the ball. To catch a wire, the meatball had to be centered, aligned with the row of green reference lights. He could see the landing signal officer standing beside it, the pickle switch in his hand.

He wobbled toward the deck with everything hanging down—flaps, landing gear, tailhook. Like a gangly crane, they were awkward, vulnerable, and on the brink of a stall. And a stall meant a watery grave. Beads of moisture ran down his face like a chilled beer mug at a poolside bar.

The meatball dropped below the reference lights. Dave could feel the black, churning sea below.

"On centerline," the LSO said, "a little low."

Water depth here was hundreds of meters, not that it mattered.

The meatball dropped lower.

"Right of centerline, you're low," the LSO said.

Nelson clicked the intercom. "Add power, Lieutenant. And get back on centerline."

Dave figured he'd probably survive the crash and watch himself drown.

The meatball turned red and the flight deck filled the windscreen.

Dave could almost see the LSO squeeze the pickle switch in his raised right hand as the radio blared, "WAVE OFF. WAVE OFF." The meatball disappeared and flashing red wave-off lights came alive.

"I have the aircraft," Nelson said as he grabbed the yoke and slapped the throttles full forward.

The engines roared, and the aircraft banked left to avoid the ship's conning tower. Only a few feet from touchdown, the hook barely missed the deck. Nelson leveled the wings. They flew over the angled deck and beyond the bow.

Nelson trimmed the aircraft for stable flight. He opened his palm toward Dave. "Let's try it again."

Dave took the controls. He climbed out, turned crosswind, entered the downwind leg, banked at the one-eighty and passed the ninety. A centered meatball came into view. "I have the ball."

"Roger, ball," came back on the radio.

Dave rolled wings level on final. The meatball dropped below the reference lights.

"On centerline. A little low."

Dave eased forward the throttles. The meatball returned to center.

"On center line, on glide slope."

The carrier grew larger.

"On center line, on glide slope."

The ship filled the windscreen. Green cut lights flashed, the fantail blurred beneath the aircraft, and Dave yanked the throttles closed. The stoof slammed firmly onto the deck, the tailhook grabbed a wire, and Dave jolted forward against his harness as they decelerated to a stop.

"Better," Nelson said.

A lineman signaled "raise hook" and "come forward." There was no rest with another hot shot always bearing down behind. Dave taxied clear of the angled deck and parked beneath the conning tower. The two passengers scrambled through the hatch as though escaping a fire, deckhands unloaded mail bags, and a new passenger climbed aboard and strapped in. The lineman directed them to the steam catapult. Crewmen secured the stoof to the launch mechanism. A yellow-shirted launch officer vibrated two fingers over his head, and Dave pushed the throttles full forward. The engines roared and the airframe shook, straining to lurch forward under the pull of the giant propellers, but held back, secured to the unmoving catapult. Nelson lowered the overhead T-bar throttle lock. Dave pushed the throttles against it, locking the T-bar and throttles in his tightly gripped fist. Nelson's hand pressed against the back of Dave's glove, his stiff arm providing added support to full throttles.

"We don't need these coming back during launch," Nelson said.

Dave pressed his helmet rearward into his headrest and swallowed hard against the rising bile. As Yellow Shirt kneeled forward and touched the deck, Dave shuddered. *BAM*! Sudden G-forces slammed him back in his seat.

"YEEEE-HAAAAA," Nelson cried as the stoof leaped across the bow and over the churning sea.

That night, Dave, Max, and Seymour lounged in their bunks drinking beer in the Da Nang BOQ. More like a warehouse than a residence, the barracks-style open space was parsed by wooden bunks and footlockers. The windows were covered, walls and ceiling dark, and the mirror behind the bar adorned with the requisite fish netting and a flickering neon Budweiser sign. A refrigerator hummed to keep the beer cold, air conditioners rattled in the boarded-up windows, and Country Joe McDonald wailed his "I'm Fixin' to Die Rag," recently recorded at some hippie love-in at Woodstock, New York. The smell of alcohol and stale cigarettes went unmasked as no transient resident of this temporary building in this inhospitable country had ever thought to bring a scented candle.

Propped up on his bunk, Max read a magazine. "Yee-haa?"

Dave nodded and took another pull on the long-necked bottle. "That's what he said."

Max shrugged. "It *is* the most fun you can have with your pants on." He held up the magazine and Miss December unfurled. "The man loves his cat shots. And his stoof."

"Especially *Double Nuts*," Seymour said. "He's probably out there stroking her tailhook right now."

"That's a disturbing visual," Dave said.

"Speaking of tailhooks," Max said, "how'd your landings go today?"

Dave averted his eyes. "Piece of cake." He downed his beer. "Piece of cake."

CHAPTER 32

Jennifer watched Dave next to her on the upholstered sofa. Half-empty coffee cups sat on the table. She shared with Gina the small one-bedroom apartment at Subic Naval Base, provided for the DOD teachers. Though the interior was basic military-stark, much like the BOQ, they had made it a home with a small sofa and coffee table, soft lighting from the lamps, framed pictures on the wall, and the scent of vanilla.

Dinner at the O club with Carol and Ken had been animated.

"Congratulations on your first Da Nang deployment," Carol had said. "I hear you're a war hero now."

Dave nodded. "That's how I'm going to spin it." He raised his glass in a self-toast.

But Jennifer knew his game face, his public display of bravado. She had seen it before. Though his mouth smiled, his eyes shone with angst. A twinge of sadness tickled her heart.

Now, in the quiet apartment, alone and reflective, he was subdued. Perhaps she could lighten the mood.

She smiled playfully. "How does it feel to be a war hero?"

His face didn't twitch. "We're not heroes. We're delivery boys. We haul people and mail from Da Nang to Yankee Station and back. Like a bus route." He bowed his head and wrung his hands. "I didn't expect any more carrier landings. That's why I chose this squadron. It's land-based."

His distress reminded her of that day by the lake in college, his eyes pleading for her help as the draft loomed over him. The vulnerable person inside made her forget for a moment the selfish, career-driven Dave in this still-evolving man-boy.

"I'm not a big fan of carrier landings, Jen."

She nodded. "I imagine it's very difficult."

"Only because I've done so few."

"Then you'll get better with practice."

"Yes, but with each landing comes risk." Fear welled up in his eyes. "They're dangerous, Jennifer. I could crash into the ship's fantail and be squashed like a dragonfly on the windshield of an eighteen-wheeler."

She took his hands in hers.

"Then there's bad weather, mechanical failure, a cold cat."

"A cold cat?"

His hand simulated an aircraft arcing off the ship's catapult into the ocean. "When the launch catapult doesn't provide enough thrust to get us airborne."

"Oh."

"And even if I survived a crash at sea, I could drown in the churning waves of the deep, black void." He shuddered. "I'm not a great swimmer."

She knew that, but he had never before admitted it. He had held it close like a shameful secret.

"Funny thing is, I'm not scared during the actual landing. I'm too busy to think about it. It's the anticipation. Drinking beer the night before to dull the ache. Tossing in my bunk. Showering that morning like it's a cleansing ceremony preparing for my suicide."

He lifted his coffee cup, held it a moment, then put it back down.

"And we're going back next week. If I survive a year of this, I'll have an ulcer for sure." He snorted. "And worst of all, the airlines don't give a damn about carrier landings. They want hours. So I'm risking my neck for nothing."

His shoulders sagged in resignation.

"Plus, I'm not that good at it."

"Then get good at it." With a finger, she lifted his chin so his downturned gaze rose to meet hers. "You can do anything you put your mind to." She kissed him lightly, then drew back. "The problem isn't carrier landings. It's managing your stress. If you live in the future, you'll always be anxious, especially in wartime. You can't change what's coming. Of course, you should be prepared. Be the best pilot you can. Don't take foolish chances. But don't obsess over what *might* happen."

He nodded as though considering her words.

"And you're not going to wash away the anxiety with beer."

"I can try."

She shook her head.

Dave expelled a long sigh of acceptance. "I guess I just need to get good at it. Crashing into the fantail won't help me get on with the airlines." He moved closer. "So I'll try not to worry about the future. I'll live in the moment." He put his arms around her. "Like Max."

She laughed. "Well, not exactly like Max."

He looked into her eyes. "Thanks, Jennifer."

He pulled her close and kissed her deeply. With the warmth of his kiss, she melted against him. Pleasure roiled up within her as he groaned with desire and pressed himself against her. She opened her eyes to his face flushed with passion.

"I need you, Jennifer. Can I stay?"

She wanted to. She had never felt this close to Dave. But she remained leery of the boy inside. They needed to wait a while. But when his hand massaged her thigh, her passion spiked. She should stop this before they went over the cliff.

She looked down and shook her head. "I have a roommate."

"We could go to my place."

"I'm not ready yet, Dave."

The lock clicked and the door popped open.

Gina's eyes widened. "Oops."

CHAPTER 33

The next two-week deployment settled into a routine of flying, drinking, and sleeping. Each day meant two or three flights to Yankee Station. Which meant two or three chances to splatter himself, but it also meant more hours toward a Pan Am captainship. So Dave endured the flying. And the evenings.

Max pulled another beer from the refrigerator. "Women are looking for a good mate." He popped the cap. "It's basic biology. An alpha male to protect the tribe."

"Nah," Seymour said. "You have to let them prattle on. They'll think you're fascinating."

Max and Seymour had this debate every night, but Dave didn't mind. The Da Nang BOQ was dark and depressing, and the background noise soothed like having a television on.

"Like being cool and good looking and muscular," Max said.

Seymour shook his head. "A woman wants a man who is open and caring and compassionate. Fortunately, that's easy to fake."

In his bunk, each time Dave began to drift off, the voices intruded. He probably should say something. Zero five-thirty came early.

"And being rich doesn't hurt, but that comes later."

"And vulnerable. They love vulnerable."

Dave pulled the sheet over his face like a shroud. The refrigerator door opened and closed, followed by a pop and a hiss.

"Confidence," Max said. "That's the ticket."

"Then why do you buy it instead of getting yourself a nice girl?"

"Supply and Demand. And I can't work at maximum efficiency if I'm all stuffed up."

Dave heard Nelson groan and turned to see him roll over in his bunk and squish a pillow against his head.

From the copilot's seat, Nelson watched Quinn hold the stoof in a rock-steady left bank, pick up the ball, cross the ship's wake, and bounce through the burble—air turbulence caused by the island, the carrier's superstructure rising from the flight deck. After two weeks of eating, sleeping, and flying with these kids, Nelson was ready to get home. But first, he had to evaluate this hotshot's landings so he could report. He knew the guy was trouble. He just had to make the Old Man see it.

He remembered Quinn's first attempt weeks earlier, an approach so unsafe that Nelson had to take the controls to salvage a wave off and avoid hitting the ship's conning tower. This time, he'd let the cocky son of a bitch screw up so Nelson could show the Old Man that Quinn wasn't to be trusted. But there wasn't a lot of room for error here. Nenita's warning whispered to him. "Be careful, Ron. I no want to see you hurt."

Sweet Nenita. He had been seriously considering requesting a two-year extension of his tour. What the hell? With his career officially in the toilet, this being his fourth dead-end billet, he didn't need to look elsewhere. He'd never make lieutenant commander anyway, and besides, he liked the PI. He enjoyed the beautiful country, got a lot of flight time, and did something worthwhile. And he could stay with Nenita. Hell, he might even extend until retirement.

"I have the meatball," Quinn said into his mic as they rolled the wings level onto the final glide slope.

Nelson refocused. How far was he willing to let this guy screw up?

"Roger, ball," crackled back. "On centerline, on glide slope."

Quinn held the controls steady as the orange ball and green reference lights remained precisely aligned. For a moment, the stoof drifted astray like the old mare that pulled at the reins when she saw the barn. The ball drooped and the master jerked her bit, demanding obedience. The ball returned to center. He could fly, but he didn't treat Nelson's girl very gently. They slammed onto the deck of the USS Shangri-La, steaming at Yankee Station, ninety miles off the North Vietnamese coast.

Quinn glanced at Nelson in a triumphant sneer, raised the hook, and taxied to the island. "That has to be an ok," he said.

The arrogant kid was now grading himself. Recently, he'd got several "oks," worth four points on the LSO's five-point grading scale. That solid score for a skillful landing contrasted to the "one" he got for the wave off, an approach so unsafe it had to be aborted.

"That gets me to a 3.2 average," he said. "And rising."

Two sailors hurried out the hatch with their duffel bags, and a deckhand pulled out a mailbag.

"Thanks for the mail, sir," he yelled over the idling engines.

"Yeah, yeah," Quinn said. "Secure the hatch."

Linemen signaled the stoof forward and attached her to the catapult. Yellow Shirt spun his finger, engines roared, and the aircraft catapulted over the bow.

As they ascended and turned toward the beach, the intercom clicked.

"Four minutes," Quinn said. "That has to be a record turnaround."

Still a cocky kid with little respect for the aircraft but pretty good at the controls. They turned toward the beach and settled in for the short ride. With the azure sea below, the emerald mountains ahead, and the thin white strand of beach that defined both, Nelson allowed the serenity to wash over him.

A radio transmission interrupted his peace. "Mayday. Mayday. I'm hit. I'm hit. Punching out."

A second voice followed. "Da Nang Control, Navy Viper Seven Seven. My wingman has ejected. He's got a good chute."

Then a third. "Roger, Seven Seven. Da Nang copies. Dispatching choppers."

The second voice again. "Roger, Control. I'll orbit as long as I can. Limited fuel. Charlie's everywhere. Please expedite."

Quinn keyed his intercom and snorted. "Those chopper pilots must have a death wish, flying low over the jungle looking for downed pilots."

Nelson just stared. "Would you abandon your comrades, Lieutenant?"

Though nothing to report to the Old Man today, with this kid's attitude, it was only a matter of time.

CHAPTER 34

After two months in country, Julio finally got his chance.

"Okay, men, listen up." Franco stood before the outdoor poker game, his face grim. "We got reports of VC activity in the area." The card game stopped as all the men looked up. "We're resuming patrols in the morning. Zero five-thirty. Check your weapons." He turned and walked away.

"Fuck," Spider said.

Sol expelled a puff of air.

Julio felt a rush of excitement. Finally. He'd be a real medic. He jumped up. "I gotta get ready."

Spider stared. "You know they shoot the medic first, right? Kill the medic and all the wounded die too."

"Baloney," Julio said. Medics hadn't worn red crosses since Korea. "The enemy doesn't even know who the medic is."

"They shoot you when you're giving aid to the wounded," Spider said. "Everybody knows that."

Julio dismissed him with a wave of the hand and headed for his hooch to prepare. He opened his field medical kit and checked his first aid field dressings. Gauze bandages, elastic wraps, small splints. Compresses and tourniquets. He checked his drugs. Surgical powder, jelly burn compound, naloxone, Benzedrine, morphine, merthiolate swabs, ammonia inhalants. His field surgery instruments. Scissors, clamps, scalpels, and tweezers. He shuffled through the rest of the kit's pockets. A tracheotomy cannula, eye dressing kit, water purification tablets, sunburn cream, Band-Aids. He zipped it closed, slung the kit over his shoulders and puffed out his chest. He was a walking hospital.

He had one more task. He withdrew a sheet of writing paper and his pen. His last letter from Mama had been distressing. Now in a wheelchair, she couldn't leave their third-floor apartment. When would he be home?

Dear Mama . . .

He told her he would soon be getting the experience he needed to be a great EMT, and when he got home he would get a good job and they would move to a one-story house with a wheelchair ramp to the front door and they would eat only healthy foods and they would get her diabetes under control and she would feel much better and they would be happy.

Sergeant Franco stuck his head in the hooch. "You're not going, Garcia."

"What?"

"I'm taking Sullivan."

Corporal Sullivan neared the end of his twelve-month tour and had seen a lot of action. He had more experience than he wanted and prayed aloud not to get any more before his tour ended. Glassy-eyed and withdrawn, Sullivan hadn't said ten words to him since Julio had arrived.

"Come on, Sarge. He's a short-timer. Give him a break. He doesn't want to go."

"No one wants to go."

"I do."

Franco eyed him. "That's because you're batshit crazy."

Frustration exploded within Julio. "Goddammit, Sergeant, I need this."

Franco looked startled. Julio knew he shouldn't take the Lord's name in vain and immediately regretted it. He lowered his head.

Franco turned and stepped out. He looked back as he walked away. "Be ready at zero-five-thirty."

Warm, clammy air engulfed Julio as he humped down the hill in the morning darkness. The straps of his kit dug into his shoulders. After playing cards for a month, he was out of shape. Also scared and excited and slathered in sunburn cream and bug juice. But he felt alive. They left the denuded hilltop and entered a narrow path overhung by the jungle. Birds sounded their protest, squawking indignantly at the intrusion.

The squad walked for hours. Franco, leading the twelve, occasionally raised his hand, and they all froze. Then they would resume the trek. They crossed several rice paddies and onto a dirt road. The path was easier, but by now the sun bore down. Julio chafed and itched and ached. They collapsed by the road and ate chow and smoked and complained. Then they humped on. When twilight finally came, and their barren hill appeared, Julio struggled forward. He forced himself the final two hundred meters up the slope and collapsed on his rack fully clothed.

The only experience he got from the ordeal was tending his own blisters.

CHAPTER 35

In town for the night, P-3 boys packed the cavernous basement bar beneath the O Club. As Dave and Max descended the stairs, familiar sounds ricocheted off the walls. *Bang. Whirrr.* Splash. Cheer. The rowdy, all-male crowd surrounded a twenty-foot track that descended into a pool of water. A wire stretched across the track just before the pool, and a mock cockpit on wheels sat on the rails. Crumpled bills filled a beer pitcher hanging on the wall.

"Catch a wire and win the pot," Max said, pointing into the cockpit. "Just pull that lever to drop the hook." He held up a dollar bill and bounced his eyebrows.

"I can't," Dave said. "Jennifer's ceremony's at six."

"Sure you can. If you catch the wire, you won't get wet."

"It's practically impossible." Dave nodded toward three soaked P-3 jocks, cheering and swilling beer.

"But those guys haven't seen a carrier since the training command. And *you* got thirty traps in just the last two weeks." He snapped the dollar bill. "And a 3.8 landing score, higher than most carrier-based pilots."

"No, thanks."

A drunken P-3 pilot sat in the contraption. The operator pressed a button and compressed air propelled the cockpit forward. *Bang. Whirrr.* The pilot pulled the lever. The hook dropped and skipped over the wire. He splashed into the water to the drunken cheers of his comrades.

"Missed again, Bernie," someone yelled.

"Who cares?" He laughed. "In four weeks, I'll be flying for Braniff."

Dave blinked. "Braniff? Airlines?"

"Yeah," someone said. "Bernie's mustering out. He's headed home."

Dave's face burned as the blood rushed in. He snatched the dollar from Max and stuffed it into the pitcher, climbed into the contraption, and fastened the harness. *Bang.* He shot down the track and pulled the lever. The hook dropped, caught the wire, and jerked the mechanism to a stop.

Silence enveloped the room.

"I've never seen anyone make it," someone said.

Max beamed. "A stoof man."

Dave dismounted, reached into the pitcher, retrieved the bills, and stuffed them into his pocket. He ascended the stairs with Max in close pursuit. "I have to risk my neck for the next year doing carrier landings, while a P-3 spaz who can't even catch a wire on a carnival ride flies for Braniff?" He sat on a stool and slapped the bar. "Beer." A mug appeared. He downed it and ordered another. "I've got to get out of here and into a P-3 squadron." He looked at his watch, threw back the second beer, and stood. "I need to go."

"Plenty of time. Let's have another."

Dave stopped. "Why not?" He sat back down. After what he'd been through, he deserved some relief.

Jennifer perched upright in the folding chair, her spine straight, shoulders back, and hands resting delicately in her lap. Only the tapping of her foot on the tile floor betrayed the poised pose. The Subic Bay School multipurpose room served as a cafeteria, gymnasium, and this evening, an auditorium. Arranged in neat rows, the chairs framed a center aisle and wooden podium in front. Children's drawings lined the walls, balloons adorned the lone basketball hoop, and a table in the rear offered cookies, chips, and Kool-Aid.

Teachers, staff, and their guests filled the room. Jennifer glanced at Carol in the next front-row seat. Her friend smiled and patted Jennifer's knee. Next to Carol, Seymour yawned. Jennifer turned around, scanned the faces of the crowd, and looked toward the door. This was important to her, would look terrific on her resume, and would help her secure a great next job on the way to her goal. He knew that, and yet, he wasn't here.

As a bow-tied man walked to the podium, the din of conversation abated. He adjusted his horn-rimmed glasses and buttoned his tweed jacket. "Good evening, everyone. For those in the audience who don't know me, I'm Principal Willard Wertz." A pensive look crossed his face. "And, I guess," he added, "even if you *do* know me." He pulled notes from his coat pocket. "We are here tonight to recognize excellence in teaching this past year . . ." He spoke for ten minutes about the wonderful school, and the wonderful students, and the wonderful teachers with whom he had had the privilege of working this term, and how dedicated Department of Defense teachers were to come halfway around the world to this remote jungle to ensure the children of servicemen receive a truly fine education.

Seymour's head fell forward and jerked back upright.

Finally, Principal Wertz called the first award. As he announced each name, the recipient approached the podium and received her award to the sound of polite applause. Mr. Wertz beamed. "And finally, our teacher of the year." He held out a hand. "Miss Jennifer Pruitt."

Jennifer stood and glanced back. Her shoulders slumped. As she turned toward the podium, the metal door slammed open. Dave and Max stumbled in, muffling snorts and guffaws, and marched up the center aisle.

"Ooo," Max said, spying the refreshment table and detouring toward it. He grabbed a handful of cookies and stuffed them into his mouth, the crumbs raining onto the seated onlookers as the men squeezed into a row.

"Excuse us, excuse us," Dave said. He tripped over his own foot and stumbled in the narrow walkway. He caught himself but not before sending a chair toppling toward a woman in the row behind. Hands sprung out to rescue her from the projectile. "Sorry, sorry," he said as others returned the chair to upright.

Dave and Max collapsed into empty seats to sighs of relief from their neighbors.

Jennifer's eyes widened as Dave grinned and flashed a thumbs-up. She hurried to the podium and received her award. Polite applause was overwhelmed by Dave's and Max's enthusiastic clapping and hooting. Max inserted his thumb and forefinger into his mouth and emitted a shrill whistle.

Jennifer touched her forehead as her face warmed.

Willard thanked the crowd. As the meeting broke up, Dave stumbled forward while Max headed back to the cookie table.

"Congratulations," Dave slurred. "Let me take you home."

She glared at him, infuriated and bewildered at the same time. Was this a United States Naval Officer or a self-absorbed adolescent?

"I don't think so."

"Sure. Come on." He grasped her elbow.

She jerked loose. "I need time to think." She grabbed her award and hurried to the door.

"What's the matter?" he called.

She raced past Max stuffing chips into his gaping maw and weaved her way through the departing crowd.

CHAPTER 36

On the metal desk guarding the commanding officer's door, a placard read *Petty Officer Archibald.* The squadron's personnel yeoman sat hunched over the four-inch-thick blue binder opened before him. He adjusted his thick glasses and turned the page with the care of an anthropologist examining an ancient manuscript, the bookcase behind him lined with identical blue binders. Engrossed in his beloved Bupers manual, he appeared oblivious to the goings-on inside the Old Man's office.

". . . and so, sir," Dave said, "it is with the greatest regret that I must request an early reassignment." He stood rigidly before the commanding officer's desk, papers in hand, reading from notes. His barely perceptible nod indicated the end of the presentation. He held out the transfer request.

The CO didn't reach or react in any way. The curving corrugated metal wall of the Quonset hut framed his head, bald save a black half-ring of fuzz, like a Roman Senator's laurel.

Dave fidgeted, then tentatively set the papers on the desk. "I've also included my top three choices for reassignment. P-3 squadrons in Reykjavik, Rota, and Naples." He refolded his notes and slid them into his pocket. The uncomfortable silence needed to be filled. "Of course, I'm willing to wait until my replacement arrives."

The CO smiled. "You've been here six months. Is that right, Lieutenant?"

"Yes, sir," Dave said, immediately on alert. The formality of a superior addressing him by rank sounded ominous, like a mother calling her child by his full given name. "I wanted to resolve this sooner than later."

"And your tour is eighteen months?"

"Yes, sir."

The CO looked him over. "Well, that *would* be an early reassignment." He leaned forward on his elbows and interlaced his fingers. "This wouldn't have anything to do with the deployments in country, would it, Lieutenant?"

"Oh, no, sir. I just feel that I would maximize my value to the naval service in a P-3 billet."

"I see." Another pause.

Dave fidgeted.

"Lieutenant, do you know how much money the Navy has invested in you?"

"Yes, sir. Two hundred fifty thousand dollars."

"And before you go on to your glorious airline career, courtesy of Uncle Sam, don't you think the Navy has the right to expect a return on its investment?"

"Of course, sir, that's why—"

"And since we've invested that kind of money, don't you think we have the right to decide where you would best serve the interests of the naval service?"

"Yes, sir, but—"

"Request denied."

Dave stood mute. The CO looked up and raised his eyebrows. "Anything else, Lieutenant?"

"Ah, no sir." He saluted and turned away, then stopped, turned back, and retrieved the papers. He saluted again and hurried out the door past the silent yeoman.

When Dave dragged into the ready room training session, Seymour tapped the chalkboard with the wooden pointer. "Casualty Assistance Calls Officer," he said slowly to the assembled officers. "CACO. Sounds like a nice insurance adjuster who comes to your house with a check for your wind-damaged roof."

Dave headed toward Max, seated in back, shook his head in a silent "no," and plopped down next to him. "I thought the Old Man would be reasonable."

"Go over his head," Max said. "Write to the Bureau of Naval Personnel. They cut the orders."

"I can do that? Bypass the Old Man?"

"Sure. Ask Arch. He knows everything. He helped me extend my tour here."

Seymour shook his head. "No, my friends. This is no helpful insurance man. This is the poor bastard assigned to tell the family that their husband/father/son is dead. Pray you never get this job. It is bad news."

Dave jumped up and hurried out the door. At Archibald's desk, he paused for a whispered conversation before knocking on the CO's door jamb.

He entered and stood at parade rest. "Captain, I formally request that my application for early reassignment be forwarded to the Bureau of Naval Personnel for their consideration."

The CO looked up. "Aren't you supposed to be in a training class?"

"Sir, Yeoman Archibald said Bupers regulations require that the commanding officer forward any request that has not been satisfactorily resolved at the unit level." Dave placed the paperwork on the desk. "Captain, with all due respect, my request has not been satisfactorily resolved at the unit level."

"You could better use your time." He raised his chin toward the door and called out. "Arch, send this to Bupers." The officious yeoman appeared and took the papers. "And recommend disapproval." The CO looked at Dave. "Lieutenant, you can't afford to skip training."

Three weeks later, Dave and Max reclined in deck chairs by the swimming pool behind the BOQ. Partially shaded in the lengthening shadows of the royal palms, they sipped from beer cans, Dave still in his flight suit and boots and Max in swimming trunks.

"I thought you had a shot," Max said, taking a huge swig from the cold, sweating can.

Dave snorted. "Hah. It was fixed from the get-go. I never had a chance. They said to reapply after I've been here fifteen months." He raised his hands. "Hell, that's my normal rotation."

Seymour, up to his chest in water, hung his arms over the side of the pool. "Let me get this straight. You're taking career advice from Max, the Navy's ranking ensign?"

Max gestured toward Seymour with a single finger while looking at Dave. "Well, *I* love it here. The flying's fun, the nightlife's great, and it's always summer."

Dave sighed. "I'm not like you, Max. I'm not here to have fun. I'm here to get hours. Period. Now, for twelve more months, I'm stuck here flying the stoof instead of getting quality P-3 hours, and tons of them. We fly out of this sorry backwater in an old jalopy that leaks in more places than my grandmother. We're target practice and delivery boys. Pan Am won't be impressed."

Max shrugged, stood, and dove into the water. He swam a lap and pulled himself from the pool. A young woman passed carrying a bundle of sheets and towels. Max smiled and ogled her up and down. "Why can't you just enjoy this paradise?"

Dave dropped his head and spoke slowly. "Because when I'm forty years old, I want to be drinking coffee from a china cup at thirty thousand feet in the captain's seat of a Pan Am 747, flying from San Francisco to Tokyo." He stood and turned toward the building. "Not peddling life insurance in Columbus, Ohio."

CHAPTER 37

They sat on her sofa, their knees almost touching, coffee cups on the table. Jennifer had selected the Rachmaninoff symphony that oozed from the phonograph. Dave's sports coat hung from a chair. The rose he gave her perched in a small vase, and new earrings glittered from her lobes. Mellow from the wine and lobster dinner at the club, she allowed him to cradle her hands in his.

This almost hadn't happened. In the month since the awards debacle, Jennifer's answering machine had recorded dozens of messages from Dave.

"He sounds contrite," Carol had said.

"Of course he does. He's always contrite. Afterwards." Jennifer remained resolute not to see him. At least not for a while. He was infuriating. Just when she thought he had matured, bam, he did something like this. "I've given him a dozen chances, and I'm tired of waiting for a selfish adolescent to grow up. He's still a boy."

Carol had shrugged. "They're *all* boys."

Jennifer felt Dave massaging her hands and looked into his wide blue innocent eyes. Dinner had been wonderful. The flowers, the earrings, the lobster.

"Thank you for a lovely evening," she said.

"I wish I could do more," he said. "I'm so sorry about my behavior at the ceremony."

"I understand, David. It's alright."

"No, it isn't." He bowed his head. "I ruined your special night. I was thoughtless and arrogant and most of all, disrespectful. I'm truly sorry."

Delighted, but still wary, Jennifer dared to hope he had finally turned the corner. He even declined wine.

"I stopped drinking. It makes me do things I regret." He squeezed her fingers. "It costs me too much."

"Thank you, Dave."

She leaned forward and kissed his cheek. Pushing off her shoes, she brought her legs beneath her on the sofa. He put his arm around her and she rested her head against him. His warm chest and thumping heartbeat soothed her.

He shifted and his lips lightly touched hers. She allowed the pleasure to linger. His tongue tickled her lips and excited her. His body stiffened as his arms pulled her against him. He kissed her deeply and groaned. She opened her eyes. His face reddened and breathing quickened. His hands roamed down her back and hips. When he put his hand on her thigh, she pushed him away.

"No, Dave."

"Please, Jen," he gasped, trying to hold on.

She shook her head and pulled back.

His hands dropped and he fell back against the sofa, panting. Droplets of perspiration dotted his forehead. He heaved a sigh. "I thought . . ."

"I know. I'm sorry."

He nodded as his breathing slowed. "Okay, we can take it slow. Can I see you tomorrow?"

There would never be a good time to tell him. She set her jaw.

"No, I have to pack."

His brow furrowed. "Pack?" he said as though he didn't understand the word.

"Yes, Dave. It's summer vacation. I'm going home."

He exhaled a deep breath. "Wow." Silence filled the room. "Okay. I'll miss you. When will you be back? September?"

"I don't know."

"You don't know when school starts?"

She took a breath. "Dave, we're two very different people. And I need time to think."

"About what?"

"About what I want."

"Then why are we here, Jennifer? Like this?"

"I don't know Dave. I want this to work. I want *us* to work."

"Then what's the problem?"

He looked bewildered. She might as well be candid.

"Dave, one moment you're a beautiful man"—she looked away—"and the next you're fifteen years old. The whipsawing exhausts me."

His brow furrowed. "*You're* being whipsawed? You just kissed me. What am I supposed to think?"

"I felt close to you."

"And now you don't?" He shifted over on the sofa, out of reach. "So you'd leave? Just like that?"

She sighed. "Dave, we don't want the same things in life."

His gaze fell to the floor. "I see." He stood and picked up his sports coat. "So I guess I'll see you in September." He opened the door. "If not, have a good life."

Bottles of San Miguel and Red Horse beer littered the table like opposing flotillas in a war game. Dave and Max spoke loudly to be heard over the music and spirited crowd in the busy Olongapo bar. The proprietress scurried about, bar girls loitered, and bow-tied teenage waiters carried drinks.

"I believe you may be right, Max," Dave slurred. "Live for today."

Two bargirls alit in chairs next to the men.

"Good evening, ladies," Dave said. "This is my friend, Max. He's a naval aviator, and he's the cream of the crop." One girl slid closer to Dave. He tilted his head toward her. "I'll bet *you're* not a judgmental goodie two-shoes, miss-perfect, are you?"

She crinkled her forehead. "I no think so."

"And you don't think my natural desires are shameful, do you?"

"Oh, no."

"And you're not full of condescending negativity, are you?"

"You friend funny," she said to Max.

Dave signaled the waiter who instantly appeared at his side. "Drinks for my friends." He twirled his downward-pointed finger around the table.

More beers appeared before the men and small glasses of amber liquid before the women.

"So," Dave said, "what's a nice girl like you doing in a place like this?"

A puzzled look scrunched the girl's face. "I work here."

A few miles away, candles flickered on the altar of the quiet, nearly empty chapel. Recorded organ music played softly. In their thrice weekly ritual, Al and Trudy kneeled in the first pew, hands folded, heads bowed.

"Thank you, Lord, for thy many gifts," Al said. He paused to smooth down his mustache. "We pray that this terrible war be over soon and the suffering end for so many people." Trudy's bowed head nodded in affirmation. "We pray for the safety of our forces and especially our pilots and their loved ones."

In the raucous bar, Dave and Max threw their heads back in laughter. The bargirl on Dave's lap poured beer into his open mouth, the overflow cascading onto his chest.

Al looked up at the crucifix. "We pray that you give our troops the strength to hold up under the pressure of this terrible war," he said as Dave fell from the chair onto his back, the bargirl on top of him, roaring in drunken laughter to the cheers of Max and the other patrons.

"And we especially pray that you look down on Lieutenant David Quinn," Al said, "and help him confront his fear, his anger, his lust, and lift the dark spot from his soul. Amen."

The bargirl rose from atop Dave. "You come with me now."

His head lolled left and right. "No, I have a girlfriend."

"Then why you here?"

He thought for a moment. "I mean, I *had* a girlfriend."

She stood and pulled him up. "Now you have new girlfriend."

As Dave wobbled to his feet, Max reached out. "Here, buddy," he said, handing him a foil packet.

A hotel clerk stood behind the desk in the small lobby. A threadbare upholstered chair, side table, and a twenty-five-watt lamp were enough to fill the room. A trail in the well-worn carpet showed the path of Dave's predecessors. His arm draped over the girl, Dave leaned against the counter and squinted against the eye-level layer of smoke.

"Twenty dolla," the clerk said, a cigarette dangling from his lip.

Dave pulled crumpled bills from his pocket and dropped them on the desk. He turned with his companion toward the stairs.

"Sir," the clerk said, "you must register." He spun the pink-paged book toward Dave and offered the pen.

"Register?" Dave slurred. "Why? Are you having a drawing later?"

The clerk stared blankly.

"It's a whorehouse, for Christ's sake," Dave said.

"All guests must register, sir."

Dave sighed and took the pen. The previous line in the book had two crossed out misspellings of *Lieutenant*, followed by *Lt. JUNIOR GRADE Alan Ross.*

Dave's brow furrowed. *What?* Then he giggled.

Ronald Nelson, he signed. *Lt., USN.* He dropped the pen, turned, and wobbled up the stairs with the girl. He passed a disheveled sailor coming down, his arm draped over a young woman.

"Sir," Petty Officer Cox said with a drunken salute.

"Cox," said Dave, returning an equally unmilitary wave.

The floor of the dark, narrow hallway creaked with each step. She led him through one of the unmarked doors into a windowless room—a walk-in closet with a bed.

As Al and Trudy kneeled in the spotless chapel before the Ornate Virgin Mary, Dave watched the girl shed her clothes onto a straight-back chair, the only other furniture, and sit on the rumpled bedspread.

This *girl* hadn't seen the sunny side of forty in some time.

"Come here, sailor," she said, pulling him toward her.

Ten minutes later, after an explosive and exhausting release, Dave lay panting as a black fog of remorse enveloped him.

Dave awoke on his own bed, his head pounding. Still dressed except for his shoes, he rose, stumbled to the dresser, and emptied his pockets. He pulled off his trousers and turned toward the bathroom. An unfamiliar object caught his eye. On the dresser lay his keys, crumpled bills, and change. And the unopened foil packet. He groaned and stumbled to the toilet. When he released the pressure, a sudden burning shot through him.

The red Corvette glistened in the small parking lot beside the Quonset hut. A simple sign read *Dispensary.* A screen door swung open and Dave hurried out. He smoothed flat the Band-Aid on his upper arm, glanced around, and looked down at the pill bottle in his hand. *Doxycycline. Take twice daily for seven days.* He hopped into Red and started her engine. Before he could move, Commander Holt's car approached. He took his foot off the brake and slid down in the seat.

Brenda parked next to him. She grunted her way out of the car and knocked on Dave's window.

"Yoo-hoo," she said.

"Oh, hi." Dave rolled down his window.

Brenda was starting to show again. "Morning sickness pills." She placed one hand on her belly.

He closed his hand around the pill bottle and forced a smile. "You know, Brenda, medical science has now ascertained the cause of your condition."

She winked. "Do they have a vaccine?"

"No, you just need to control your behavior."

"You mean Phil's."

Dave forced an even broader smile.

"So Dave, did you ever snag that gorgeous teacher?"

He looked down and shook his head. "It didn't work out. She went home."

Brenda rested her hand on Dave's shoulder. "She'll be back in September."

"I wouldn't count on it."

She smiled. "I would." She glanced down at the pill bottle peeking out from Dave's fist. Her eyes radiated concern. "Just take care of yourself until then."

CHAPTER 38

After two months marching on patrol through the countryside, Julio still had never encountered the enemy. The war had become routine, and depression descended on him like the morning mist. At this rate, he would go home with no more medical experience than when he arrived. Sure, he was grateful that his friends hadn't been injured, and for his own safety, but he didn't come eight thousand miles just to survive.

They humped down a narrow jungle path and into a small clearing.

Spider hadn't stopped talking since base camp. "Got some R&R coming up. Going to get me some more of that sweet Saigon poontang."

He turned to face Julio, made a two-finger V, brought it to his mouth, and wiggled his tongue. As he grinned, his shoulder exploded, followed by a loud rifle crack. Spider spun around from the impact and landed face down on the path. Suddenly, small arms fire filled the air. Julio stood staring at Spider's contorted body. A hand grabbed him and pulled him down behind a tree.

"Goddammit, Garcia," Sergeant Franco said, "get the fuck down."

Julio lay on the ground and covered his head. Bullets whizzed through the undergrowth, thumping into the earth and whacking into trees, one just inches above his head, sending a shower of splinters raining down upon him. For several moments, he lay frozen. Then he realized he couldn't stay like this. He had to do something. He raised his head and peeked from behind the tree. Spider lay motionless, blood pooling beneath him.

"He's going to bleed out, Sarge."

"We're pinned down."

Bullets thwacked the earth in the clearing. Julio crossed himself. "Cover me."

"Cover you? We can't see shit. We don't know where they are."

Julio dashed into the opening, kneeled before Spider, and turned him over. He took off his pack and opened it.

"Fuck," Franco said and started firing blindly into the overgrowth. The other men joined in.

Blood pulsed from the hole in Spider's shoulder. Julio stared at the gore, unmoving. He looked into Spider's eyes, then at the blood-spurting, gaping shoulder wound. He shuddered in horror.

Spider groaned and his eyes half opened. "I hope I'm not as bad as *you* look."

That jolted Julio into action. He stuffed dressing into the wound, trying to stanch the massive bleeding, but the blood kept coming. It had to be an artery. He found his clamps, pulled the blood-soaked gauze from the wound, and the squirting resumed. He stuck the clamp into the gaping hole, but he couldn't find the bleeder. Blood kept spurting out. He took a breath, plunged his fingers into the hole, found the vessel, and pinched it off. He clamped it, then stuffed in clean packing, and bandaged the hole. Hunched over Spider, his knees in the mud, Julio found himself hyperventilating. He realized the chaos had gone silent. He pulled out the morphine.

Spider stared into his eyes. "Ah, the good stuff."

With shaking hands, Julio injected Spider.

Franco emerged from behind a tree. "Charlie bugged out." He kneeled before Spider. "Hey, buddy, you just got your ticket home." He turned and put his hand on Julio's shoulder. "Good work, Garcia. He'll make it."

Julio stared at his blood-covered arms and started shuttering uncontrollably.

A medivac chopper arrived and the others loaded Spider in as Julio sat shivering on the ground. He had seen a comrade almost bleed to death. This wasn't like bandaging dummies. He couldn't watch God's creation being hideously mangled.

"I don't have the courage for this."

"Are you shitting me, kid," Franco said. "That was fucking heroic."

"I mean the blood. I can't . . . I can't deal with it." He looked at his blood-encrusted hands. Could he really be a medic? Or an EMT?

CHAPTER 39

Heading back across the South China Sea in the copilot's seat, Nelson studied the distant thunderheads towering over the Philippines. He looked left and right. The wall of storms blocked their path as far as the eye could see. This looked bad.

"Cubi Tower," Quinn broadcast, "Checkertail Zero Zero. What's your weather?"

"Welcome home, *Double Nuts*," the radio responded. "Light rain, overcast, ceiling at one five hundred feet. Radar shows a line of CBs off the coast."

"Any holes in the storm?"

"Negative."

"How wide's the line?"

"Off the radar in both directions."

Quinn turned to Nelson. "It doesn't look so bad. I say we punch through."

Nelson stared at him. Was he serious?

Quinn grinned. "Gotta get back to the lair."

"The what?"

"The lair. My room."

Nelson shook his head. "What's with the names? Your room is the Lair, your car is Red, your adolescent monkeypod figurine is Woody. You got a name for your pecker?"

Quinn shrugged. "What do you say, Lieutenant? Can we go through it?"

Nelson remembered Nenita's words of caution, but this could be the learning moment he'd been waiting for. He took a deep breath.

"It's your call."

Dave was getting very tired of taking crap from Nelson. What was his problem? First, he busted his chops about the way he talked, then he wanted Dave to spend another hour in this crate going around the storm because he didn't have the balls to fly through a little rain?

Dave keyed his mic. "Roger, Tower, Zero Zero inbound. ETA one five minutes."

As the stoof approached the line of gray clouds, the sun disappeared behind the shadow of a towering thunderhead. Moisture formed on the windshield, coalesced into streams, and raced up the glass. The aircraft buffeted. Dave gritted his teeth as he penetrated the clouds and went on instruments, his view outside obscured by gray gauze.

Rain splattered against the windshield. The aircraft vibrated, the yoke shaking in Dave's clinched fist. As they bore deeper into the storm, the cockpit darkened. Perspiration beaded on Dave's forehead. After a few moments, the buffeting slowed, the rain subsided, and the sky lightened.

Dave smirked at Nelson. "Piece of cake," he said just as they entered a second storm cell.

The airframe responded to the new assault, shaking the pilots and rattling the flight instruments against the console. Their rotating red beacon flashed back at them from the darkness. Dave struggled with the yoke. His eyes burned from perspiration, and his sweat-soaked flight suit clung to his skin. Again, the air smoothed out and rain lessened. They broke out into a clear patch.

Dave looked at Nelson and smiled weakly. When he turned back, he saw the black wall. They pierced the veil and entered the netherworld. Sheets of water obscured the windshield. The interior darkened to night. The yoke bucked and raged to break loose of Dave's grip. Hail beat the stoof like it was an intruding piñata. A violent downdraft hurled them toward the earth. Dave's stomach leaped to his throat as he watched the altimeter unwind in the sudden plunge. His muscles ached and his head throbbed as he wrestled the beast. As quickly as they had dropped, the aircraft jumped heavenward in a violent updraft.

A flash on the control panel caught Dave's eye.

Nelson pointed. "Fire warning light. Starboard engine."

Dave jerked his head to the right to see the engine trailing smoke and then flames erupting. The sudden movement induced dizziness as the spinning fluid in his inner ear sent his head tumbling. He put a hand to his temple.

"Vertigo," he said as a wave of nausea overtook him.

"Stay on the gauges, Lieutenant," Nelson said.

Dave released the yoke. "Take the controls."

He leaned forward and vomited. Nelson grabbed the yoke. Dave lifted his head, then heaved again.

"I've got the controls," Nelson said, pulling the right throttle closed.

The engine slowed to idle, but the fire continued as the aircraft's nose pulled to the right in a sharp yaw, like a car with a blown right front tire. Nelson slammed the left rudder pedal to straighten the aircraft.

"Put out the fire," he said.

Dave reached up tentatively.

"M-F-E," Nelson said as he struggled with the yoke. "Mixture-Feather-Emergency." The aircraft continued to buffet violently, now with only one engine. Smoke entered the cockpit. "Put out the fire, Lieutenant."

Dave reached up, grabbed the left mixture control lever, and pulled it back. The good engine sputtered.

"NO!" Nelson yelled, slamming his hand against the back of Dave's and pushing the lever forward. "The *starboard* engine," he said, "not the port." Nelson slapped Dave's hand away. He curled his fingers around the starboard red knob. "One," he said, "starboard mixture—OFF." He pulled the lever smartly aft. The flames diminished, but still burned. "Two, starboard feather button—PUSH." He shoved the red button up with his palm, the propeller blades feathered, and the aircraft yawed back to the left. "Three, emergency switch—ENGAGE." Nelson reached up and jerked back the red switch cover, breaking the safety wire and revealing a toggle beneath. He flipped the switch. A cloud of white powder puffed out of the engine cowling, extinguishing the flames. The fire light went dark.

The plane continued to buffet in the storm. Dave could see Nelson watching him wipe the vomit from his mouth with the sleeve of his flight suit.

"You have the aircraft," Nelson said.

Dave hesitated.

"Take the aircraft, Lieutenant."

Dave put both hands on the yoke and his feet on the rudder pedals. He focused his eyes on the flight instruments.

"Cubi Control," Nelson broadcast, "this is Checkertail Zero Zero declaring an emergency. We've had an engine fire. Request immediate vectors direct Cubi Point."

"Roger, *Double Nuts*. Come right to one five zero. Descend to and maintain two thousand five hundred feet."

The aircraft dropped to the assigned altitude but continued in a slow descent, unable to maintain altitude with a lost engine. Suddenly, they entered another powerful downdraft. Dave watched the altimeter unwind a thousand feet.

"*Double Nuts*," the controller said, his pitch rising, "come right to two zero zero immediately. You won't clear the mountain at that altitude."

Dave looked at Nelson.

"DO IT," Nelson yelled, "NOW."

Dave jerked the yoke to the right just in time to see the mountain-top jungle foliage appear out of the mist. He could count the palm fronds as he passed within fifty feet of the earth, turning parallel to and then away from the mountain ridge. The clouds once again enveloped them. With insufficient power, the aircraft continued its slow descent.

"Unable to maintain altitude," Nelson broadcast. "Say our position."

"Roger, *Double Nuts*, you're one mile out. Come left heading zero seven zero. Field now overcast at four hundred feet."

Dave turned to the new heading. The altimeter read eight hundred feet, and they were still in the soup. Then seven hundred . . . six hundred . . . five hundred.

"We're landing blind," Nelson said. "We have only one shot at this, Lieutenant. There's no power for a wave off."

Four hundred feet. Three hundred and fifty. Still in the soup.

"You're over the numbers," the radio crackled.

"Go for it," Nelson said.

Dave jerked closed the throttle of the good engine. At two hundred feet they dropped below the overcast, already past a third of the runway. Dave pushed the nose over. His airspeed increased as he dove for the deck. He hit long with less than one thousand feet of runway remaining. His airspeed too high, the aircraft porpoised back into the air, stalled, and came down hard. Dave stomped on the brakes as the end of the runway, and the drop-off into the bay approached. They overran the concrete, breaking off several approach lights, and slid into the grass. They skidded to a stop just short of the seawall. Rain pelted Dave's face as he scrambled through the hatch. Smoke rose from both tires. One burst into flames. The men ran clear to the rising sound of sirens. Emergency vehicles appeared and sprayed foam on the smoldering engine and wheels.

At the ready room table, Dave sat hunched forward in a straight-back chair, his head pounding. Both hands clutched a mug of coffee. His wet flight suit clung to him where he had washed off the vomit. Nelson sat on a corner of the table.

"We have two problems, Lieutenant," Nelson said. "First, you don't know your emergency procedures. Probably because you have a piss-poor attitude. You think being able to nail a carrier landing makes you a good pilot? It doesn't. If you don't know procedures, you're a time bomb. You may have survived this one, but when you fuck up badly enough, you won't get a second chance." His eyes bored into Dave as he pointed to the scar on his chin.

Dave stared at the table and took a sip of his coffee. "I got vertigo."

"Shut up and listen." Nelson held up two fingers. "Second is something I can't teach you—good judgment. Some people just don't have it. You might be one of them. You chose to fly directly through a violent storm. And for what? Because you had a sore butt and didn't want to take the time to go around? To get a beer a few minutes sooner? Don't you know how to weigh risk against gain? Next time you put yourself and others in jeopardy, you'd better have a damn good reason." Nelson stood and picked up his helmet. "But what is most important here is that you accept responsibility for your actions and learn from your mistakes."

"P-3s have radar," Dave said. "I could have picked my way through the cells in a P-3."

As Nelson walked out shaking his head, Max rushed in from the flight line. "We heard the radio chatter. You okay, buddy?"

Dave nodded, still holding his coffee mug.

"This calls for a beer," Max said.

Dave sighed. He knew he had blown it big time. He'd almost killed himself. And Nelson was sure to rat him out to the Old Man. And that would mean bad orders. Maybe it was time to try a different tac—play their game, study his procedures, and suck up to the powers that be.

"You go, Max. I'm beat."

"Really? No beer?"

"I'm going to hit the sack."

In his room, Dave reached to the top bookcase shelf and pulled out a volume. He blew the dust from the top and settled on a barstool. The lava lamp undulated. Woody watched from within his barrel. A table lamp cast a circle of light on the book as Dave turned a page of the Natops Procedures Manual.

CHAPTER 40

It was hot. And muggy. Typical Shaker Heights in July. Living in one of the most upscale neighborhoods in Ohio didn't protect you from the weather.

Jennifer sat by the pool behind the mini-mansion where she had grown up. The wrought-iron table sprouted a large umbrella, its green-embroidered top matching the pattern of the back awnings. She shifted on the cushion protecting her from the metal chair and flipped through the *Time* magazine. *Nixon orders invasion of Cambodia. Four students shot by National Guard at Kent State. Beatles split up.* She tossed the magazine onto the table and looked into the sparkling pool water.

If she didn't renew her DOD contract by Friday, Principal Wertz would hire her replacement. Should she go back? Certainly not for Dave, still an immature, self-absorbed man-boy. But she did love her work. And her friends. And Dave's blue eyes, boundless curiosity, and biting wit, quoting Democritus and Herodotus and Curly Joe Howard. *Who does that?*

Daddy had spent the last three weeks trying to convince her to stay. "Apply to law school. You got great grades in college." He'd been singing this tune for years. She'd join the firm. As a senior partner, he could assure her a position. "There are practically no women lawyers. You could write your own ticket. And, you'd make triple a teacher's salary." Law school brochures had been carefully arranged on the coffee table. Ohio State. Case Western. Duquesne. "All great schools," he'd said. She had nodded. And all nearby.

She stood and pulled the beach coverup over her head, exposing the bathing suit beneath and her sensitive alabaster skin. When she dove into the pool, the jolt of the brisk water sent a shiver through her. Under water, she swam the length of the pool, pushed off the other side, and swam back. As she approached the wall, two blurry figures coalesced through the last two feet of water. She broke the surface, gasped for breath, and smoothed back her hair with both hands. Squinting into the sun, she saw Daddy and a young man she didn't recognize, both in business suits. She glanced at her coverup on the chair ten feet away.

"Have you met Winston? He's an associate with the firm." Daddy smiled his fake work smile. "He's assisting me on a case. We were nearby so we came over to take a break."

Daddy never came home during the day.

"Could you entertain him while I get some files together?" He turned and disappeared into the house.

Jennifer forced a smile.

"Would you like to sit down, Winston?"

He would.

When he turned to sit, she popped out of the water and donned her coverup.

Winston said he loved the law, didn't mind working sixty hours a week, and hoped to make junior partner next year and have a piece of the action.

Jennifer glanced at her watch on the table.

"With bonuses, junior partners can make six figures," he said.

She smiled. "Happiness resides not in possessions or in gold. Happiness dwells in the soul."

Winston blinked. "What?"

"Democritus," she said.

"Where's that? Syria?"

Mother appeared carrying a tray with a pitcher of lemonade, two glasses, and a plate of finger sandwiches. She smiled sweetly as she set them on the table.

Jennifer shot her a glance. *Et tu, Mother?*

"Daddy, please stop trying to set me up," Jennifer said, looking across the dinner table.

"Your mother wants grandchildren."

Mother watched her food and ate quietly.

Jennifer's father cleared his throat. "Jenny, you're twenty-three. I thought you would have come around by now."

"Exactly, I'm only twenty-three."

He pointed his fork at her. "Winston would be a good match."

Jennifer stared back. "What about his brothers Marlboro and Chesterfield?"

His forehead wrinkled like a confused Shar-Pei. "It's time to get a sensible job, marry a suitable man, and put aside your childish idealism."

"You mean quit a job I love for a mind-numbing one, marry a boring man because he has the right pedigree, and become a baby machine so Mother has someone to play with?"

"I had hoped I could convince you."

"You have, Daddy."

CHAPTER 41

Dave entered the hangar and approached the damaged aircraft. Chief Malloy stood on a lift, working on the starboard engine of *Double Nuts*. The grizzled maintenance chief was ancient. Fifty, at least. They said he served in WWII and saw Doolittle launch from the USS Hornet in '42. A seasoned sailor, the no-nonsense, hands-on, get-it-done maverick had little patience for stupid questions or green junior officers. But he was tight with Nelson and the Old Man. It wouldn't hurt to get him in Dave's corner.

The cowlings had been removed, and the engine disassembled. Tools lay about the platform. A young sailor handed him a wrench from below.

"Scotty," the chief said, "get me a fire sensor switch."

"We're out, Chief," the sailor said.

"Then scavenge one from Helen." As the sailor hurried out to the flight line, the chief noticed Dave loitering. "You lost, Lieutenant? The officers' club is up the hill."

Dave smiled. "No, not lost. Just wanted to see how the repairs are coming."

The older man stared. "You're the hotshot that burned up my engine."

Dave glanced away. "We caught some bad weather."

"Uh-huh." The man could see through him like a pane of glass.

Dave showed his palms. "I'm sorry, Chief. I made a bad call. It didn't have to happen."

Chief eyed him for a moment. "Okay." He returned to his work.

Dave examined the blackened cylinders. "Any idea what caused the fire?"

"Of course. A broken fuel line."

"How'd that happen?"

"You tell me, Lieutenant. You were there."

Dave shrugged. "Vibration? We penetrated a storm cell." He thought for a moment. "Could hail break a line?"

"Sure could." He put his hand on a cylinder. "I hate to see her like this."

"Sorry about that, Chief, but parts can be replaced."

Chief squinted like a one-eyed pirate. "So can pilots." He nodded at Red in the parking lot with its shredded fiberglass and missing bumper. "You need to take better care of my girl, Lieutenant. Be gentle with her and don't try any hot-shot funny business."

Dave could have been in the chief's living room, picking up his daughter for a date.

"Not to worry. I won't be doing that again."

Chief took a deep breath and stroked the cowling. His eyes shone. "She's like a good woman. You treat her right, and she'll take care of you."

The sailor trotted over and handed him the fire sensor switch. "It's the last one. Helen out there's pretty near stripped naked."

Chief took the part and resumed his work.

Dave walked around the platform, inspecting the damaged engine. "Can you fix her?"

Chief snorted at the junior officer. "Shit, son, we can fix anything." He wiped the sweat from his forehead with his sleeve. "I mean, shit, *sir*."

The chief was an enigma. Dave couldn't read him. It was time to move up the food chain.

Dave scribbled on the ready room chalkboard.

He looked over the assembled officers. "One," he said. "Mixture—close." He yanked back the mixture lever on the overhead mockup. "Two. Feather Button—press." He pressed the button. "Three, Emergency Switch—engage." He flipped the toggle switch. "MFE." He tapped the chalkboard with the wooden pointer. "Short of a wing falling off, an engine fire is the worst thing that can happen in flight."

"You ought to know," Seymour jeered. "That's why you're teaching this class."

Seymour didn't know the half of it. MFE was Nelson's mantra. It represented all he held dear. Know your procedures. If this didn't ingratiate Dave, nothing would.

After the class, Dave filled his mug from the coffee pot in the back of the Quonset hut. Seymour and Max played acey-deucy.

"He never showed," Dave said.

Seymour looked up. "Who?"

"Nelson. I put on a dog and pony show, and he couldn't be bothered to come."

"Why? Does it matter?"

"If a tree falls in the forest and no one's there to hear it, did it make a sound?"

Seymour turned to Max. "What's he talking about?"

"He's trying to build bridges."

"So *you're* into riddles now too?"

Dave sat down. "You're mighty feisty today, Seymour. Isn't Carol back?"

"Of course. It's October. School started four weeks ago." He stared at Dave as though waiting for the next question.

Dave wouldn't ask.

"Look," Seymour said, "if you want to see Jennifer, why don't you just call her?"

"I don't have time for a social life."

Max rolled the dice and Seymour snorted. "Yeah, right."

From a gray navy Jeep a hundred yards from the school entrance, Dave had watched Jennifer leave the building and walk to her apartment a block away. Since nearly crashing, he thought of her constantly. He should approach her. His hand squeezed the door handle and started to pull. No, she needed her space. She *wanted* her space. But she had come back. That had to mean something. He sighed. It did, but not for him. She loved her friends, her job, her kids. He released the door handle.

"Are you bringing Carol to the thing tomorrow?" Dave said.

"I could." Seymour looked up. "Oh. Yeah, I'll bring her." Seymour rolled the dice and moved his checkers. "What are you waiting for? Jennifer to walk up and grab your package?"

Dave snapped. "Don't talk about her like that."

Seymour's eyes widened and Max grimaced. The game continued in silence save the rolling of the dice.

On Saturday morning, Dave stood atop the maintenance lift. With a wet sponge, he glided a dollop of Turtle Wax onto the nose of *Double Nuts*. He drew small circles until the wet goo dried. Then he buffed away the white haze with a clean cloth. The "00" gleamed. This would impress the Old Man. With repairs completed, Dave would make sure *Double Nuts* sparkled.

"This time, we'll do it right," he said. "From nose to tail. Let's make her shine."

The gang moved along the aircraft like washing a baby, from one part to the next. Half the squadron had turned out. Seymour had brought Carol, who invited Jennifer.

Dave slathered wax over the engine cowling. He watched Jennifer perched atop a ladder. Her small hand glided a soft cloth, gently buffing the waxy haze beneath the copilot's window, and revealing *LTJG DAVID QUINN* gleaming in the sunlight. She glanced toward him. As he nodded, movement in the shadows of the hangar caught his eye. Nelson and Chief Malloy watched the crew pamper their girl. While Dave would like them as allies, in this game only one man made the decisions.

But on Monday morning, when the CO marched into the ready room, he didn't mention the newly waxed aircraft. No thank you, no nod of appreciation, no nothing. Just an announcement that fitness reports were ready, and he marched out.

CHAPTER 42

Dave rattled the dice within the leather cup and tossed them so hard that one ricocheted off the table and careened into Max's chin.

"Hey." Max rubbed the red mark. "Take it easy, buddy."

"Sorry, Max, but this really sticks in my craw."

Seymour, in the on-deck chair, stared blankly. Playing acey-deucy may have been mindless, but watching it induced catatonia. He came out of his stupor. "That sucks. I never got a 'satisfactory' fitness report. It sounds okay, but, like grade inflation, it's really a D, maybe a D plus."

"Or like grading olives," Max said. "'Jumbo' sounds big, but it's really the smallest." He rolled doubles. "I got a 'satisfactory' once."

"Yeah, when you flew into Mexico," Dave said. "What did *I* do?"

Max shrugged. "You made a boneheaded decision to fly through that storm."

Seymour raised a finger. "You tried to bail from the squadron after six months, then appealed the Old Man's 'no,' making him look bad."

Max moved his checkers across the board and rolled again. "And the flight with Gina's cat."

"That was a favor to you, Max."

Dave risked his life every day and for his trouble got a lousy fitness report.

"Nelson's fingerprints are all over this. Now he'll use it to cut back my hours."

Dave's face flushed. Getting the flight hours he needed could no longer be left to the grace of the scheduler. He knew what he had to do. He'd beg, borrow, and steal every flight he could, even deployments to Da Nang and the dreaded carrier landings. Satisfactory, hell. He'd fly so many hops, he'd be indispensable to the squadron or die trying. And when he left here, his logbook would be jammed with hours.

He surveyed his opportunities to accumulate more flight time. Ted had no hours to surrender, barely flying the four-hour monthly minimum required for flight pay. And Max, of course, would no more give up flight time than he would women or beer. Seymour, on the other hand, would rather cuddle with his honey than fly off for a week, so he'd gladly relinquish an assigned hop from time to time. As for the other pilots, Dave snagged their hours easily, especially the Da Nang deployments. Going to war in another man's place was an easy sell.

But Al surprised him.

"Want me to take your hop, Al?" Dave said.

"Oh, no. It's my duty."

So another approach became necessary, and scheduler Cox was a willing confederate. Thus, with an occasional stroke of the grease pen on the scheduling board, Dave had one more hop and Al one fewer. Each morning, Al marched into the ready room, looked at the board and scratched his head.

He finally pulled down his logbook and examined it. "I only flew twenty hours last month," he said.

Cox's downcast eyes remained riveted on important paperwork.

For the next several months, Dave woke most mornings to the stale-beer-and-cigarettes smell of the Da Nang BOQ. He donned his flight suit, fore-and-aft cap, and aviator shades. He admired himself in the mirror, went to the head, and often as not, vomited. He hopped between Da Nang and the ships of Yankee Station like a ping pong ball. His logbook filled—eight hundred, nine hundred, one thousand hours. But no matter how many landings and cat shots he made, the knot never strayed from his gut. Fear, stress, and loneliness fermented a rancid brew. Though he thought about Jennifer often, he had no time to pursue her. With back-to-back deployments, he rarely came home. And when he did, he barely had time to crash for twelve hours before starting all over again.

By his fifteenth month, he had logged twelve hundred hours, and his troubles would soon be over. No more Da Nang, no more carrier landings, and no more stoof.

Sunken into an over-stuffed ready room chair, Dave scribbled on the clipboard on his lap. A sweaty Max entered in his flight suit, carrying his helmet and flight bag, and collapsed in the next chair.

"What'd you ask for?" Max said.

"VP-22 in Rota, VP-14 in Naples, or VP-1 in Keflavik."

"Ooo," Max cooed. "Those Icelandic girls are babes."

"You been there?"

"No, but I hear things." Max winked. "They have geothermal heating."

"That's the houses, Max, not the girls."

"Well, I hope you get your first choice."

"I should. I put my ass on the line with twelve deployments, eighty-one traps, and twelve hundred hours, most of it in-country." He popped the paper from the clipboard and stuffed it into a manila envelope. "In three months, it's sayonara PI and the stoof, hello Europe and the P-3."

Three weeks later, just back from Da Nang, Dave lay propped up on his bed, his legs crossed and fingers interlaced behind his head, admiring his vanity wall and its symbols of achievement—the beautiful monkeypod wings, flight certificates, photographs of his aeronautical exploits, and especially the picture of *Double Nuts* with *LTJG DAVID QUINN* painted under the copilot's window. He looked at the P-3 and the Pan Am 747 posters, the final mountains yet to be conquered.

The black telephone jangled.

"Hello?"

Twenty minutes later, Dave rushed into the Quonset hut.

"You got good news for me, Arch?"

Yeoman Archibald looked up. He grunted to his feet, rifled through the file cabinet, and came out with a manila envelope.

Dave ripped it open.

CHAPTER 43

Sol lay face down in the undergrowth. Julio hovered over the slit-open pantleg. His fingers shook as he held the leg and brought the tweezers to the wound.

"Ow," Sol cried. His leg spasmed and kicked open Julio's medic kit. "Hurts like a son of a bitch."

"Goddammit, Sol, don't move." Julio often took the Lord's name in vain now. The months with these guys had rubbed off. Mama would be shocked. He poked the tweezers into the back of Sol's calf and came out with a dime-sized piece of shrapnel. He cleaned, medicated, and bandaged the wound. He showed the metal to Sol. "Want to keep it?"

"Fuck," Sol said, "where's my morphine?"

"Sorry." Julio zipped up his kit. "That's only for going-home wounds."

Julio had assumed not only the profanity of his squad, but also its casual indifference to pain. But it was an act. Last night, alone in his hooch, he shuddered uncontrollably, then wept.

Back when the patrols had started, he was weak. He thought he'd get over it. And he did, physically. His calves and thighs were now as hard as steel cables, and his stamina allowed him to go all day. But inner strength did not come.

He had thought that too would pass. Spider had been shipped to Japan to recover, and then home. His first patient. And his introduction to the horror of war. But after months on patrols, patching up his friends still sickened him. They'd been in a dozen skirmishes with the Viet Cong, the local black-pajama-clad guerrilla fighters. They were mostly small bands and lightly armed. They could kill you just as dead, but they didn't have the numbers or firepower of the NVA, the North Vietnamese Regular Army. And in every battle, he became sick. Yes, he could be wounded or killed on any day, but he could push that down deep. Whatever happened to him would be God's will. But playing God with other men's lives horrified him.

Several months passed before it finally sank in. After treating a neck wound, he turned his head and vomited. In front of half the squad. At that moment, he knew it wouldn't get any better. Holding him back might have been God's plan, or fear of the war, or terror that he might not come home to Mama. He didn't know, so he prayed to the Lord for guidance.

But God didn't show him the light. Sergeant Franco did.

He knelt beside Julio as he wiped the vomit from his mouth.

"You're a good medic, Garcia," he said, resting his hand on Julio's shoulder. "And one goddamned brave son of a bitch. You have no fear for your own safety, dodging bullets and shrapnel to treat your fallen comrades. You'll end up with a Silver Star. Or dead."

At that moment, Julio knew. Franco had it right. What made him sick wasn't his fear for his own safety, or the war, or playing God over other men's lives. It was his revulsion to blood, to injury. And that would never change. He could no more do this in civilian life than he could fly a chopper.

Shame overwhelmed him. As much as he wanted to be a man, to help his fellows, and to return home victorious and save Mama from her wretched circumstances, he couldn't. He could only pretend, do his job, and, when he left, never look back. When he got home, he would take care of Mama as best he could, even if that meant a career at Whataburger.

CHAPTER 44

Dave's forehead rested on one of the papers that littered the O Club bar. A torn manila envelope lay nearby.

Max held a sheet of paper. "BOQ officer at NAS Saufley Field," he read. "That's not even a flying billet."

"You're very astute," Dave slurred. "I'll be wet nursing newbie flight students, making sure they have clean sheets and full bellies."

"Pensacola's a hopping town," Max said.

"I'll be lucky to get four hours flight time a month in the T-34 trainer. The mighty Teeny Weenie." He drained another bottle and signaled the bartender. "Christ," he muttered. "It's the end of everything." He dropped his forehead to the bar.

"Hello, David," a voice said from behind.

He lifted his head and saw Jennifer smiling nervously in the mirror.

"How have you been?" she said.

He spun around and stared at the angelic figure.

"I understand your tour is up soon," she said, "and the school term is almost over, so I guess we'll both be leaving. And I wanted to say goodbye before . . ." Her voice trailed off. "Can we keep in touch?"

"I'd like that, Jen." He took a long blink. "Where will you be?"

"Ohio."

"Maybe I can get a job selling life insurance in Columbus."

Jennifer furrowed her brow and glanced at Max.

He shook his head.

She took a deep breath. "The teachers are having an end-of-the-year gathering after last classes on Friday. I wondered if you'd like to come."

"I can't, Jen. I'll be deployed again. Besides, I wouldn't be good company. I'm not in my happy place right now."

Max pointed to the paper he held.

She shrugged her shoulders.

"Bad orders," Max mouthed.

"Oh, no. I'm so sorry, Dave." Her fingers touched his arm.

"Me too," he mumbled.

She hesitated. When he didn't move, a sigh escaped her lungs. "This is my parent's number." She slid a card across the bar. "If you want to call me." A sad smile crossed her lips. "Goodbye, David," she said and hurried away.

Slumped over the bar, he watched in the mirror as she left the club. He gulped his drink and ordered another.

Max put his hand on Dave's back. "Don't you have an early hop?" he said, waving off the bartender. He stood and helped Dave to his feet.

When they got to the BOQ, Dave's arm draped over Max's shoulder for support as they stumbled down the hall. They stopped in front of Dave's door, and Max propped Dave against the wall.

"Your key," Max said.

Dave searched his pockets, came up with a key, and tried to insert it into the lock. He fumbled it, dropped it to the floor, and giggled.

Max retrieved the key and opened the door. "There you go, buddy."

Dave stumbled in and toppled onto the bed.

"No answer, sir," Cox said, holding up the phone. The clock above the duty office desk read 6:00 a.m.

Commander Holt stood in his flight suit clutching his helmet with "Melissa & Sophie" stenciled across the back. He stared at the scheduling board with the maintenance flight he and Dave were to fly. "No sweat," he said. "It's just a twenty-minute test hop. I can handle it alone."

"Are you sure, sir?"

Holt nodded. "Procedures allow maintenance test hops to go solo." He lifted his flight bag and walked through the door to the flight line.

Cox erased *Quinn* from the whiteboard.

Sunlight streamed through the bedroom window. Dave slept atop the bed, fully clothed. The phone rang. He groaned, reached over, fumbled with it, and dragged it onto the bed.

"What?" he said.

He listened without speaking.

Twenty minutes later, he rushed into the ready room. Several pilots milled about. Dave looked at Al, who nodded toward the acey-deucy table. Upon it rested a flight helmet, the visor shattered and the shell cracked open by a gash bisecting *Melissa* and *Sophie*. Several others stared at the motionless object like bewildered animals faced with the carcass of one of their own, touching it, nudging it, trying to coax it back.

"That's all the divers found," Al said in barely more than a whisper.

At the desk an officer spoke into the phone while others waited. "Yeah, honey," he said. "It was Phil. Yeah, I know. I have to go. Others need the phone. I love you, too." He hung up, and another married officer dialed.

Seymour sat in an overstuffed chair, bent forward with his head in his hands.

"The Old Man assigned him CACO," Al whispered. "He has to tell Brenda." Al looked at the floor. "Poor bastard," he said, the only profanity Dave had ever heard him utter.

Dave stared at Seymour, then hurried from the room.

In his office, the CO sat, staring at his hands folded on the desktop. Dave knocked.

Commander Jensen glanced up. "Come."

Dave stepped in. The CO's gaze returned to his hands, his face furrowed, his skin sallow.

"I'll tell Brenda," Dave said.

The CO didn't move. "Take the padre with you."

Dave turned to leave.

"And Lieutenant—"

Dave turned back.

"—you're grounded."

Dave sat before the modest one-story block house, pale green like the others but with flowers lining the sidewalk, a woman's touch in an otherwise testosterone-fueled outpost.

Dave wore his tropical whites. Next to him, the base chaplain sunk deep in the red vinyl bucket seat. Neither spoke while the hidden jungle inhabitants sang their chaotic melody. At the house across the street, a window curtain moved. Someone, half hidden, peeked out. Next door, another curtain moved. The other husbands had all called home. Only the Holt phone had not rung that morning. Dave hoped Brenda's curtain would move so that she might be forewarned. But it did not. Finally, the chaplain turned to Dave and raised his eyebrows.

Dave swung his door wide and lifted himself out of the Vette. He brushed his white trousers to allow them to uncrumple into a razor-sharp crease and donned his cover. Dave always loved wearing his tropical whites—the white hat perched atop his sharp haircut and barely regulation-length sideburns, golden wings shining on his chest, and LTJG epaulettes on his shoulders. A babe magnet, he had always thought. But now, a beacon.

He stepped onto the curb to join the chaplain. His shades remained in his pocket. The officers marched between the flowers to the front door. They heard laughter from inside and looked at each other. Dave took a breath and knocked. He heard stirring and approaching footsteps.

Brenda partially opened the door and saw Dave. She smiled flirtatiously. "Why, Dave," she said, "what a surprise. Is this a date?"

Her smile held for a moment awaiting a grinning, wise-crack response. Dave's face didn't twitch. Her eyebrows furled. Then she saw the chaplain.

She cocked her head. "Hi Roger. To what do I owe this—" She stopped and her smile evaporated. Her jaw dropped open. She looked back at Dave.

"Phil crashed," he blurted out.

His words stunned her like a blow to the chest. She stood frozen. She didn't breathe. The color drained from her face. Her knees buckled, and the men reached out to arrest her fall. As she steadied herself, tears welled up in her eyes. Dave watched his friend, a thirty-two-year-old naval commander's wife, now mother of three, full of all the joy life had to offer, suddenly become a shattered child.

Dave had meant to say, "We lost Phil. I'm so sorry," and hug her. But he just stood there, his arms limp, watching her, not moving, too exhausted to even berate himself.

Melissa came up behind Brenda. "Hello, Mr. Kin," she said to Dave. But even a four-year-old can sense tragedy. "What's wrong, Mommy?"

"Nothing, baby." Brenda kneeled down and hugged her. "Go back inside."

For thirty minutes, Dave sat in Brenda's living room, dwarfed in a large papasan chair, staring at a framed photograph of the family. The chaplain spoke softly to Brenda amid her hushed sobs. Another wife arrived. Then another. Dave sat and stared.

A shadow from the fading evening light drifted through the open hangar door across the concrete deck and onto a small circle of men standing in silent reverence. The cavernous structure dwarfed the group and the object protected within their perimeter—a canvas tarp on the hangar floor. Upon it rested a battered radio, a seat cushion, a parachute harness, and unrecognizable twisted metal.

Investigators traditionally assembled wreckage in a hangar, but in this case, it wasn't really necessary—so little remained. Divers had retrieved these few remnants within hours of the crash, and the search had ended. They surrendered one of their own back to nature in the churning dark water of the bay. No one could have survived the impact, and sharks quickly removed all traces of flesh and bone. Nature is indifferently efficient.

Some men still wore their flight suits, the sweat from the day having long since evaporated, but not the fatigue. Others were in uniform, and still others in civvies, their evening plans long since forgotten.

Dave stared transfixed at a small glint of gold almost obscured in the debris, the golden frame of a pair of aviator's sunglasses. No lens. No strap. No case. Just the mangled frame, obscenely contorted.

Dave put his hand to his pocket and felt his shades within the protective case. He glanced around at the other faces. Some looked up and quickly away. Others refused to meet his eye. His shades, once a symbol of all that he wanted, all that he had worked for, indeed, all that he *was*, were now his badge of shame.

As the light faded, a sudden tropical storm blew through. The hangar groaned against the raging wind, and the metal roof became a tympanum for a billion drumming raindrops. Beyond the open hangar doors, the wind peppered the rain against the concrete tarmac. Nature's deluge bubbled up and washed away the deposits of oil and grit left by man. The lights from the hanger illuminated the flight line just outside but quickly faded into the darkness that cloaked Subic Bay and the Philippine jungle beyond.

Dave couldn't help imagining Phil's last moments as the aircraft stalled and spun out of control—the disorientation, bracing for impact, and then panic when all hope evaporated. He imagined the terror of one's imminent and certain death, and the sorrow for all that he left behind.

Dave gazed through the open hangar door into the night and the runway beyond. As suddenly as it had begun, the drizzle on the roof fell silent, the clouds parted, and a full moon shone through. An F-8 fighter taxied onto the runway and began its takeoff roll. The afterburner exploded into a roar as it ignited and the jet leaped into the air. Hangar doors vibrated in sympathy. The whine of the engine and the blue cone of flame from its tailpipe faded as another soul lifted off the earth and hurtled into the darkness.

Nelson lay splayed on the futon, his chest pressing into its surface, almost to the hard bed frame beneath. Everything felt damp in the oppressive humidity—the air, the sheets, his skin. The bed took up most of the small room. Without air conditioning, the open window let in the sounds and smells and sorrows of the warm, dark city. He lay unmoving, arms at his side, his energy drained from him. The knot that had locked his gut all day refused to leave. Even speaking the words aloud did not provide relief.

"It's my fault."

Nenita rose from his side and straddled the small of his back, kneaded her thumbs up each side of his spine, and massaged his neck and shoulders.

"No, Ron, it not your fault. You no control everything."

He shook his head. "I knew this was coming, and I couldn't stop it."

"You blame yourself for everything. Your friend make choice. You no control that. Your friend twenty years ago make choice too. You no control that either. But you still blame yourself." Her thumbs dug into his back in a beat accompanying her words. "That why you so angry." She collapsed onto his back, their perspiration joining to form a seal. She kissed his neck. "You good man, Ron. You need to forgive yourself."

He sighed into the darkness. That would be very hard to do.

The two men sat silently at a table in the quiet officers' club. Dave's hands enshrouded a coffee mug, while Max sipped a beer. Dave was transfixed by the lobsters moving slowly in the tank. Bound by bands on their claws, they undulated slowly within their glass cage, oblivious to the outside world and their fate in it. A waiter hurried by and stopped at the tank. He reached in, grabbed a lobster, and carried it through the kitchen door. Dave watched the remaining crustaceans stir at the disturbance, then return to their normal lethargy.

"How'd he choose?" Dave said.

"What?" Max said.

"The waiter. How'd he choose which lobster to take?"

Max shrugged. "The fat one?"

Dave shook his head. "They all look the same."

Cars overflowed the chapel parking lot and lined the road. Inside, every seat was taken. An enlarged photograph of Lieutenant Commander Philip Holt stood on an easel by the altar. He smiled broadly in his tropical whites, with ribbons across his chest capped by golden wings. The chaplain stood at the podium, his words scant solace for the mourners.

". . . and so we salute Commander Holt," he said, "for the ultimate sacrifice he made in service to his country." He stepped down and presented a folded flag to Brenda, seated in front. She looked up, her face red and puffy, and accepted the banner.

Others rose in turn and offered tributes. Finally, Dave stood and walked to the podium. He looked at the sea of faces and recognized every mourner. Each couple—Commander Jensen and Margaret,

Seymour and Carol, Al and Trudy, and others—clasped hands tightly. Jennifer and the other teachers huddled in a protective pod. Max, Norm, Nelson, Ted, and the other pilots stared stoically. And Chief Malloy, Cox, and the other enlisted men and officers of the squadron filled the sanctuary.

But they all appeared clouded in a fog. Dave's gaze settled on the only clear faces, sharp images in an otherwise blurry photograph. Brenda, with eyes downcast, held her daughter's hand. Melissa looked bewildered. Only Sophie and the new baby were not there. Dave took a piece of paper from his pocket and unfolded it. He looked at Brenda again, at Nelson, at Jennifer, then down at his notes.

"Commander Holt was my mentor," he read, his voice quavering. He paused, then continued. "He showed me how to fly safely, how to deal with the unexpected, how to be a professional in the air."

He glanced up toward the assemblage and attempted a reassuring smile. But he couldn't lift the downturned corners of his mouth. He returned to his notes.

"But as my friend, Philip Holt taught me trust. He taught me respect." He looked at Brenda and Melissa. "And he taught me love." He looked at Jennifer. "Phil loved more than I thought possible."

A soft sob arose from the assembled. Dave stopped reading and measured his breathing, then continued. "When the hand of fate reaches down and takes a man like that, we ask ourselves the question, 'why?' Why take from us a loving husband and father, a superb naval officer, and a remarkable human being?" He looked up at all the faces. "Is it a random event? Does someone choose who is taken and who remains?"

His eyes fell back on his script. The next words read, "It is God's will," but he couldn't bring himself to utter such a blame-shifting lie. He stiffened his spine.

"No," he said. "No one decides." He cleared his raspy throat and swallowed hard. "But it's not random, either." He wiped his eyes. "It's the actions we take."

A rising lump choked off his throat, and his hand crumpled his notes.

"Our choices have consequences," he croaked.

He met Brenda's eye. "I . . . I . . ." He looked away. "I'm so sorry," he said, eyes downcast as he stumbled from the podium.

A recording of the "Navy Hymn" welled up through a loudspeaker as the mourners filed out of the chapel. The rising roar of approaching jets slowly displaced the music. Everyone looked skyward. Three Air Force Phantoms in tight formation flew directly overhead with an empty slot off the leader's wing.

"The missing man formation," Max said softly.

As the jets boomed past, Nelson returned the salute that no one could see but all knew was there. The mourners watched the tribute disappear over the horizon.

Dave and Max walked down the BOQ corridor.

"Good night, Max," Dave said in a monotone voice as he unlocked his door.

"Are you okay, buddy?" Max said from behind, reaching out and putting his hand on Dave's shoulder.

Dave didn't answer. He pushed the door open and stepped inside, leaving behind his friend's touch. The door closed with a terminal click. Dave stood silently facing the Pan Am poster. Suddenly, a convulsion shuddered through his chest, and a guttural howl erupted from deep within. He ripped down the poster and shredded it. He threw himself against the bar, toppling it and sending the lava lamp shattering against the block wall, and Woody twanging in midair, having ejected his barrel. Dave attacked the embankment of stereo gear. Speakers and tape decks and amplifiers crashed to the floor. He yanked the monkeypod wings from the wall and beat them against the bookcase, scattering books and tapes and records. His chest heaving, he dropped the splintered weapon, tore the naval aviator wings from his chest, and crumpled to the floor. He drew his knees to his chest, buried his face, and sobbed.

CHAPTER 45

A taxi squealed to a stop in front of the BOQ. Jennifer jumped from the cab and hurried into the building. As she approached Dave's room, the adjacent door cracked open and Max peeked out. He nodded, then receded into the darkness accompanied by the faint click of the latch. She knocked lightly on Dave's door.

No answer.

She knocked again.

"Go away," came a voice from within.

"It's me." A pause. "May I come in?"

"No. I don't want you here."

She stared at the door, then expelled a sigh. "I'm coming in." She turned the knob and eased the door open.

The room in shambles, Jennifer surveyed the damage and found Dave on the floor in the corner, as tattered as his surroundings. His shirt was torn, his arms bruised, and his hands scratched and bleeding.

"What do you want?" he said, barely visible amid the debris.

"Max called. He was worried."

"About me? Hah. What for?"

She walked in and closed the door. "I was worried too."

"Why? You don't owe me anything, Jen. I dumped on you like I did everyone else around here, with Commander Holt being the apex of my career." He choked and looked away. "And Brenda." He wiped his eyes with his sleeve and took a deep breath. "You couldn't swing a dead cat around here without hitting someone I've dumped on."

She looked down at him. "Yourself, most of all."

He met her eye. "Why are you here?"

She moved aside a toppled bar stool, brushed away Woody, his spring sans appendage, and sat on the floor beside Dave. "Because you're in pain." She took his hand. "And because I care about you."

Dave shook his head. "You don't even know me."

"I know you're chasing something that doesn't make you happy." She stroked his palm. "What happened to the boy I knew in college? The one who knew what he wanted, who pondered the big questions, who recited Nietzsche and Kant and Camus? The one who grew grapes and made wine in the basement of his dorm? The one who—"

"He threw a snit and killed a good man, destroyed a wonderful woman, and left three children fatherless forever." He pulled his hand away. "I don't want you to see me like this, Jen." He wrapped his arms around his knees and squeezed. "Please leave."

She slid next to him and put her head on his shoulder. "I don't want to leave. I want to be with you."

He didn't move.

"What you did in the chapel took a lot of courage."

"Courage. Hah. I'm afraid of everything. Of the water. Of the carriers. Of being a failure."

"Courage isn't about not being afraid. It's about acting in spite of your fears."

A breeze blew through the windows, billowing the curtains. A beam of the street light illuminated the couple. Blood shone on the floor. Jennifer took both his hands and examined the cuts. She stood, went into the bathroom, and returned with a washcloth and bandages. She felt his gaze as she tended to his wounds. When finished, she kissed the back of his bandaged hand.

"Better?" She placed his hand on her heart and peered into his deep blue, defeated eyes. All doubt vanished as she realized that a career without love was only half a life. One doesn't foreclose the other, and she wasn't willing to sacrifice either. And marriage wasn't servitude. It was partnership.

She rose, sat on the bed, offered her hand. "Come."

"No, Jen. Not now. Not when I'm like this."

She smiled. Men could be so stupid.

Dave reclined in the back row of his college classroom watching Jennifer's ponytail bob as she took notes. The professor droned on, the lesson an incomprehensible blur. Familiar faces filled the room.

Beside him, a voice said, "I told you so." Dave turned. Brenda sat in the next seat. "I knew you'd get together."

Jennifer looked back from the front row and winked.

"Isn't this better?" Brenda said.

Dave's Adam's apple bobbed. "Better than what?"

"Better than lying to yourself." She nodded toward Jennifer. "Isn't this what you really wanted?"

Dave's eyes blinked open. Wedges of moonlight cut through the jalousie slats and onto the rumpled sheets and intertwined bodies. The wicker blades of the ceiling fan whirred to the slow cadence of Jennifer's rhythmic breathing and sent down a gentle breeze to kiss and cool their moist skin. He had no doubt. He had found what he wanted.

Though he joined the Navy to avoid the jungle, he stayed to revel in the status. No longer a geek, a protestor, a misfit, he had become a naval aviator. When he put on those wings and shades, he became *somebody*. He let his pride take over. And now . . . He swallowed hard. Phil had died and Brenda had been destroyed. He tried but couldn't blink away the tears.

Jennifer's face pressed into his side. He turned his head and kissed her hair, then fell back and stared at the ceiling.

If he couldn't be a pilot, he would find something else. As long as they could be like this. Let love replace his ambition, his fear, his anger. He had always treated his fear like an alarm clock, as though ignoring it would make it go away. But it never had. He exhaled a long breath. Then blinked in surprise. Something had happened. The knot in his gut. That ever-present, ever-aching part of him. It was gone.

With his free arm, Dave reached for the Natops procedure manual perched atop the nightstand and silently slid it onto the bed. He opened it and read slowly.

She stirred and he froze. She slid her arm across his chest. A minute passed before her soft cadence resumed.

"I didn't expect this," he whispered.

She opened an eye. "Me neither." She kissed his chest. "I used to be Snow White, but I drifted."

He furrowed his brow. "Mae West?"

She nodded. "You're not the only one with pithy quotes." She took the book from his hand and dropped it to the floor.

On the other side of the eight-inch-thick block wall, Max's room glowed with its usual eeriness of black lights, undulating lava lamp, and seductive music. Disheveled black silk sheets exposed the curved back and buttocks of a slender sleeping woman, her olive skin adding to the ambiance.

Max stood in a silk kimono, a beer bottle in one hand. In the other, he held a glass to the block wall and pressed his ear against the bottom. As he listened, his eyes widened and his mouth dropped open.

Eight officers half reclined in the ready room chairs.

Dave stood before them, holding a model stoof. "There's an upside to being grounded," he said. "You have a lot of time to study your procedures." Guffaws arose from the seated. "So I've boned up on a few things." He tapped the numbers written on the board. "Short field procedures get you in and out of some of these podunk fields around here." He gestured with a stoof model approaching the desktop. "Full flaps, eighty knots on final, approach power. You could land in six hundred feet on a dirt road if you had to." The model landed smoothly. "Takeoff is trickier. Two-thirds flaps, rotate at seventy knots, climb out at seventy-five. You can clear a fifty-foot obstacle in a thousand feet." The model lifted off the desk with inches to spare.

"What if you're heavy?" Al said.

"It takes longer, of course. At max gross of twenty-nine thousand pounds, rotate at eighty knots and climb out at eighty-five. Takeoff distance is fourteen hundred feet."

Nelson entered in the back, poured a coffee, and stood watching.

"What's your stall speed at max gross?" Seymour said.

"Seventy-seven knots at a fifteen-degree angle of attack. So you're right on the edge of a stall. You have to be precise in your speed control." He held up a copy of the manual. "It's all in the book."

"How about short field *and* max gross *and* hungover?" Max said.

They all laughed.

"Okay," Dave said, "that one's not in the book." He looked at each man. "The point is, you have to know the numbers. Because when you need it, you won't have time to look it up."

Nelson sipped his coffee as he watched Dave absorb the friendly barbs of his peers. Shamed, grounded, and guilt-ridden, Dave had accepted responsibility for what had happened and had moved on, using the experience to better the lives of those around him rather than becoming a bitter loner, angry at life for twenty years.

He remembered Nenita whispering to him in the dark. "You must forgive yourself before you can forgive others."

He set down his cup, left the ready room, and headed for the commanding officer's office.

Dave spent his afternoons wandering the hangar and observing the repairs. Chief Malloy noticed.

"Did the O Club close, Lieutenant?" he asked as Dave watched him working on a dissembled engine.

"It's still early, Chief."

Max tromped over in his flight suit. "There you are, buddy." He tapped his watch. "Let's go. It's happy hour."

Dave smiled at the chief and shrugged. What could he do?

Hours later, Dave, Max, and Seymour hunched over the bar. From a distance, the Filipino bartender scowled at the pyramid of beer mugs he was not allowed to remove.

Dave examined the glass structure. "Do you know why the skyscraper towers over the rude hut?"

Seymour scrunched his face. "What?"

Max didn't react.

"Because it stands on beams of steel. Beams hardened in the inferno of the blast furnace."

"Yeah," Seymour said, "that would have been my guess."

"Liberty stands on beams too, but those beams are forged in blood."

Seymour held up Dave's beer. "What the hell are you drinking?"

"He talks that way a lot now." Max sipped his beer. "He had an epiphany."

Seymour blinked. "A what?"

"An epiphany. It's like a kick in the head."

Seymour nodded. "He also got laid."

Dave ignored the ramblings of his friends. "The tragedy is that the price is paid by others."

"Is there a point here?" Seymour said.

"Yes. We can pursue our dreams only because others sacrifice theirs. We sit here, clean and dry and cool, drinking beer with friends, while grunts bleed in the mud." Dave downed his beer and balanced the empty mug at the apex of the skyscraper.

"Max's only dream is getting laid," Seymour said.

"Bangkok," Max said. "That's the place to go for action." His eye followed a Filipina waitress as she wiggled by. "I should take some R and R out there."

Dave turned to his friend. "Don't you ever slow down?"

"I'll slow down when I'm dead."

"You know, Max, hookers might not be the best way to go. Maybe you should find a sweetie you can stick with."

"Besides," Max said, "the girls around here are always in a big hurry. Like they have someplace to go."

Dave raised his mug. "Lord Chesterfield said the pleasure of sex is transitory."

"Who?"

"Lord Chesterfield. An Englishman. A couple hundred years ago. Famous for his pithy quotes. He said the pleasure of sex is transitory, the cost abominable, and the position ridiculous."

"The cost isn't so bad around here. I never pay more than twenty."

"I don't think he meant money, Max."

"And what position was he talking about? Or did they only have the one back then?"

"Probably," Dave said.

Max took another sip and belched. "What else did he say? Transitory? Like doing it on a bus?"

Dave put his hand on Max's shoulder. "I'm going to miss you, buddy."

CHAPTER 46

"You want Lieutenant Quinn back on the Da Nang deployment?" Cox asked, seated at the ready room duty desk. "The Old Man grounded him."

Nelson stood by the scheduling board. "He changed his mind."

"But he wouldn't do that." Cox scratched his temple. "Unless you—" He pursed his lips, looking at Nelson again before filling in Dave's name on the board:

Time	Pilot	Copilot	Aircraft	Mission
0800	*Nelson*	*Maximillian*	*UE32*	*Da Nang*
0800	*Quinn*	*Ross*	*UE00*	*Da Nang*

The next morning, two stoofs flew in loose formation, *Double Nuts* a hundred yards to the starboard. Dave could see the outline of Nelson's and Max's helmets in the other cockpit. As they crossed the water toward Viet Nam, a sense of regret surprised him. His last deployment. In three weeks, he shipped out.

Mesmerized by the drone of the engines during the long flight, Dave gazed at the horizon, his eyes hidden beneath the tinted visor. Serenity washed over him. Although the South China Sea seemed immense when flying over, it was only a small corner of the grand expanse of the Pacific Ocean. He heard distant outposts communicate. The long undulating waves of the low-frequency radio band bounced between the surface and the ionosphere, carrying radio messages over many miles. He heard Anderson on Guam, Clark in the Philippines, and Tan Son Nhut in Viet Nam. Because of the huge distances, the frequency modulation ebbed and waned with atmospheric conditions, giving the voices a singsong quality, like the melody of a whale calling to the pod over the miles.

"Even whales need companionship," Dave said.

"What?" Al said from the copilot's seat, eyeing Dave.

"No man is an island. We need others."

"Who said we didn't?"

Dave stared at the vast ocean. "I did."

On landing, the cool air of their lofty perch yielded to damp tropical heat. As they trudged from the Da Nang flight line, the sun bore down. They passed the fortified bunker kneeling low in the sand, corrugated metal forming its walls and roof, and fifty-pound sandbags lining every surface. Next to it stood the bachelor officers' quarters, a stark wooden building as unwelcoming as the war-torn country, and inside, more a bar than a home.

They crashed on their cots. As sweet oblivion washed over Dave, Commander Holt's face appeared.

"I'm sorry," Dave said.

"For what?" Holt said.

"I killed you."

Commander Holt chuckled. "You didn't kill me. My choices killed me. Just as yours could kill you. Or save you. You're in command of yourself."

Dave stared, blinking.

"It's not too late, Dave." Holt tilted his head and looked skyward. "Incoming."

A siren shrieked and Dave bolted upright. An explosion outside sent the far wall collapsing inward, toppling the refrigerator and sending three cases of cold beer bottles shattering on the floor. Shards of glass flew and foam hissed. The men leaped from their bunks, scrambled out the door and into the bunker. In the cramped, dark space, they settled onto low benches, the air warm and dank. Clad only in their underwear, they listened to distant explosions rumble. Dave's pounding heart slowed and his breathing became measured. He stretched his legs, crossed his bare ankles, and leaned back against the sandbag wall. A small packet on the bench caught his eye. He reached for it and drew out one of the narrow tubes. He slid the matchbook from beneath the cellophane. A match flared and he drew the flame into the cigarette, igniting the tobacco in an orange glow. Dave inhaled deeply, and blew the smoke across the still air.

"Since when do you smoke?" Max asked.

"Since a minute ago."

Max picked up the pack and squinted at the warning label. "That's bad for your health."

Dave raised his palms. "We're in a bunker, Max. I'm not worried about getting cancer at sixty."

A mortar exploded close by. Dave froze as the ground shook, sandbag walls shuddered, and the metal overhead vibrated. Loose sand drizzled down, and the smell of explosives wafted in. Dave's shaking hand returned the cigarette to his lips. He took another long drag and the glowing ember illuminated the darkness. Soothing, long-absent nicotine washed over him. He gazed at the Chesterfield with affection. "I forgot how good these taste."

Max smelled the pack.

"Carpe diem," Dave said. "You taught me that, Max."

"Fish of the day?"

Dave smiled. "Enjoy each moment."

"Oh, yeah, that's mine." Max flicked his wrist to pop up a cigarette.

Three flew out and landed on the sandy ground. He retrieved them, stuffed two back in, and hung the third from his lip. He struck a match, ignited the tobacco, and inhaled. The coughing lasted several seconds, before he leaned back against the wall, next to Dave.

Side by side on the bench, they watched their smoke cloud the bunker, while distant flashes flickered through the door.

"Max," Dave said, "why are we here?"

Max's forehead furrowed. "So we don't get blown up outside."

"No, I mean the big picture."

Max tried another drag and coughed again. "To support the war effort."

"Bigger."

"Are you going all cosmic-spooky on me again?"

"Is your only purpose in life to drink and get laid?"

"And fly," Max said. He examined a bleeding scratch on his forearm and extracted a small shard of brown glass. "I'll bet I can get a Purple Heart out of this. The ultimate babe magnet."

Dave sighed. It must have been settling to have purpose. "I don't know why I'm here, Max."

When the all-clear blew, Dave emerged to find an entire wall of the BOQ collapsed inward onto his bunk, their belongings strewn about. He had dodged yet another bullet.

For the next two weeks, the pilots and aircraft of Fleet Composite Squadron Five hauled people, mail, and supplies to the carriers of Yankee Station. Each morning, Dave, Nelson, Max, and Al rose in the dark and headed to their planes. Dave briefed his passengers and checked that the mail and other cargo were properly secured. The sky always hinted of pink as he took off and flew over the beach and out to sea. He landed on the *Constellation*, and the *Shangri-La*, and the *Bonnie Dick*. Passengers scrambled out, crew unloaded mail, and other passengers climbed aboard. Shot from the catapult, he returned to Da Nang, only to do it all again.

No longer the master of his steed, Dave respected the aircraft. Two lovers dancing the minuet. Swaying together amidst heaven's beauty, he touched her gently as he guided her through the waltz. She responded to even the most subtle movements of his fingers. His hands and feet made fine adjustments to her yoke, throttles, and rudder pedals as she followed his lead.

Nelson watched most mornings in silence.

"I have the meatball," Dave said, approaching final.

"Roger, ball," the LSO said.

The orange ball remained fixed in the center of the mirror, aligned with the reference lights as they slid down the glide path together.

"On centerline, on glide slope," the LSO said thrice in soothing repetition.

Dave's thumb stroked her yoke. He whispered inaudibly to her as they rode through the burble, anticipating the exhilaration of their arrival as the courtship built to its crescendo. Then, the wheels slammed onto the deck, the tailhook grabbed the wire, and the lovers shuddered as the ballet reached its climax.

"Nice landing," Nelson said.

The next morning, Dave, Nelson, and Max emerged from the maintenance shack for the trip home.

"Jesus, Dave," Max said. "The LSO gave you a five on your last landing. That's unheard of. You practically have to make a perfect landing in a typhoon to get a five. I never got one. I don't *know* anyone who ever got one."

"Most pilots never do," Nelson said. "Great deployment, gentlemen."

"Yeah," Max said to Dave, "you're smoking hot now." Max turned to Nelson. "You should tell the Old Man, Lieutenant."

"I may," Nelson said, looking at Dave. "He might wish to review those orders."

Max grinned and winked. Dave nodded modestly.

Nelson turned his head toward the BOQ. "Is Al still sick?"

"Yeah," Dave said. "He's been puking all night. He said don't wait. There's a P-3 heading back this afternoon. He'll hitch a ride."

Nelson pondered. "Okay. Max, you come with me. Dave, you'll have to take Zero Zero solo, so stay close on my wing."

"Count on it."

Nelson and Max headed for their aircraft.

"And Lieutenant—" Dave said. Nelson turned. "—you were right."

"About what?"

"About me naming everything. I call him Big Jim." He turned for his airplane.

Nelson's eyebrows furrow. "Who?"

Dave looked back over his shoulder. "My pecker."

CHAPTER 47

Julio was grateful that things had been quiet for some time. The squad hadn't been on patrol for a while, and his tour ended in a week. He had expected to spend his last few days in country hanging out within the fire base perimeter, playing cards, and drinking beer. And when he got home, he'd be discharged. With his medical career over, and his time in the army a fiasco, he had achieved nothing. A year of his life had been wasted on his foolish dream of becoming an EMT and providing for Mama in a way she deserved and needed. At least he was still alive.

Julio had already packed his gear when Franco made the announcement. "We're headed to Quang Tri in the morning."

Okay. One more patrol.

In the morning darkness, Sergeant Franco led the eight men down the barren hill. Julio brought up the rear. The sergeant had reupped, and the other six were recent draftees. After only a year, Julio was the veteran. The kids looked to him for leadership.

They'd been to Quang Tri before, a peaceful village five miles away. All the young, fighting-aged men had left, either conscripted by the Saigon government or recruited by the Viet Cong guerrillas. Only women, children, and old men remained. No sweat. But it would be a long day.

After marching two hours, the sun had risen, and Julio could see the village ahead. They stepped onto a long, straight road leading into town—a hell of a lot easier than slogging through rice paddies and jungle.

After a dozen paces on the road, Franco held up his hand and stopped. His head turned upward as though hearing distant music.

Julio heard it too.

Franco's face contorted. "Incoming."

The world exploded. Something thumped Julio's chest and threw him backwards. His ears rang. When the smoke cleared, he found himself on his back in the ditch beside the road, a man on top of him. Warm rice paddy water trickled onto him. No, not water. Blood. Julio pushed the soldier off, unloaded his medical pack, and opened it.

Another shell exploded on the road. Franco opened fire from the ditch, and the others followed suit.

Julio secured a tourniquet around the man's mangled arm. He needed a medivac. Now.

In the distance, men appeared, firing and advancing down the road from the village.

Franco squinted. "Jesus."

Julio had never seen Franco look scared.

"That ain't VC. It's NVA regulars. There must be a hundred of them." He turned to Julio. "We've got to bug out of here. Now."

He waved his arm and started scooting down the ditch on his haunches. The others followed. Suddenly, he jerked forward and went down. When Julio got to him, the hole in his back oozed blood. With no time for proper care, Julio stuffed gauze into the wound.

Franco grunted. "Get these men out of here."

"Me?"

"No, my grandmother."

"I can't do it."

Franco snorted, then grimaced in pain. "Fuck, Garcia. Don't you get it?"

Julio hit him with a shot of morphine.

"You can do anything you put your mind to." Franco exhaled as the drug kicked in.

Julio thought of Mama. Without him, she'd die sick and alone in some squalid poverty ward.

He turned toward the squad. "Follow me, men," he said, dragging Franco down the ditch. The six men crouched low pulling the injured. "Call for help," he yelled at the radioman. The kid looked fifteen and terrified. Small arms fire hit all around. The North Vietnamese regulars were gaining.

Julio's thighs burned from running in a crouch. Just as they got to the end of the ditch where the road became a jungle path, another man went down. Now five men carried three. They couldn't outrun the troops. They had to take a stand. He turned to the men. “Choppers are on the way,” he said. “We’ll set up a perimeter here and hold until they arrive.”

The remaining four laid a wall of fire back toward the advancing army. As Julio worked on Franco and the other casualties, he saw Mama, alone and destitute. At least she’d get the $10,000 from his Army life insurance.

CHAPTER 48

Dave strolled around Zero Zero, stroking her faded fuselage. The years of wear only added to her matronly grace. He squeezed through the hatch, entered the solitary cockpit, and settled into the familiar contour of the pilot's seat. He slid into his parachute and tightened his harness until he was as snug as a swaddled infant.

The aircraft's massive engines fired on his command, and he taxied out behind Nelson and Max and took the runway as soon as they were airborne. He lifted off into the morning sky, banked, and raced after them in a climbing turn. He caught them over the beach and settled comfortably in tight formation. Together they met the dawn as they flew east across the South China Sea toward the Philippines and home.

With the copilot seat empty, the cockpit seemed cavernous. Dave hadn't flown without a copilot since the training command, but he still recalled vividly his first solo flight and the exquisite liberation of floating alone in the sky. He also remembered standing on the steps of indoctrination battalion, suitcase in hand, as Sergeant Walker handed him his dog tags. Dave brought his hand to his chest and felt the medallions under his flight suit behind the zippered pocket containing his shades. He heard the grinning drill instructor's words. *Just in case, you know, something should happen.*

As the white strand of beach passed behind them, the ships on Yankee Station appeared in the distance, their wakes cutting lines into the sea.

Dave looked down and made his final salute. "Adios, Connie," he said, bidding the *USS Constellation* goodbye forever.

The rising sun bathed the cockpit in an orange glow, melting the tension that flowed out of Dave's shoulders. As he tucked himself snugly under Nelson's wing, a faint, static-filled transmission crackled weakly in Dave's headset.

". . . Bravo . . . Quang Tri . . . RVN . . ."

Dave reached down and adjusted the sensitivity dial to boost the weak signal. Must be a handheld transmitter.

"Anybody . . ." punctuated with more static ". . . this is Bravo Foxtrot two klicks south of Quang Tri. We're engaging a large force. We need help. Fast."

Dave straightened up. He adjusted his throttles to keep in tight formation.

"Roger, Bravo Foxtrot," came in loud and clear, "this is Da Nang Control. No choppers in your zone. Dispatching evac from Da Nang."

"Hurry . . . eight of us . . . three wounded."

"Roger, Bravo Foxtrot," said control, "ETA three zero minutes."

Dave looked at his watch.

"Thirty minutes?" The faint voice grew increasingly frantic. "We can't hold for thirty. Charlie is everywhere."

"Keep it tight," Nelson blared, the powerful transmission only fifty feet away. The two-stoof formation overflew the fleet.

"Sweet Jesus," the young voice cried. "Isn't anyone closer? Please help us."

"Negative, Bravo Foxtrot," control said. "Three zero minutes is the closest we have."

"Oh, God." Then static.

Dave looked at the rising sun reflecting off the South China Sea, but he saw young men being slaughtered in the jungle. He saw uniformed servicemen marching up flower-lined sidewalks in Mobile and Denver and Tucson. He saw wives and parents answering their doors. He saw Brenda and Melissa. He saw Nelson pointing to his chin. "If you fuck up badly enough, you don't get a second chance."

Dave bowed his head and closed his eyes. *God help me.* He jerked the yoke sharply to the right. *Double Nuts* fell out of formation, banking steeply.

"Lieutenant, what are you doing?" Nelson broadcast.

Dave continued his turn for 180 degrees, advanced the throttles to full, and pushed the yoke forward. The nose dropped into a dive toward the beach. As the altimeter unwound, the airspeed indicator rose—one hundred fifty, one hundred seventy, one hundred ninety knots.

"There's nothing you can do," Nelson said. "We're not search and rescue."

A loud broadcast, enunciated clearly and with dispassion, filled Dave's headset. "Naval aircraft Uniform Echo Zero Zero, this is Da Nang Control. Be advised you are not cleared in-country."

Dave's airspeed continued to wind up: two hundred, two hundred ten, two hundred twenty knots.

"Lieutenant, return to formation," Nelson said. "You are disobeying a direct order."

Dave's yoke started to vibrate.

"Dave, you're throwing everything away," Nelson said. "Please. Don't do this."

Dave keyed his mic and spoke softly. "It's my second chance, Ron."

His dive continued. Two hundred thirty. Two hundred forty. Two hundred fifty knots. He looked back through the bulbous side window. Just as Nelson and Max passed out of sight, their wings rocked in a salute. Or a farewell.

He keyed his mic. "Control," he said, "this is Checkertail Zero Zero, request vectors to Bravo Foxtrot." The radio was silent. "Control, do you copy?"

"Roger, Navy Zero Zero, be advised you are not authorized in-country. Repeat, you are *not* authorized in-country."

Dave squeezed the yoke hard. "Copy that. Now gimme the goddamn vectors."

A long silence filled his headset. Finally, a mic click became the controller's voice.

"Roger, Zero Zero, come right heading two niner zero. Bravo Foxtrot at two three nautical miles."

Dave turned the yoke and banked to the new heading, the airspeed indicator continuing to climb. Two sixty, two seventy, two eighty. It crossed the two hundred ninety red line. The airframe began vibrating. Three hundred. Three hundred ten. The shaking became more violent. As the airspeed topped out at three hundred and twenty knots, the yoke rattled in his fists like a machine gun spitting six hundred rounds per minute.

Dave's thumb massaged the yoke. *Easy, girl.*

Continuing her dive, the aircraft blazed across the beach.

"Bravo Foxtrot," Dave broadcast, "I'll be there in niner minutes."

A mic clicked to loud static punctuated by rapid gunfire. "Please hurry."

Dave could barely read the vibrating instrument panel. He keyed his mic. "Where can I land?"

Static and gunfire accompanied the response. "There's a clearing about fifty meters in diameter. You can put down there."

"I need a strip to land on. This isn't a chopper. It's a stoof."

"A *what?*"

"A stoof. A fixed wing aircraft."

"Jesus," the young voice said, "there's no runway here."

"I don't need a runway. Just a strip. Is there a field, a long field?"

"Some rice paddies."

"I can't land in a swamp. I need a hard surface. A field, a road." No response. Dave waited. "Are you there?" he finally said.

Static. "You can land on a road?"

"A road? Yes. Where?"

"Just south of the village."

Dave's eyes raced across the horizon. Within minutes, the village appeared. Then the road, only a narrow trail, but straight for a few hundred yards with low growth on both sides. *Was that even possible?* He remembered the steep dive into Da Nang to avoid enemy fire. But here, he would have to come in low and slow like an arthritic clown in a carnival shooting gallery.

North Vietnamese Army soldiers advanced on the road toward a small squad. Dave yanked closed both throttles and approached at tree-top level as his airspeed bled off. He dropped his landing gear and full flaps and banked sharply. He rolled wings level over the road and slowed to minimum landing speed. As he descended, he awaited the certain gunfire, but there was no other way to land on such a short strip.

The North Vietnamese soldiers turned from the besieged army squad toward the metal descending from above. Rifles pointed skyward. Rapid small arms fire filled the air. Cracks appeared in the windshield. Bullets pinged through her skin. Seventy-two knots. Too slow. Dave felt the stall shudder. Wham. He landed hard. His wheels barely fit on the edges of the road, and his wings just cleared the growth on either side. He saw the U.S. Army squad ahead squatting in the ditch where the road petered out. He locked his brakes. NVA soldiers dove off the road just ahead of the skidding stoof. She slid to a stop barely short of the squad. Dave found himself hyperventilating.

Let's see a P-3 do that.

Out of the ditch scrambled five U.S. Army soldiers carrying three wounded. They opened the hatch and started squeezing through. Soldiers filled the back and aisle into the cockpit. Dave turned to watch the port wheel strut sink under the weight as the men piled in. Maybe an inch of clearance remained, seriously overloaded according to Max's four-inch safety margin. And as the last man climbed aboard with his pack and radio equipment, the aircraft's nose lifted from the weight imbalance, and *Double Nuts* sat in the dirt on her tail, like a begging dog.

"Dump your equipment," Dave yelled above the rumbling sputter of the idling engines.

"What?" said the soldier squatting next him.

"Your gear. Toss it out the hatch."

"We'll be defenseless if we do."

"We'll be dead if you don't," Dave said. "We can't take off with all this weight. Unless someone wants to stay behind."

From the hatch flew flack jackets, canteens, ammo belts and canisters, rifles, radios, medical supplies, and anything else that wasn't bolted down.

"Is everyone aboard?" Dave yelled.

The soldier in the aisle gave a hand signal to go, go, go. Dave stomped on the port brake, revved the starboard engine, and tightly spun around on the narrow road, the tail drawing an arc in the soft roadbed. He now faced the NVA troops who were scrambling from the ditches and back onto the road. They continued firing. Soldiers swarmed over his runway and advanced directly toward the stoof. What a prize she would be. Along with her crew.

A sledge hammer whacked the side of Dave's head. His vision blurred, time slowed, and the chaos of the moment faded to silence, save the sound of his heartbeat. Ba-boom. Ba-boom. The army ahead advanced toward him in slow motion. *Ba-boom. Ba-boom.* "Be careful," Jennifer whispered. *Ba-boom. Ba-boom.*

"SIR," he heard, "SIR." The pungent smell of rifle fire permeated Dave's consciousness as fingers of white smoke wafted through the cockpit. "SIR." Someone was shaking him.

As the crescendo of gunfire returned, the approaching army resumed its full speed assault toward the waiting aircraft and the nine souls on board. Dave pushed both throttles full forward. The engines roared. Under their powerful thrust, the nose again lowered and the overloaded tail rose from the dirt road.

As the stoof rolled and accelerated, NVA soldiers again dove off the road to escape the lethal propellers. One didn't make it. The whirling guillotine splattered what remained of his head and torso on the copilot's window. Dave had no time to reflect on the horror, it being no more surreal than everything else going on around him.

The stoof ran the gauntlet of heavy fire from the surrounding rice paddies. A shower of metal peppered the airframe, and bullets ripped through the cockpit. Dave's right leg exploded in pain. He cried out. Blood soaked through his flight suit. No time for pain now. *What's the rotation speed? What's the liftoff speed? Seventy? Two-thirds flaps? Are we over gross weight? Is it even possible to fly at this weight?*

The end of the straight road approached rapidly. *Well, we can't fly through trees. Here goes nothing.* At sixty-eight knots he eased back on the yoke. The stoof's nose rose, but her wheels remained firmly on the ground. She rolled and rolled like a shooting gallery target. Just short of the tree line, Dave had no choice. He yanked the yoke back. She shuddered but lifted off. He released a little back pressure, but the shudder continued. He held just enough yoke pressure to keep her on the verge of a stall. Palm fronds swatted the underbelly as she barely cleared the first line of trees. He lowered the nose to gain speed and limped away mere feet above the tree tops.

Dave turned east. *Get to the beach, then follow it south to Da Nang. If we go down, better crash land on the beach than in this godforsaken jungle.*

Finally, the beautiful sea appeared. He turned south, low over the beach. He winced as the pain crept up his leg.

"Control," Dave broadcast, "Navy Zero Zero inbound to Da Nang at one hundred."

"Roger, Zero, Zero. Understand inbound at one thousand."

"Negative, Da Nang," Dave said, "we're at one hundred feet. We've taken fire. The aircraft is damaged. One engine is in trouble. And we've got nine souls on board, four of whom are wounded."

"Roger," the controller said, "report field in sight. Emergency vehicles are standing by."

Dave's thumb stroked her yoke. He just might pull this off.

A wide swath of white appeared in the distance. Dave gazed at the beautiful sight.

"Da Nang tower, Checkertail Zero Zero has the field in sight. Approaching from the north."

The starboard propeller began wobbling. Dave inched back the right throttle and the vibration subsided. *Hold on, girl, we're almost there.* He turned directly for the field.

"Da Nang control, Checkertail Zero Zero inbound at three miles. Request clearance to land."

"Negative, Zero Zero, negative. Abort your approach," the controller said. "Da Nang is under mortar barrage. Repeat, abort your approach."

Even at this low altitude, Dave could see plumes of smoke rising from the field.

"Divert to Cam Ranh Bay, heading one seven zero at two five zero nautical miles."

Cam Ranh? "I can't make 250 miles. I need something closer."

The stoof continued south over the beach, the jungle to the right, the sea to the left.

"Negative, Zero, Zero. Cam Ranh's your best bingo field."

"That's too far. There has to be something closer."

"Negative. No other fields are close."

Dave grimaced in pain. No *Air Force* fields. He turned sharply left. The stoof banked, crossed the beach and headed out to sea.

Dave turned to the baby-faced soldier crouching next to him. "Do me a favor, will you Sergeant?" he said, wincing. "Could you tie off my leg?" Blood covered the deck. Dave grunted in pain as the soldier pulled off his belt and tightened a tourniquet on the leg. "Do you have anything for pain?"

"We tossed it, sir."

Dave pointed to a first aid kit mounted on the bulkhead. He turned back to the controls and tried to focus. The soldier suddenly stuck him with a needle. Within seconds, the pain lessened.

"You might have a concussion too, sir." The soldier pointed at Dave's head.

Dave reached up and touched the flattened bullet embedded in his dented and cracked helmet but felt unconcerned. A calmness overcame him. "What's your name, Sergeant?"

"Garcia, sir," the soldier said. "I'm a private."

"Garcia. That Mexican?"

"No sir. It's Texan."

Dave nodded. "Ever fly an airplane, Sergeant?"

"No, sir."

"Want to learn?"

"No, sir."

"Great," Dave said. "Have a seat." He pointed to the empty copilot seat.

Garcia hesitated, then sat.

"My leg doesn't seem to be working," Dave said, "so we're going to need yours. Understand?"

"No, sir."

"Put your feet on those pedals."

Garcia rested his feet on the rudder pedals.

"You work the pedals," Dave said. "My arms, your legs. Okay?"

Garcia stared at him, slack-jawed.

"She's great. You'll love her."

"Who?"

The starboard propeller started wobbling again. Oil leaked from the prop hub and splattered onto the copilot's blood-stained window. Finally, one blade separated, and like a spear, penetrated the fuselage just behind Garcia. With a loud rush of air, the stoof yawed sharply to the right and vibrated violently.

"Left rudder," Dave said, "left rudder." Garcia pushed on the right rudder. The plane yawed further right. "Your other left," Dave said calmly. Whatever drug the sergeant had stuck him with was good stuff. Garcia pressed the left rudder and the plane straightened out.

Under the cowling, prop oil hit the engine's hot cylinders and burst into flame. The fire warning light illuminated.

"Ooo," Dave said. "I know this one." His hand moved with his words. "Mixture off. Feather button—push. Emergency switch—engage."

The prop feathered and stopped. White powder puffed from under the cowling and the flames went out. With the loss of the right engine, the stoof descended, the engine still smoking. They entered ground effect, which supported them only feet above the waves.

Soothed by the painkiller percolating through his brain, Dave turned to the soldier. "Ever land on an aircraft carrier, son?"

Garcia's eyes widened. "No, sir."

"It's fun," Dave said. "You'll see."

Garcia pressed hard on the rudder pedal.

"But first, we have a little problem. We can fly on one engine with this weight, but we have to be close to the water to utilize ground effect. This gives us the little extra lift we need. Unfortunately, the carrier deck is, oh, I don't know, a hundred feet above the surface. So we have to get from down here to up there." Dave pondered the options. "Full power on the one good engine will put us in a hellacious yaw, and flaps will slow us to stall speed. What to do?"

Garcia put both hands on his left knee and pushed. Dave cranked in full left rudder trim to ease the pressure.

"There she is," Dave said. A ship appeared in the distance. The stoof followed her wake, skimming the wave tops, smoke trailing from the right engine. "*USS Constellation*," Dave broadcast, "this is Checkertail Zero Zero, seven miles out for landing."

"Roger, Zero Zero, we have you in sight." A pause, then the static returned. "Are you on fire?"

"Negative," Dave said, "just smoking a little."

"Roger, Zero Zero. You are not authorized to land. Divert to Da Nang, heading two four zero, two seven nautical miles."

Dave chuckled. "No can do, Connie," he said, and then in his W.C. Fields voice, "Da Nang is *closed*."

Garcia's eyes grew huge. "Are you all right, sir?"

Dave imagined the scene in the conning tower with the Air Boss, Mini-Boss, and Potted Plants all watching him through binoculars and chortling at his casual humor in the face of danger. But no such gaiety came through the transmission.

"I repeat," the air boss said, "you are NOT authorized to land. Divert immediately."

Dave motored on. Another voice broke in. "This is the captain of the *USS Constellation* speaking," he said. "Look, *Double Nuts*, you are not landing a burning aircraft on this boat."

Dave looked at Garcia.

"I can't swim, sir," Garcia said.

Dave nodded. "Good morning, Captain. I've got nine souls on board. Four are wounded. We won't survive a ditching."

Dave knew the captain was watching through binoculars.

The Old Man uttered a curse, then ordered, "Rig the barricade." Sirens wailed, and netting popped up above the deck like a giant tennis net ready to catch an errant ball. Men and machines scurried about, clearing the deck.

Dave approached the ship's stern, skimming the waves just above Connie's wake. Two miles. Then one.

"Call the ball," the LSO said.

Dave was so far below glide slope, he saw no ball at all. He grimaced as a sharp pain shot up his leg. "We're going to need more altitude," he grunted to Garcia. "Push on the left rudder pedal to hold us straight."

Dave added power on the good left engine. The plane yawed to the right. Garcia pressed the left rudder pedal, and the airplane straightened a little. As the stern approached, Dave added more power. They again yawed to the right. Garcia put both feet on the left rudder pedal, pushing, sweating, and grunting. Headed for the fantail. Dave added full power. As the plane again yawed right, Garcia screamed, his body horizontal and wedged like a log between his seatback and the left rudder pedal.

The aircraft rose a few feet. A red ball peaked from the bottom of the mirror.

"I have the ball," he said, still well below the flight deck.

"You're too low!" the LSO yelled. "WAVE OFF. WAVE OFF."

All lights on the mirror flash red. Dave slapped down the flaps lever. Valves turned, redirecting hydraulic fluid, the pressure lowering the flaps and changing the camber of the airfoil. The lift vector pulled upward, but the drag vector pulled back. They rose, but the airspeed indicator moved from one hundred to ninety to eighty knots.

The fantail filled the windscreen. Sailors on the stern scrambled to avoid the stoof's collision. As the flaps lowered, giving her the added—but temporary—lift she needed, the stoof popped up and began a stall shudder. Her nose peeked over the fantail. The flight deck flashed beneath as they almost cleared the stern, clipping off the right wheel. The plane shuddered violently, stalled, and pancaked onto the deck. It slid into the barricade and skidded to a stop at the side of the angled deck, balanced on the edge. Netting wrapped across the windshield, the right engine smoldered with its propeller bent back, and the severed wheel rolled past and off the angled deck into the sea.

Fire crews rushed out and doused the smoldering engine with foam. Soldiers scrambled from the hatch. Sailors extracted the wounded on stretchers.

"Good work, Sergeant," Dave said.

"I'm not a sergeant, sir."

"You should be."

Dave was carried on a stretcher across the deck, surrounded by Garcia and other soldiers.

The ship's loudspeaker blared. "This is the captain. We have inbound recovery in two minutes. Get that debacle off my deck."

Men and deck tractors pushed *Double Nuts* toward the edge. Two Phantom F-4 jets flew over the deck and broke sequentially to the downwind leg. Dave shivered with a chill. He could barely lift his head.

A soldier squeezed his hand. "God bless you, sir," he said. "And God bless the United States Navy."

"Hang in there, sir," Garcia said.

Dave saw the blurred faces and heard the garbled voices, but his attention was riveted behind them on the words beneath the cockpit window. *LTJG DAVID QUINN*. Before he could take another breath, the yellow lettering tilted upward and slid from view as *Double Nuts* toppled into the sea.

CHAPTER 49

Julio had arrived in paradise. Subic Bay Naval Hospital stood amid lush, manicured grounds. Its red-barrel tile roof crowned the white-washed walls, and ancient royal palms, their bases painted white, cordoned the stately structure like the palace guard. Within, gossamer curtains billowed into a large, bright room. In the corner beneath the window, Julio sat dwarfed in an overstuffed chair, sinking into the soft, comfortable vinyl upholstery. He was clean, dry, and without fear for the first time in twelve months.

When the carrier had docked at Subic, Julio disembarked. His tour was over and the Army was sending him home tomorrow. The Navy had flown Franco and the two other injured Army buddies here from the ship, and Julio had spent yesterday with them. But this morning, he wanted to spend time with the man who had saved his life. And to ask him something.

Lieutenant Quinn lay in the only occupied bed in the four-bed room. His girlfriend Jennifer sat in a straight-back chair next to him, her hand resting on his as they spoke in hushed tones. Julio hoped he might someday find the love he saw between them.

The lieutenant caught him staring and smiled. "So how do you like flying, Sergeant?"

Julio's face warmed. He shouldn't have been intruding on their privacy.

"Corporal, sir," he said, pointing to the new chevron on his arm. Then he surprised himself. "I like it." He thought for a moment. "The flying part, not the crashing part."

This was his chance. He rose and approached the bedside.

"Sir, I've been thinking about using my VA educational benefits when I get out for flight training."

Lieutenant Quinn's face blossomed into a broad smile. "That's terrific."

Julio looked at the floor. "Do you think that's possible, sir?"

"A career in aviation? Of course. You wouldn't have military training, but you're young, and time is on your side. And if you want something badly enough and go after it, you can achieve it. I'm sure of that."

That's the same thing Momma had always said. "Julito, you can be anything you choose." Sergeant Franco had said it too, though differently than Mama. "Fuck, Garcia. Don't you get it? You can do anything you put your mind to." And Julio wasn't yet twenty. With his VA benefits, he could work part-time, support Momma, and go to school. It would be difficult, but he knew he could do it.

An officer stuck his face through the door with a conspiratorial smirk. "You dog," he said as he entered the room.

The bandage on Lieutenant Quinn's forehead tugged at his skin as his face lit up. "Hey, Max," he said warmly.

Julio retreated to his corner chair under the window.

"Talk about a turn-around." Max was giddy. "From squadron pariah to war hero."

"The Navy doesn't think so. I disobeyed a direct order, flew into an unauthorized area, and landed on a carrier when the captain wanted me to go away."

Max waved his hand.

"And I wrecked the Old Man's plane," Quinn said.

"So what? You saved eight soldiers from certain death. You think they can ignore that? You're a hero, man."

"Thanks, Max."

"And here's the best part," Max said. "The Old Man says I can extend for another year. He says we can't afford to lose two experienced pilots at once." He grinned broadly. "Another year in paradise."

"That's great, Max."

"AND . . . you're not going to believe this one . . . I got a date with Gina. Maybe I *will* settle down."

"I'm happy for you."

"Not as happy as you should be for yourself. You have your pick of jobs now. A war hero moves to the front of the line." He grinned. "Pan Am, here you come."

Jennifer brought Quinn's hand against her cheek, then kissed it.

"Max, I'm afraid Pan Am is no longer in the picture."

"Sure it is. You're a war hero."

Quinn sighed and shook his head. "I lost my leg."

Max's brow furrowed. He looked down at the blanket that lay flat below the Lieutenant's right knee.

"The airlines are not in my future."

Though Quinn's voice was relaxed and reassuring, Max looked like the wind had been knocked from him. He stumbled back and collapsed into a chair.

Another officer entered the subdued gathering and nodded to those present. His nametag read *Lt. Ron Nelson*.

"The Old Man is right behind me," he said. "I want to say something before he arrives." He stepped to Quinn's bedside. "First, the LSO gave you a zero on that last landing, Lieutenant. That's going to bring your average way down."

The corners of Quinn's mouth twitched upward. "It doesn't much matter now."

Nelson looked down and cleared his throat. "You taught me something, Dave."

"*I* taught *you* something?"

"Yes. Your selfless act taught me that sometimes rules need to be broken." He stood in silence, nodding.

"Thanks, Ron."

"Attention on deck," someone called from outside as the door swung open and a Navy commander strode in.

"Don't get up," he said to Quinn. "The rest of you, at ease." He wore a stern commanding-officer face. "Well son, I see your judgment is as bad as ever."

"Sorry about your plane, Captain."

The CO walked to the bed. "I have something for you." He opened a small box and withdrew a heart-shaped medallion on a purple ribbon. He pinned the Purple Heart to Quinn's gown. "For wounds received in combat, I thank you, Lieutenant. And a grateful nation thanks you."

Quinn and his Jennifer smiled at each other.

"Thanks, Captain."

"That's the good news. The bad news is Navy JAG recommended you be court-martialed." He paused, letting the gravity of it sink in. "For insubordination, destruction of military property, and willful violation of a direct order. *Several* direct orders."

Quinn nodded. Nelson looked on, stone-faced. The others listened stoically.

"But the Army put you up for the highest honor in the nation, the Congressional Medal of Honor." He scratched his bald head. "So we compromised." He reached into his pocket and produced another small box. "The official paperwork will be rattling around Washington for a couple of months, but I wanted the honor of presenting it to you before you left." He opened the box revealing the Navy Cross on a blue and white ribbon. He offered it to Jennifer. "Would you like the honors?"

She stood and lifted the medal and ribbon from the box.

The CO opened the citation and began reading. "The president of the United States takes pride in presenting the Navy Cross to Lieutenant Junior Grade David L. Quinn, United States Navy, for conspicuous gallantry at the risk of his life, above and beyond the call of duty, while serving as an S-2 pilot attached to Naval Fleet Composite Squadron Five in action against enemy forces."

Jennifer lay the medal on Quinn's chest and put the ribbon around his neck.

"During a routine mission," the CO continued, "Lieutenant Quinn monitored an emergency call that eight American soldiers were being overwhelmed by a large North Vietnamese force. He flew to the scene and found fifty to seventy enemy soldiers advancing on the squad. Lieutenant Quinn displayed exceptional airmanship as he landed his aircraft on a narrow dirt road while under constant attack by the enemy force."

He looked up and inspected each solemn face. Nelson nodded quietly.

"Using his aircraft as a shield, he loaded eight men, three of whom were severely wounded, successfully maneuvered about, and took off directly into intense enemy fire."

The CO swallowed hard and took a deep breath. "Despite injuries to himself and damage to his aircraft, Lieutenant Quinn maneuvered out to sea. Displaying superb airmanship, he successfully landed aboard the *USS Constellation* . . ."

He cleared his throat, brought his handkerchief to his mouth, then briefly to his eyes. "Well, you know what happened."

"I want to hear it," Jennifer said. She looked at Quinn and squeezed his hand with both of hers.

The CO nodded. "Lieutenant Quinn's extraordinary heroism coupled with his outstanding flying skill prevented the annihilation of the small force. His courageous actions reflect great credit upon himself and uphold the highest traditions of the U.S. Naval Service . . ."

Quinn's and Jennifer's fingers intertwined as the commanding officer read on, and Julio looked out the window at an F-8 Crusader rising off the runway across the bay.

CHAPTER 50

October 2013

Even with a lopsided gait, Dave outpaced Max as he led his army of one among the vines and up the hill.

"Slow down, Dave," Max said. "Jeeze, we're not kids anymore." He stopped and leaned over to catch his breath. "You move faster on one leg than I do on two. Where do you get the energy?"

"What can I say? I love my grapes."

"It's the footwear," Max said.

Dave wore work boots, Max sported shiny, tasseled loafers, now covered with the dust of the dry earth.

Max's gaze scanned the vineyard, spread across the valley floor and up the rolling hillsides. A gentle breeze fluttered the leaves. The arch over the gate at the highway read *D&J Winery, Sonoma Valley—Since 1972.*

"You started this right when you got back?"

Dave smiled. "Jennifer insisted. Follow your dream, she said." He sighed and stared at the rows of vines. "She's always been the strong one. Her teacher's salary supported the winery in the early years before she opened the school. She just retired last year and turned the academy over to our oldest, Marcia, to run."

"Well, you've built quite a place here."

"We reap what we sow, Max." Dave put his hand on his friend's shoulder. "We had a good year."

"The harvest up?"

"No, about the same. But Jennifer got a good report from the oncologist, and we had another grandchild. So, a good year. Great, really."

"Well, you look terrific. I guess doing what you love leads to a stress-free life."

Dave smiled. "Hardly. We raised four girls. But, yeah, it beats waking up every morning with a knot in your gut. I sure don't feel sixty-six."

Dave surveyed Max, his high forehead with hair pulled back into a gray ponytail and nails well-manicured and shining with clear polish. A gold chain on his neck and a large diamond pinky ring sparkled in the sun.

"You still dealing?"

Max nodded. "The casino doesn't have a good retirement plan. But I like the work. Always have." He shrugged. "I'm on my feet eight hours a day. But that leaves sixteen for sitting. Or lying down." He bounced his eyebrows. "And I meet interesting people."

"Like Tempest?"

Max smiled. "Yeah. Like Tempest."

"Wedding bells in your future?"

Max snorted. "Nah. Three divorces are enough."

As they approached the white, two-story farm house on the knoll, a red-haired woman, forty-something and far too busty for her petite waist, smoked a cigarette on the porch swing.

When they waved, she nodded a perfunctory acknowledgment and flicked her ash over the porch rail.

Dave looked at his watch. "It's time to call him."

When they entered the kitchen door, Jennifer was leaning against the counter, a phone in her ear. Dave put his arm around her waist and kissed her cheek.

She pushed him away and mouthed, "Melissa. Boy trouble."

Dave turned to Max. "Our granddaughter relies on Grandma for dating advice."

"He's only seventeen, sweetie," Jennifer said into the phone. "It takes boys a while to grow up." She winked at her husband.

As Dave set up his laptop on the living room coffee table, Max admired the wall photos of a young Dave and Jennifer holding a newborn, then a newborn and a toddler, then a tweener. High school and college graduation pictures, wedding photos, grandchildren.

Max sat on the sofa as Dave clicked the touchpad. A Skype screen popped up. An older Filipina woman squinted into the camera.

"Hello, Nenita," Dave said.

Recognition crossed her face and she smiled. "Oh, hi David." She wiggled her fingers in a wave. Max tilted into the frame. Her face soured and she grunted. "I get the commander."

Her laptop camera rotated 180 degrees, scanning the room. Beams of sunlight streamed through the curtains into the study. Oak bookcases lined the wall. End tables were littered with mementos and pictures. The camera settled on an old man in a wheelchair behind the large desk, slowly turning the pages of a photograph album. His wispy strands of white hair reached for the sky. The scar on his chin had faded little. Behind him, plaques and certificates covered the wall and chronicled the thirty-eight years of service of Commander Ronald Nelson, USN, Retired.

Nelson looked confused, trying to focus on the screen, but when he recognized Dave and Max, his face lit up. "It's my boys." He turned his head. "Look Nenita, it's my boys."

"Yes, dear."

They talked for ten minutes, mostly Nelson wistfully recounting his Navy days.

Dave smiled. "You've become quite mellow, Ron."

Nenita swatted Nelson's shoulder. "He not that mellow." Then she kissed his balding head. "The commander needs his nap. Thanks for calling, David." She scrunched her nose in a sneering goodbye to Max.

She rolled Nelson off camera, revealing the centerpiece of his memorabilia wall—a framed black and white photo of young Nelson and Dave in uniform, arms draped over each other's shoulder. Both grinned broadly. Dave wore the Navy Cross around his neck. The photo was signed, "Big Jim."

In the morning darkness, Max leaped from the cab, looked at his watch, and hurried into the terminal. "We're late."

Dragging her rolling overnight bag, Tempest strolled behind, her cleavage straining the too-tight blouse, and her legs running from her short leather skirt to the stiletto heels clicking on the terrazzo floor. "At least we're out of the boondocks."

"They're old friends, baby. I rarely see them. Besides, it was a nice minivacation."

She snorted. "A weekend with Farmer Brown ain't no vacation."

Max sighed.

An airline captain marching past caught his eye. Max turned in a double take and stared.

"What?" Tempest said.

"I thought—" He shook his head. "Nothing."

The captain strode down the concourse of San Francisco International, his uniform crisp, shoes shined, and haircut immaculate. His leather flight bag swung in his firm grip, and an expensive watch peeked from his sleeve. Passengers nodded and smiled. He passed two attractive female flight attendants. They glanced flirtatiously.

"Good morning, Captain," they said in unison.

He nodded back. As he arrived at the gate, the attendant looked up from the counter and smiled. "Have a great flight, sir."

He passed through the door and down the gangway. A flight attendant stood inside the open aircraft hatch.

"Welcome aboard, Captain."

Taxiing onto the runway, the pilot squinted against the first rays of sunlight. Reaching into his shirt pocket, he removed his aviator shades and slipped them on. As he pushed the throttles full open to the roar of the mighty engines, the aircraft surged forward. And with a gentle pull on the yoke, Captain Julio Garcia lifted the jumbo jet into the dawning new day.

DEDICATION

On August 27, 1970, naval aviators of Fleet Composite Squadron Five (VC-5) practiced carrier landings aboard the *USS Shangri-La* cruising in the South China Sea. Returning to Cubi Point Naval Air Station at night in a driving rainstorm, naval aircraft US-2C 133344 crashed into Subic Bay, Philippines, killing the four young naval aviators aboard. News of the event was barely noted, dwarfed by the two hundred plus American military deaths each week, five hundred miles to the west in Vietnam.

This novel was inspired by that event and is dedicated to those young naval officers: Quentin Gunn, Glenn Spar, Jack Dripps, and Bob Hollingsworth. It was written out of affection and respect for those men. Since they perished outside Vietnam, their names do not appear on that solemn black granite wall in the nation's capital, along with the fifty thousand who died in that conflict. But their loss is no less grieved. And so, this is their memorial.

Ken Hubona
November 2019
Richmond, Virginia

FINAL WORDS

The events leading to the actual Subic Bay crash were chronicled by Commander (then Lieutenant Junior Grade) Larry Nevels, USN, Retired, in his autobiography *Course Corrections.*

On April 11, 1970, Commander Philip R. Holt, Executive Officer of Fleet Composite Squadron Five, lost his life in the crash of an F-8 Crusader. Later that day, his cracked flight helmet, fished from Buckner Bay, was returned to the VC-5 ready room.

The novel's rescue scene was inspired by the exploits of Major Stephen W. Pless, USMC, for which he won the Congressional Medal of Honor.

About the Author

Da Nang, Vietnam
1970

Ken Hubona earned his Navy wings in 1969. Stationed in the Philippines, he deployed to bases throughout the Far East, including Da Nang and Cam Rahn Bay, Vietnam, and logged carrier landings aboard the *USS Constellation, USS America,* and *USS Shangri La.* This novel was inspired by that experience. He now lives and writes in suburban Richmond, Virginia.

If you enjoyed this book, please consider leaving a review on Amazon.
Thank you. Ken

KenHubona@comcast.net

Made in the USA
Columbia, SC
25 October 2020

23435611R00150